# BURNIN'
# FOR YOU

MONTANA FIRE
SUMMER OF FIRE TRILOGY **3**

# BURNIN' FOR YOU

## SUSAN MAY WARREN

**SDG PUBLISHING**
*A division of Susan May Warren Fiction*
Minneapolis, MN

# Praise for Playing with Fire by Amazon.com readers

**Strength For Today & Bright Hope for Tomorrow**

Once again I have been captured and made to feel as if I've lived in Susan's novels! I am continually amazed at how well-written and well-developed her stories are! They build me up, and yet humble me, and this one is no exception. Not only have I laughed, cried, and sat on the edge of my seat, waiting to see what would happen, but I found myself singing, "Great is Thy Faithfulness" all the way through the book. I fell in love with the wonderful characters of sweet Gilly & strong Reuben, who learn that "the only way we can have peace with our decisions & choices, is if we trust God." One of my favorite quotes is: "...as if creation was made to flourish even under suffering. Starting anew, despite the ashes." "Strength for today & bright hope for tomorrow" accurately describes this book! LOVED THIS BOOK!!!! ~ *Becky Smith*, Amazon.com reader

**Burnin' For You~Exciting inspirational romantic fiction at its finest!**

This much anticipated third book in the Montana Fire series left me breathless! When I first started reading, I had two choices. read slow and savor the story, or read as fast as I could to find out WHAT HAPPENS! I ended up with a combination of both. The first portion I read slowly as Warren laid the groundwork for events in this installment of the ongoing firefighting series. Petite smoke bomber pilot Gilly Priest and big guy smokejumper Reuben Marshall have quite a story to tell and tell it they do, exposing all their strengths and weaknesses along the way.

From the time Gilly fires up her plane for takeoff, the story really takes off, too, leaving me unable to stop reading until I finished it. I was at times nervous, calm, scared, relaxed, horrified, hyperventilating, charmed, thankful, feeling the love, well, you get the picture. On and on the emotional rollercoaster went, but I couldn't stop reading until the story ended (the middle of the night is not a good time to end up with this big of an adrenaline rush!)

Suffice it to say, Warren once again delivers an amazing, heart stopping, romantic story while bringing the goodness and trust-worthiness of God to the forefront. Her use of old familiar hymns had me singing along and remembering the truth of their words. Peace for today and bright hope for tomorrow from Great is Thy Faithfulness figures prominently in the story, and rightly so, but at one point I found myself singing, He hideth my soul in the cleft of the rock, That shadows a dry, thirsty land, He hideth my life in the depths of His Love and covers me there with His hand.

Burnin' for You is an exciting, phenomenal, breathtaking pag-eturner. I was captivated from the start and didn't want it to end, even when my heart was pounding. ~*Tracey*, book corner fan, Amazon.com reader

**This series has spoilt me forever!**

Oh me, oh my! I think this whole series has spoilt me forever when it comes to the romantic suspense genre, because I'm not sure I will ever find another book that will make me feel like these books have. Reading these books is like an intravenous dose of romance and action. Somehow, Susan May Warren knows exactly the right words to use to tap straight into my visceral senses, and my poor heart doesn't know whether to pound, stop, melt, or some strange combination of all three. How will anything else ever compare with that?

Rueben and Gilly . . . *sigh* I loved Jed and Kate, and I loved Conner and Liza, but there was something about Rueben in particular that tugged at my heartstrings. I think it was his vul-nerability; his lack of confidence around Gilly. He's quieter than his smokejumping teammates; a man of action more than words. But his emotions run deep, and he feels like he's let a lot of people down in his life: his father, Jock and the other teammates who lost their lives in a forest fire almost a year ago. His friendship with Gilly, meagre though it is, means too much to him to risk spoiling it by making a fool of himself and pursuing his attraction to her.

Gilly once had aspirations of being a smokejumper herself, but her fear of heights held her back. And yet, put her in a pilot seat and she'll fly into what feels like hell if she has to. And that is exactly what she does at the beginning of this novel, on her first official day as a firebomber. She pushes herself to prove that she is capable and fearless, in spite of her size and gender, and she most certainly does NOT need a man in her life; someone who would feel compelled to protect her all the time, or worse, would end up trampling her heart.

Meanwhile, it looks like the arsonist who has been lighting fires and trying to pin the blame on Conner's drones has given up. But when their plane crashes, leaving one of their team members dead(!) and two seriously wounded, Gilly and Reuben learn they couldn't be more wrong. I was surprised that they learned who was behind the sabotage and arson halfway through the novel, but don't think for one minute that it means the tension lets up! I guarantee your adrenaline will be pumping right up to the end.

Susan May Warren seems to have taken 'show, don't tell' to a whole new level in this series. She doesn't just show; she recreates the experience. And in a novel with raging forest fires, plane crashes, an escape-for-your-life trek through forest land, and a dangerous air rescue, that's a lot of experiencing!

She's also one of the handful of writers I've found who can create emotional intensity in her romances (and I don't just mean the kissing bits!) without it coming over as cheesy or overdone. Her characters connect on a soul level and their attraction is anchored by that connection, making the romance a completely organic part of the story. And maybe that's why I loved Reuben's character so much. It's always the quiet ones that have the hidden depths!

Seriously, if you love romantic suspense, you are missing out big time if you don't get your hands on these books. *~Fiction Aficionado*, Amazon.com reader

**Montana Fire**
**Summer of Fire Trilogy**
Book Three: *Burnin' for You*
ISBN-13: 978-1-943935-15-4
Published by SDG Publishing
15100 Mckenzie Blvd. Minnetonka, MN 55345
Copyright © 2016 by Susan May Warren

This book is a work of fiction. Names, characters, places, and incidents are either products of the author's imagination or used fictitiously. Any similarity to actual people, organizations, and/or events is purely coincidental.

Scripture quotations are taken from the King James Version of the Bible.

Scripture quotations are also taken from the Holy Bible, New International Version®, NIV®. Copyright© 1973, 1978, 1984, 2011 by Biblica, Inc®. Used by permission of Zondervan. All rights reserved worldwide.

For more information about Susan May Warren, please access the author's website at the following address: www.susanmaywarren.com.

Published in the United States of America.

For Your glory, Lord

I F THEY STARTED RUNNING now, they just might make the lake before the fire consumed them.

At least that's what Reuben Marshall's gut said when the wind shifted and rustled the seared hairs on the back of his neck, strained and tight from three days of cutting line through a stand of black spruce as thick as night.

After a week the fire in the Kootenai National Forest had consumed nearly twelve hundred acres. And as of breakfast this morning, his team of smokejumpers, as well as hotshot and wildland firefighter teams from all over Montana and Idaho, had only nicked it down to sixty percent contained.

Now the fire turned from a low crackle to a growl behind him, hungry for the forest on the other side of the twenty-foot line that his crew—Pete, CJ, and Hannah—had scratched out of the forest, widening an already cleared service road. CJ and Hannah were swamping for Reuben as he mowed down trees, clearing brush. Between the two of them, they worked like an entire crew, still determined to prove themselves. Pete worked cleanup, digging the line down to the mineral soil.

Reuben's eyes watered, his throat charred from eating fire as he angled his saw into the towering spruce—one more tree felled and it would keep the fire from jumping the line or candling from treetop to treetop.

Chips hit his safety glasses, pinged against his yellow No-mex shirt, his canvas pants. His shoulders burned, his arms one constant vibration.

In another hour they'd hook up with the other half of their crew—Jed and Conner, Ned, Riley, and Tucker—dragging a line along the lip of forest road that served as their burnout line. They'd light a fire of their own to consume all the fuel between the line and the active fire and drive the blaze to Fountain Lake.

The dragon would lie down and die.

At least that seemed the ambitious but attainable plan that his crew boss, Jed, had outlined this morning over a breakfast of MRE eggs and protein bars. While listening, Reuben had poured three instant coffee packs into one cup of water and tossed the sludge down in one gulp.

Deep in his gut, Reuben had expected trouble when the wind quietly kicked up early this morning, rousing the team tucked in their coyote camp—a pocket of preburned space, their safety zone on the bottom of the canyon near a trickle of river. Already blackened, the zone shouldn't re-ignite, but it left ashy debris on Reuben, the soot probably turning his dark-brown hair to gray under his orange hard hat. His entire team resembled extras on the *Walking Dead*.

He felt like it too—a zombie, barely alive, fatigue a lining under his skin. Ash, sawdust, and the fibers of the forest coated his lips despite his efforts to keep his handkerchief over his mouth.

They'd worked in the furnace all day, the flame lengths twenty to thirty feet behind them, climbing up aspen and white pine, settling down into the crackling loam of the forest, consuming bushes in a flare of heat. But with the bombers overhead dropping slurry, the fire sizzled and roared, dying slowly.

He'd watched them—the Russian biplane AN2, which scooped water from the lake, and the Airtractor AT, dropping red slurry from its white belly. And, way overhead the C-130 circled for another pass, a loaner from the National Guard.

Reuben wondered which one Gilly piloted—a random thought that he shoved away. But not before imagining her, dark auburn hair tied back and cascading out of her baseball cap, aviator glasses over her freckled nose. Petite at just over five feet, the woman had don't quit all over her when she climbed into a cockpit.

But it did him no good to let his thoughts anchor upon a woman he could barely manage to speak to. Not that he had any chance with her, anyway.

Keep his head down, keep working—wasn't that what his father had always said?

They all had expected the Fountain Lake fire to fizzle out with their efforts.

Until the wind shifted. Again.

And that's when the fine hairs of Reuben's neck stood on end, his gut began to roil.

He finished the cut, released his blade from the trunk of the tree, hollered "Clear!," then stepped back as the massive tree lurched, crashed into the blazing forest.

The fire roared, a locomotive heading their direction.

It seemed Pete, twenty feet behind, hadn't yet alerted to the shift. Reuben couldn't account for why his gut always seemed to clench with a second sense that scented danger. The last time he'd felt it, he'd known in his bones that teammates were going to die.

And they had.

*Not again.*

Reuben did a quick calculation. They'd completed about

twenty-four chain lengths in the last six hours, about a quarter mile from the safety zone. They could run back to their strike camp in the burned-out section—a theoretical safe zone.

However, he'd known forests to reignite, especially loam that had flashed over quickly, hadn't scorched the land down to the soil. There was plenty of fuel to burn in the so-called safe zone if the fire got serious. Not to mention the air, searing hot in their lungs as it cycloned through the area.

If they turned and ran another hundred yards along the uncleared forest service road, they'd be over halfway to the lake, less than a half mile away.

But they'd be running into unburned forest with nowhere to hunker down if the fire overtook them.

Reuben listened for, but couldn't hear, the other team's saws.

Through the charred trees, the sun backdropped the hazy gray of the late afternoon, a thin, blood-red line along the far horizon.

Jed's voice crackled over their radios. "Ransom, Brooks. We're battling some flare-ups here, and the fire just kicked up. How's your position?"

Reuben watched Pete toggle his radio, gauging the wind.

"Must be the lake effect. She's still sitting down here," Pete said.

Reuben frowned, nearly reaching for his own radio. But, despite his instincts, Pete was right. Except for a few flare-ups, the fire *behind* them seemed to be slow moving.

Maybe—

"Right," Jed said, confirming Pete's unspoken conclusion that they were safe. "Just don't turn into heroes. Remember your escape route. To the fire, you're just more fuel. We're going to start bugging out to the lake."

Which, probably, was what they should be doing, too.

As if reading his mind, Pete glanced up at Reuben. For a second, memory played in Pete's eyes.

Only he, Pete, and Conner had survived being overrun nearly a year ago in a blaze that killed seven of their team, including their jump boss, Jock Burns.

That had been a case of confusion, conflicting orders, and hotshots and smokejumpers running out of time. Fingers had been pointed, blame assigned.

The what-ifs still simmered in low conversations through their small town of Ember, Montana. Thankfully, this summer had been—well, mostly—injury free.

Reuben wanted to keep it that way. But if their safety zone wasn't completely burned to the ground, it could reignite around them, trap them.

If they left now they could probably make the lake. But what if the fire jumped the road, caught them in the middle of a flare-up?

If Reuben should mutter his suggestion, he could end up getting them all killed. And if he was wrong, God wouldn't exactly show up to rescue him.

Reuben couldn't help shooting a look back at Hannah and CJ, still working, unaware of the radio communication.

Sparks lifted, spurted out of the forest, across the line, lighting spot fires near the edge of the road. Reuben ran over, stomped one out, threw water from his pack on another.

Pete joined him. "We'll head back to the black."

Reuben glanced at the route. Clear, for now.

"Roger," he said.

Pete yelled to CJ and Hannah as Reuben shouldered his saw, started jogging along the road to their safety zone. The air swam with billowing dust and smoke. His eyes watered, his nose thick with mucus.

*Why is being a smokejumper so important to you?* His brother's words of disbelief after their father's funeral smarted in his brain.

Why indeed? Reuben coughed as he ran, a blast of superheated air sideswiping him, peeling a layer of sweat down his face. Sane people had normal jobs—like ranching or even coaching football. They didn't bed down in ash, drink coffee as thick as battery acid, smell like gas and oil and soot, and run *toward* a fire, hoping to find refuge.

If Reuben lived through this, he'd take a serious look at the answer.

Behind him, he heard Pete yelling to CJ and Hannah. "We're not on a scenic hike! Move it!"

Around them, sparks lit the air, the roar of the fire rumbling in the distance.

*We should be running the other direction.* The thought had claws around his throat.

As if in confirmation, a coal-black cloud rolled down the road, directly from their safety zone, a billow of heat and gas.

Reuben stopped cold.

Jed's voice burst through the radio, choppy, as if he might be running hard. "Pete. The fire's jumped the road. Head to the black *right now.*"

Except the black—their safety zone—was engulfed in smoke, embers, and enough trapped poisonous gases to suffocate them.

Reuben whirled around and Hannah nearly ran him over. He caught her arm. "Not that way!"

Pete ran up to him. He still held his Pulaski, his face blackened behind his handkerchief, eyes wide, breathing too hard. "We're trapped."

Reuben stifled a word of frustration.

He knew it—he should have said something. But again, he'd kept his mouth shut, and people—*his* people—would die.

He glanced at Pete who was staring down the road, at the flames behind him. Pete shot a look at Reuben and nodded.

The past would not repeat itself today.

Reuben toggled his radio, searched the sky. "Gilly? You up there?"

*Please.* He might not be able to talk to her face-to-face in the open room of the Ember Hotline Saloon and Grill, but that wasn't a matter of life and death.

"Priest, Marshall. I'm here. Starting my last run right now—"

"Belay that. We're making a dash for the lake and we need you to lay down retardant along the forest road. We're about one click out, but the fire jumped the road a quarter mile in."

Static. Then, "Roger that, Rube. I'll find you. Start running."

Pete had taken off with CJ, running along the still-green fire road toward the lake, some five hundred yards away.

"You miss this, we're trapped, Gilly." Reuben started running, still holding his saw.

More static, and probably he shouldn't have said that because Hannah, jogging beside him, looked at him, her eyes wide.

He didn't want to scare her, but they couldn't exactly run through a forest engulfed in flame. If Gilly could drop water or retardant on the road, it might settle the fire down enough for them to break through, all the way to the lake.

The fire chased them, crowning through the trees, sending limbs airborne, felling trees. Sparks swirled in the air, so hot he thought his lungs might burst.

A black spruce exploded just to his right and with it, a tree arched, thundered to the ground, blocking the road.

Flames ran up the trunk, out to the shaggy arms, igniting the forest on the other side.

Hannah screamed, jerked back just in time.

Pete and CJ had cleared the tree. The flames rippled across it onto the other side of the road, into the forest, a river of fire.

"We're trapped!" Hannah screamed.

Reuben grabbed his backpack of water and began to douse the fire, working his way to the trunk. "C'mon Hannah—let's kill this thing!"

She unhooked her line, added water to the flames. The fire died around the middle, the rest of the tree still burning.

Reuben grabbed his saw, dove into the trunk.

Sweat beaded down his back, his body straining as he bore down—*faster!* He could do this—he'd once won a chainsaw competition by sawing through a log the size of a tire in less than a minute.

The saw chewed through the wood, cleared the bottom.

He started another cut, a shoulder-width away, from the bottom. "More water, Hannah!" The flames flashed up toward him.

He turned his face away, let out a yell against the heat. Then hot, blessed water sprinkled his skin as Hannah used the rest of her water to bank the flames.

The saw churned against a branch. "Use my water!"

She grabbed his hose, leveled it on the fire biting at the

branches, the bark.

The fire had doubled back along the top, relit the branches around him. He gritted his teeth, standing in the furnace, fighting the saw.

*Don't get stuck.*

He broke free, the wood parting like butter.

The stump fell to the ground, an escape through the trunk. Reuben grabbed Hannah and pushed her through, commandeering the hose and dousing the flames with the last of his water.

Pete and CJ, on the other side, had banked the flames with the last water in their canisters.

Ahead of them, the fire edged the road—beyond, a wall of flame barred their escape.

Reuben dropped his saw. "We can't deploy here. We'll die."

He looked up into the sky, saw nothing but gray, hazy smoke.

He scooped his radio from his belt. "Gilly, where are you?"

Nothing. He looked at Pete with eyes blurry from smoke and ash. Hannah was working out her shake-and-bake fire shelter—he didn't have the heart to repeat himself. CJ had run ahead, as if looking for a way out.

They had a minute—or less—to live.

"Gilly," he said into the walkie, not sure if she could hear him. His voice emerged strangely distant, vacant.

Void of the screaming going on inside his head.

"If you don't drop right now, we die."

Her first day officially flying bomber planes just might be her last.

"Tanker Five-Three, and I'm talking to you, Gilly, abort. I say again, abort. Alter course northward and climb. The wind gusts are too strong."

The voice came through the radio—their lead plane pilot, Neil "Beck" Beckett—and he sounded just on the edge of furious.

If she could, Gilly would shut the radio off. Having their lead plane pilot Beck bellowing in her headphones did nothing for her focus as she held her course into the canyon, her flaps extended, aiming directly for the road.

Nobody died today. Not if she could rescue them.

Best case scenario, air command grounded her. But if her smokejumpers survived, she'd gladly spend the rest of the summer turning a wrench and gassing tankers at the Ember Fire Base, home of the Jude County Wildland Firefighters.

Gilly toggled the radio switch. "No go, Lead Four. I'm already in the neighborhood."

"You're going to kill us," Jared, her co-pilot, snapped. "Just because you've been flying smokejumpers around for years doesn't mean you can handle a bomber."

"No, I'm not."

Except during the last pass she'd taken, searching for the road Reuben had frantically described, the super-heated wind roiling out of the canyon had nearly flipped the plane. She'd barely missed trees as she pitched the plane up, fighting the washboard turbulence that seemed strong enough to rattle the teeth from her mouth.

When they hit the blue sky, her heart restarted.

Now, as she banked, headed around for another run, Jared used a word her pastor father wouldn't approve of and actually made a grab for the controls. "You've got to be kidding me!"

"Those are my jumpers down there."

"You know these wings could rip right off—I've seen it happen. This old Russian Annie is a tin can of rivets and patches. If we go down there again, we die."

"If we don't, our friends die," she said, her voice tight. "We've already had too many close calls this summer." She didn't bring up the tragedy from last fall, the one that killed seven smokejumpers.

The price of living in a wildland firefighting town—you grew up with and knew the people who put their lives on the line. Friends who died gruesome, horrific deaths when the flames trapped them.

She might not be a smokejumper, but it didn't mean she wasn't down there with her team. She'd dropped them off— and she planned on getting them all back in one piece.

"Stop and think for a second before you get us killed!" Jared snarled, finally fighting on her team to control the plane as it bucked and kicked its way into the canyon. "What are you trying to prove?"

That was a question for a different day. But even if she hadn't made it as a jumper, she did possess one talent that might keep her friends alive.

She wasn't afraid to fly into what felt like hell to save the people she loved.

"I'm going to bring us along the edge, then bank right, use the left rudder and slide slip down into the canyon. That way we'll avoid the gusts coming from the center of the fire. Then I'll bank hard again and release the load, roll right, and we'll fly out back over the ridge. Okay?"

She didn't look at Jared, her gaze instead on the fifty-plus-foot trees near the summit of the ridge. They crowned with brilliant red flame, the fire most definitely having jumped the service road.

Heat enveloped the plane, the smoke black, blinding. The controls of the old Russian tanker shimmied in her grip as she forced the plane through the ridgeline updrafts. Jared's words flashed in her brain. She'd seen bombers—especially the old DC-6s—come apart under the violent gusts of a fire, and Jared was right. The forty-year-old plane had seen better years.

The world's largest single-engine biplane, the Annie was made to survive in the Siberian wilderness. But it was all they had, and frankly, she would have flapped her arms carrying a bucket of water if it meant saving lives.

"Gilly, clearly you're not listening." Beck snapped over the radio. "But you're flying blind up there. Let me help you—I'll tell you when to release."

She found his little lead plane, an OV-10 Bronco, off her right side. She could nearly make him out in the observation canopy, probably glaring at her.

"Roger, but we need it right in the pocket, Beck."

She glanced at her airspeed—one hundred forty-five knots. Slow enough to spread out her drop, make it effective enough for Reuben and the team to escape, but hopefully fast enough for the kinetic energy to affect her lift and bank.

But it wouldn't work at all, however, if she lost a wing.

*Please, God.*

She wasn't ashamed to pray for help, especially when it meant saving others.

"Ready, Jared?" He'd better have his hand on the red release button.

She spotted the road, downslope three hundred yards

ahead. Flames engulfed it, and a fist hit her gut as she nudged the rudder left. The plane slid down the ridgeline—too fast, perhaps—but she suddenly leveled out and aimed for the road.

A washboard of air currents jolted hard, ramming them against their restraints, tightened down so hard she might have the seat folds imprinted in her bones.

Her stomach rose to her throat, filled it with bile. *C'mon ,Annie, hold together.* The air inside the cockpit reeked of campfire, burning resin, and oils.

From the air, the breadth of the fire could turn her weak. As she flew along the edge of the ridge, flame and ash, gray and black smoke billowed into the blue sky now bruised with the fading sun. Below in the canyon, a pit of ashes glowed red, as if the land had been raked by the breath of a dragon. It cast an eerie aura into the twilight.

And into that furnace ran her people.

Gilly glanced at her instruments.

"You're nearly there, Five-Three—" Beck's voice, steady in her ear.

"Ten seconds, Jared," she said, her eyes on the road, the finest parting of forest before smoke obscured it.

*Please, God, let her hit this right.*

She counted down, then, "Now!"

Her words echoed Beck's, and Jared thumbed the drop switch.

The AN-2 released her load onto the forest. A plume of white smoke rose, engulfing them, and the windscreen turned white.

Jared let out a word, that yes, put a fine point on the fact they could be aiming straight for a mountain ridge and not know it.

"Help me with the yoke!" Gilly pulsed it back as she goosed the throttle.

The heated air shuddered the plane, the updrafts throwing it into a roll. The airplane shook with such violence, she couldn't make out the instruments. She banked hard, flying blind while her plane rattled apart around her.

"Five-Three, I've lost you!" Beck's voice.

Gilly fought to hold her bank into the blue, but the wind currents raked the plane, the airframe whining.

"She's coming apart!"

With a shriek, the metal twisted. The aircraft recoiled in the air, as if jolted.

"We hit something!"

Maybe. Whatever happened, they'd lost lift on the right side, the plane pitching over. She rolled the yoke to counter, her brain fighting through checklists to keep them airborne. "Check the wing!"

Jared stared out the window. "It's the lower right wing— it's partially sheared off and dangling!"

Which meant, with the weight and drag, the entire wing might detach.

"METO power on—all the way, Jared! We need to get out of this chop." Probably he'd already turned the "maximum except takeoff" setting on full.

Her arms ached with the tension of holding the plane out of the roll. They burst out into a patch of blue, and for a second she got a good look at their tragedy. The lower right wing of the biplane lay in shreds, probably caught on one of the flaming lodgepole pines at the top of the ridge.

They didn't have enough lift to keep climbing out of the canyon.

But they might make the lake. Over the ridge and back into the canyon, she could practically cut the engine and glide them in.

With the plane on floats, she could save the plane.

"We're setting her down in Fountain Lake."

"What? You're crazy, Gilly Priest. On a bright sunny day, maybe, with the wind at our back. But you're already fighting to stay at altitude. We'll never make it over the ridge."

"We're going down the other side, through the—"

"Don't say fire."

She looked at him. A three-year veteran, Jared was used to flying bigger planes, like the Lockheed Hercules 130, the kind that dropped slurry from higher altitudes with double engines and multiple loads, so if they didn't get it right the first time...

But Gilly preferred the smaller, more aerodynamic planes like her Otter, which she used for dropping off her jumpers.

"We can do this," she said.

"Have you lost your mind? Even if we survive another run into the canyon without busting apart, the sun is nearly down—there's no way you'll be able to judge the distance to land on the water. Please stop trying to kill us!" Jared unstrapped himself.

"What are you doing?"

"I'm jumping. There's a reason we have chutes—"

"We're not jumping." She said it quietly, her decision made years ago. Besides, she wasn't ditching her plane—not when she'd worked so hard to finally be more than a glorified taxi driver. Sure, the Jude County Smokejumpers considered her a part of the smokejumping team, but they all knew— even if they didn't say it—that she *wasn't* one of them. Not brave enough, not strong enough, and certainly not risking her life with them.

But now that she had her rating as a bomber pilot, she could support them from the sky. Be a real teammate, finally.

And she certainly wasn't going to crash on day one.

Jared had found the chutes. "C'mon. We're going." He stormed back up to the cockpit. "Now."

"No!" Her arms burned, her eyes watering from the smoke that wheedled its way into the cockpit. "I'm not jumping." Better to say, she *couldn't* jump, but she didn't have time for that now. "If you want to jump you can, but I'm staying here."

The ridge approached, flames licking along the top. "But you'd better do it now, before we're over the fire again."

"Bomber Five-Three, suggest you bail." Beck's voice came through the line. "You're losing altitude; you're drifting back over the fire."

Silence as she fought the wind currents.

"Now or never!" Jared snapped. "Let's go!"

Frankly, she could use Jared's help on the yoke to keep the plane from rolling, or worse, stalling and pancaking them right onto the side of the ridge.

But she wasn't going to beg for help. That's the last thing she needed—if they survived—a reputation for not being able to handle the plane on her own.

Jared threw down the chutes with another dark word and slid into the copilot seat. "Fine. This better work."

She angled them back over the ridge, into the smoke, but she had a bead on the lake, rippling crimson and burnt orange under the setting sun and the glow of the flames. "I can get us there."

"I'm never flying with you again." Jared had strapped

himself in again, his voice tight.

She didn't want to cheer, but...

Their airspeed barely held at one forty-five, the canyon floor rising, a bed of embers. Flares shot into the sky, igniting the smoky horizon.

*Please, God—let the jumpers have gotten to the lake.*

She knew Reuben—at least what he let them all know of him—and the panic in his voice over the radio just before she dropped her tank shook her.

Not prone to emotion, Reuben, if anyone, could get the team to safety. Something about him exuded strength. Power. And it wasn't just his size. Yes, as sawyer for the team, he had the girth of one of those bulls he rode off-season, was probably six foot two, had ropy, wide shoulders, and a solid pack of muscles from carrying his chainsaw around the forest. But he also had a quiet, get-'er-done spirit about him.

If only she didn't have the kind of baggage that kept her at arm's length from men, especially big ones like Rube, they might be friends.

She knew better than to get tangled up with a smoke-jumper. Not only that, but aside from the occasional thank-you when she let him sit in the copilot seat, she barely registered on his radar.

What did she expect? She certainly wasn't the kind of girl who attracted male attention.

Anymore.

They were close enough to the falling edge of the ridge to watch the candling effect—flames climbing up eighty-foot lodgepole pines only to burst into flame at the crown, the fire leaping from tree-top to tree-top.

"You'd better call in the emergency, tell them we're putting down into the lake."

"Roger." Jared snapped.

The plane sank lower as she throttled forward, listening to him call in their sit rep. She dropped them toward the lake, the plane washboarding over the air currents, her arm aching with the jarring.

The fire had now consumed any remnant of the road, a storm of flame below.

Jared finished calling in their position.

Beck came on the line. "Your entire lower wing is hanging by a thread. You lose that, you lose the plane."

"That's a helpful bit of advice," she said into her headset. "Jared, run the before-landing checklist."

They'd fallen to fifty feet above the tops of the trees, the flames shooting sparks against their windshield. The rutting of the plane could jackhammer her teeth from her skull.

No wonder her sisters had cornered her at the beginning of the summer, offered her, yet again, a position at their bakery.

She might choose making cupcakes over flying a rattle-trap Russian Annie over a sea of flames.

Or not.

Because as the plane cleared the edge of the forest, dropping toward the platinum-and orange-lit waters of Fountain Lake, she couldn't escape it—this feeling of triumph sluicing through her.

"Flaps thirty," Jared said, his tone biting.

"Flaps coming to thirty."

Gilly used all her remaining strength to keep the plane steady as they broke free of the fire's windstorm. The sudden change in pressure dropped them ten feet, and if she hadn't been strapped in, she might have hit the roof of the cockpit.

"Geez—flaps forty!" Jared yelled.

"Roger, forty."

Landing a plane on water required just a bit more finesse, the attitude of the plane sharper, the speeds lower, so as not to nose into the water. She throttled back to one-thirty, slowing as they drifted down.

In the encroaching darkness, she fought to gauge the distance to the surface. Choppy and white-capped, it would be a bumpy put-down.

*Please, Lord, don't let the wing catch before we hit the water.*

She nosed the aircraft up, fighting the drag of the plane, searching for something that might give her a reliable distance check.

"We're going to cartwheel!" Jared said. "I swear, if we live through this—"

"Shut up, Jared."

There—a streak of orange from the flames lit the dark water. She did a rough estimate, throttled back, nosed up.

She glanced at Jared. He sat in white-knuckled silence.

They hit the water with a jolt. Water sprayed against the window, off the floats of the plane. They bounced hard, skipped, and landed again. She kept forward pressure on the controls to stop the plane from bouncing along on the back of the floats.

The lower wing nicked the water, jerked the plane, and nearly nosed them down. Gilly kept the attitude up and righted them.

Still, as they settled into the water, the wing caught, whipping them around.

A wave pitched them up, threatened to flip them.

"Retract flaps!"

Jared braced his hand on the ceiling but somehow retracted the flaps. The plane slammed back onto the water.

Gilly cut the power, not wanting to encourage another near flip, her heart in the back of her throat.

"Lower water rudders."

The addition of the rudders stabilized them, and for a second they rode the waves, rocking in the water.

Then she simply tasted her adrenaline pooling in her chest, felt the hammering of her heartbeat in the purple light of the cabin.

Silence fell like a rock between them.

Only then did she realize she couldn't move her hands—stiff and hard, affixed to the yoke.

Finally, "I don't know whether to hate you or kiss you," Jared said.

Kiss her? Hardly, even if she couldn't exactly remember the last time she'd been kissed.

Oh, wait...yes she did.

"Keep your lips to yourself." She unwound her hands from the yoke, eased the burning from them, and looked over to shore.

Only then did she spot the group of smokejumpers silhouetted against the bright flame of the forest. A forest service boat had pulled up to shore, clearly on site to pluck them off the beach.

She did a quick count, then her gaze landed on a form standing slightly apart from the group. Tall, broad shouldered, he stood as a darkened, soot-covered sentry against the maelstrom of the fire. Even without his saw, and thirty feet away, she knew him, could feel the intensity of his gaze, the way he stared out over the waters at her.

Reuben Marshall.

And for the barest of seconds, everything dropped away—the fear roiling in her gut, the tension lining her shoulders, the deep, rooted ache of failure, desperation, and longing.

Leaving only a queer breath of peace, the slightest sense of right.

The unexpected stir of warmth in her chest.

Then Jared let out a long sigh, jarring her free. "Now what? Swim to shore?"

"No," she said, unstrapping herself. She opened the window, waved to the boat now turning its light to them. "We join our team and catch our ride home."

# CHAPTER 2

J UST WHEN A GIRL saved lives, she got benched. Or at least that's how it felt from Gilly's perch at the dispatch bench in the Ember Fire Base.

The weather map displayed satellite heat signatures with live updates of the dying fire, and the map on the wall pinpointed with tacks the current location of the deployed Jude County Hotshot teams, along with members of the Bitterroot, Lolo, and Flathead hotshot teams.

The wind had finally died, turned in their favor, and with a sortie of bombing runs, they'd managed to stop the fire just over the ridge, kicking it into submission.

Monday night's storm—not a drenching, but enough to slow the fire down—worked in their favor too. Now, with the teams doing mop-up, packing up their gear, and heading home, everyone hoped the fire season might be dying. With two weeks left before Labor Day, maybe they could end the season without any more flare-ups.

Which meant her flying season was over.

Gilly tried not to let that sink into her like a stone, tried not to glance over at the flight list hanging on the wall next to the hotshot dispatch list, again searching for her name.

Which wasn't there.

Thank you, oh, so much, Jared. Although, the man hadn't been back in the cockpit once since their put-down in Fountain Lake nearly a week ago, so maybe she'd rattled him more than she'd thought.

It couldn't have come as a surprise. Firebombing was one of the most dangerous professions within the firefighting community.

Still, she could admit to being unnerved when she'd gotten a good look at the damage to the Annie as they'd dragged the biplane from the lake, put her on a truck, and ferried her back to the base.

The lower right wing strut had completely blown apart, the wing hanging at a forty-five degree angle. With the wind chop and the heat, Gilly knew that a hotshot team of angels had kept them aloft.

Something her father—the Reverend John Priest—suggested in Sunday's sermon about the difference between living dangerously and living dangerously for the Lord. Got it, Dad. She didn't have to dig deep to find the thinly veiled reproach.

Except, she'd had everything under control. *Really.*

Although, she had appreciated God showing up to lend a hand to the rescue.

"The Lolo team is hiking out for pickup," Miles Defoe said now, running operations from the Ember office. "Let me know when they connect with their buggies. Then you can take off." The incident commander had met them on the tarmac when the plane came in. Had given her a thin-lipped look and shook his head.

Even Patrick Browning, their mechanic, was speechless as he inspected the damage. His family ranched a piece of land to the north—protected a herd of buffalo on their property, which he often surveyed with his own Cessna. The fact he worked for the Forest Service on an on-call basis even after the death of his son last year showed a commitment to saving lives despite the brutal reminder of all he'd lost.

She well remembered Tom Browning, a few years younger than she was, too young and brave to die. It was guys like Tom that made Gilly drop into the canyon. Guys like Tom... and Reuben.

Which brought her, for a second, right back to that enigmatic look he'd given her across the lake. She hadn't exactly been close enough to see it as much as *feel* it.

Gratitude?

Respect?

She didn't care that they'd grounded her. Because her jumpers were safe. For now, maybe even for the rest of the summer.

Sadly, that meant she would be relegated to the machine shop for the winter. Or worse...

Roped into making cupcakes. Her gaze fell on the large bakery box of chocolate cupcakes decorated with the Ember Fire base emblem, sent over by the Hot Cakes Bakery.

She just wanted to roll her eyes.

How embarrassing to have her sisters involved in something that made them look like stereotypical women... Soft, sweet, and silly.

She would never, *ever* be one of those girls who swooned in a man's arms and let him carry her off into the sunset.

She could carry herself into the sunset, thanks.

"Dispatch, Lolo One here. Our pickup has arrived." The radio lit up, and Gilly confirmed their position, updated the map, and surrendered her chair for the evening shift.

She grabbed her shoulder bag and headed outside into the balmy late afternoon, the smell of pine and loam in the air, roused by last night's rain.

They could use a lot more of it. The hills around Ember still bore evidence of the parched summer, the pastures brown, the trees dark and dry, some turning to bronze. They'd fought over a dozen fires just in the upper northwest alone—a few that the National Interagency Fire Center out of Boise suggested might be arson.

They'd nearly arrested Conner Young, one of the Jude County Smokejumpers, as a suspect. As if. The thought of one of their own—or *anyone* who knew firsthand how a fire could kill a person, their lungs boiling, their skin peeling off, or worse, literally roasting to death under their fire shelter—deliberately setting a fire, destroying a forest, wildlife, and threatening lives was—

Well, simply unthinkable.

Thankfully, it seemed they weren't being chased by an arsonist anymore. Conner had been exonerated when the NIFC determined that he hadn't been responsible for any possible blazes caused by his experimental firefighting drones. And then the so-called arsonist had vanished.

They didn't need an arsonist around to increase the risk to their lives.

Gilly headed for her car, the classic red Mustang with the brown ragtop, shiny under the sun like a beacon of joy in the parking lot. So what that she spent more time fine-tuning it than she should—at least it was dependable. And a sweet ride with the top down on a sunny summer day.

A girl who'd spent most of her high school years restoring a car would never spend her life baking cupcakes.

She opened the door, tossed in her satchel, then walked to the hangar.

The massive garage door stood open, an old Douglas

DC-6 in for a repair on the left outboard engine. A red Snap-on tool chest was rolled up under the wing, a ladder extending to the double wasp, radial engine.

She only saw the gray coveralls of the mechanic and took a guess. "Patrick?"

"Sorry, Gil." Hudson Rich, one of their full-timers, leaned down from his perch. "Patrick finished up the airframe on the Annie and took off for the weekend, the lucky dog."

"He finished repairing the wing?"

"Worked all week on it." He gestured to the plane parked outside the hangar, beyond the lot. "It's been inspected—no test run yet—but he patched up the wing, remounted the struts, and riveted her back together. He did a good job."

"Of course." She waved at him and headed outside to where the Annie sat in the shadow of the giant hangar. Fresh rivets banded the new main strut with the bracing wires also taut and re-attached. The wing looked reconstructed, patched, although still not painted, the metal bare and shiny in the fading sun.

Gilly ran her hand over the wing. "Good job, Annie. Thanks for holding together." And for a second, she was back in the sky, feeling the world shake apart.

She shook her head. Nope. She wasn't the kind to go back, relive her near misses. If she did, she'd probably end up on the ground in the fetal position.

"Gilly!"

The voice made her turn, and she spotted Kate waving to her from the back of Jed's motorcycle, her hand on Jed's shoulder.

Jed and Kate's budding romance had roared to full flame over the summer, and Jed had put a ring on her best friend's finger a couple of weeks ago.

Gilly tried not to be jealous—but it must be nice to trust someone enough…

No. She certainly didn't need a man to wrap her arms around or lay her head against his chest and sway to music on the dance floor.

She didn't *need* a man at all.

Gilly lifted her hand to Kate and walked over to her red-headed friend. Kate wore jeans, a flannel shirt tied around her waist, a Jude County Smokejumpers gray T-shirt. She had probably spent the day in the ready room repairing chutes, packing supplies, refolding packs. After a fire entrapment at the beginning of the summer, she went part-time as a jumper and spent most of her time as a fire behavior analyst, jumping only when the roster was slim.

Jed was always calling the team in for more training, assessing fire scenarios. Gilly guessed he had probably spent the day going over their plan of attack on the Fountain Lake fire, trying to figure out how to keep them out of situations that nearly cost them lives. Now, he sat on the bike, his dark hair cordoned back with a baseball cap, his eyes hidden by a pair of aviator sunglasses.

"Hey, Gilly," he said.

"What's up?" Gilly asked.

"We're headed over to the saloon to catch the Ember End-of-Season Roundup semifinals." Kate answered. "Reuben's riding a bull, and I think CJ's doing some roping."

"Just because we live in Montana doesn't mean we're all cowboys. What is it with those two? They spend a week busting their backs fighting fire and the weekend getting them broken on wild animals?"

Jed hiked his glasses down his nose. "We all decompress different ways. Rube's pretty good. You should check him out."

Kate waggled an eyebrow at her fiancé's words.

"Stop it."

"No, really, Gilly," Kate said. "Neither Jed nor I are blind. We see the way you look at Reuben."

"What—no, listen, I'm not interested in—"

"All that muscle wrestling, as you say, a wild animal?"

"All that *misplaced testosteron*e. I pull him out of a fire just to see him break his skull? I don't think so."

"Oh, so that's it. You don't want him getting hurt." Jed grinned.

"No—-I mean, yeah, but—listen." She swallowed, found her footing. "Reuben barely knows I'm alive. He's practically a caveman around me. And, we're teammates—sort of."

"Gilly. Reuben is just shy." Kate said. "Trust me, get him going, and he's got plenty to say."

"To you, maybe." Although she could admit that maybe he spoke more with action than words, given that look from him after the Fountain Lake fire.

The mystery behind it could still light an odd fire deep in her bones.

She felt the burn of a blush spread across her face.

Jed's face turned solemn. "Reuben is a great guy—a little tight-lipped, but he definitely knows you're alive, Gilly."

And what did he mean by that? But Jed, pushing his aviator's back up, added, "You *did* save his sorry hide."

Oh. Right. That made sense.

"Maybe it's time to celebrate that with your team, huh?" Kate asked.

And Kate, her best friend since childhood, knew just how to hook her.

She gave Kate a wry smile. "We'll see."

"That's a yes. I expect to see you there." Kate winked as she fitted on her helmet. Jed gunned them away.

Gilly cast another look at the AN2 then wandered back to her Mustang and headed home to her tiny bedroom in her parent's rambler next to the Ember Community Church.

The sun lay just over the horizon, a shimmering line of amber across the jagged western mountains.

Hopefully, she wouldn't stay grounded forever. Maybe Miles's memory would dim over the winter months.

She parked the Mustang on the basketball court and headed inside, the garlicky smell of a roast in the Crock-Pot filling the house. An old-fashioned woman, her mother produced dinner on the table every night at six p.m. and raised her daughters, well, two out of three of them, with the cooking and baking skills to feed an army of starving firefighters.

Of course her kid sisters, Juliet and Isobel, had taken those skills and parlayed them into a thriving business—a bakery that kept the entire town of Ember in cupcakes, muffins, and designer wedding cakes.

If only they might have picked a different name, Gilly might be willing to occasionally take them up on their prodding to swoop in and help.

*Hot Cakes.* The last thing she wanted to be known as was "one of the girls down at Hot Cakes."

No, thank you. She already had enough trouble keeping up her reputation as a fearless pilot, thanks to her less-than-fierce frame. Sort of like Mighty Mouse behind the controls.

She headed downstairs to her basement bedroom and shut the door.

"Gills—open up." Juliet tapped on the door.

Gilly opened it a crack. "What?"

It simply wasn't fair that her sisters nabbed all the good looks. Especially Juliet, with her curves, her long brown hair, those big hazel-green eyes. Isobel was a near clone but with blonde hair, hazel-brown eyes, and just a little shorter. Juliet and Belle were beautiful, smart, and sweet—the perfect pastor's daughters, the kind men most wanted for wives.

The only reason Juliet, at age twenty-five, hadn't yet settled down was that she couldn't make up her mind which fella to choose. As for Belle, she'd inherited the same hard-work genes Gilly had and spent most of her time perfecting her cake-decorating skills.

"Let's go to the rodeo," Juliet said.

Really? If she wouldn't go to the rodeo with Jed and Kate, why would she even think of being seen there with Juliet, a walking magnet for male attention? Gilly opened the door the rest of the way and found her sister dressed in a patterned dress and a pair of black cowboy boots.

"Jules—" Gilly started.

"Aw, c'mon. I love rodeos. They're so...tough guy. Besides, I heard a couple of your smokejumper friends were competing." Her eyes glowed.

"My smokejumper friends? Juliet, you have a lineup of fresh hotshots every season. You don't need my help to meet my"—she finger-quoted the words—"smokejumper friends."

Juliet made a face. "Yeah, well, those hotshots aren't here to stay. Besides, when I tell them I'm the preacher's daughter, they run for the hills."

Gilly laughed, although that never seemed to slow down the firefighters she had known.

"Fine. But please don't embarrass me." Gilly moved away from the door and Juliet came in to sit on her bed. Gilly shed her JCWF T-shirt and green Nomex pants—her uniform for the day—and grabbed a pair of faded jeans.

"Wear a dress," Juliet said.

"What? Are you kidding?No." Gilly jerked on the jeans. Oh, what she wouldn't give for just a few of Juliet's curves. "I don't do dresses."

"C'mon. Just because you run in a guy-dominated world doesn't mean you're a guy." Juliet got up and went to Gilly's closet, raked through it. Sighed. "I'll be right back."

Juliet exited and Gilly was left to stare in the mirror at her reflection. She'd never been the type to go in for the girly stuff—okay, well, once, a very long, ancient history time ago, she might have been the epitome of the word girl. A ballerina. But that all had changed one dark summer night.

Fast.

Forever.

And there was no going back. So she was left with this—a sunburned face that outlined white raccoon eyes from her aviator glasses, freckles across her tiny nose, unexciting lips, dark auburn hair that never cooperated, hence always the ponytail, and a body that felt most comfortable in a bomber jacket, jeans, and a baseball cap.

There was a reason she didn't work for Hot Cakes, besides her pride. She simply wouldn't fit in.

"Ta-dah!" Juliet returned, holding a dress, light blue with a lacy top and hem. "I bought it a few years ago, but it doesn't fit me, and I was thinking..."

"What? No—are you kidding me? So—"

"Girly? Yep." Juliet held it up to Gilly. "And if you think you'll get cold, you can just add a denim shirt over it, tie it around your waist."

"I'm not worried about getting cold, Jules—I need the shirt for modesty! This dress barely covers my backside."

"That's not true. Hold up your arms."

Gilly frowned at her but obeyed. Juliet dropped the dress over her. Billowy and soft, it accentuated her thin, muscular legs and distracted from the fact she didn't have much in the back *to* cover up. "Now, we'll put up your hair, add some boots, and you'll be adorbs." Jules winked at her. "Maybe catch the eye of one of your jumper pals."

"That's what this is about—I don't need to catch the eye—"

"Stop it. Don't tell me you haven't noticed any of the cute guys on your squad."

"They're *teammates*, Juliet." She made to pull off the dress, but her sister grabbed her hand. Gilly surrendered. "Fine. But no—I haven't noticed any of them." She opened the door, walked down to the bathroom, grabbed a brush for her out-of-control hair.

Except. Well. But the last thing she'd do is fling her heart out for some man to trample on.

Or more.

Besides, Reuben was just so…well, she'd have to stand on a bench to kiss him. And how that thought drifted in, she didn't know, but…okay, yes, it wasn't exactly random, or rare.

She'd wondered more than once what it might feel like to be swept up in those massive arms, to know the quiet man who often ended up in the copilot's seat, fighting his sensitive stomach during a flight.

And she found it *oh-so* interesting that he hadn't dated one—not *one*—girl since arriving on base seven years ago.

Seven years was a long dry spell.

Oh, for cryin' out loud.

She ran the brush through her hair, and Juliet appeared to put it up in a messy bun. She handed Gilly some mascara and lipstick, and soon Gilly was in over her head.

"We're taking your Mustang," Juliet said.

Reuben just needed a way to burn the frustration away. To jolt free of the residual hum of fear, the panic that gripped him around the throat when he thought of their run to freedom.

Regret did that—lived deep in his gut, an ember, smoldering.

He needed something bigger than himself—a fifteen-hundred-pound black-and-white Plumer bull named Custer, a beast with so much mean in his eyes he didn't need the horns to make a man's gut roil. But he had them—cut off on the ends, just in case—and tonight he'd already tried to tear up everything that got near him—the horses, the stalls, the barrels.

Even the cowboy trying to ride him.

Reuben straddled the chute, breathing hard, trying to remember what he'd learned about this bull. Just a junior bull in the big world of PBR, this animal was known as a sunfish bucker—twisting up his belly, mid-kick. If Reuben managed to stay on longer than four seconds, the bull might settle into a spin. Throw Reuben off like a top.

Not tonight.

Reuben simmered with a restless energy, something dark and brooding lit by the fire, still seeing Hannah nearly perish as the wall of flame bore down on them. He could still smell the sizzle of flame in water, feel his boots on the superheated embers as he and Hannah ran down the road.

He still heard Hannah's scream as she fell, tasted his heart in his throat as he grabbed her by the scruff of her jacket, boosted her up, dragged her into the open toward the cool water of Fountain Lake.

How they'd survived, he still couldn't work out, although he knew it had mostly to do with Gilly's miraculous rainstorm of rescue as he'd run toward the wall of flames.

He'd never been a fast man—not even in football. Well, a lineman didn't actually have to be fast, just sturdy. But he ran like he could have gone to state, his regret—no, his *stupidity*—ringing in his ears like the brutal wind.

Why hadn't he stopped Pete earlier, listened to his gut, told them to head the other direction? They would have cleared the fire before it jumped the road.

And then he wouldn't be waking from his sleep, nightmares piling one over another.

First his dad, then Jock, and now this.

And all were his fault for not speaking up, for letting someone else make the decisions.

Not tonight. Tonight he was in charge. Tonight he would do what he did best—tighten down his grip, hold on, be the master of his fate.

Reuben settled himself on the bull and worked his gloved hand into the bull rope, the bell beneath the animal's chest ringing. He worked his fist into the rope, pounded his fingers down, closed.

Already his muscles burned, adrenaline rippling through him.

Custer snorted, slammed against the back of the chute.

"You sure, Rube?" This from CJ, his gate man perched on the rail, holding the nylon rope to swing the door open. CJ shed his smokejumper attire for a good-ole cowboy aura, including a Stetson and faded jeans, cowboy boots. He wore his dark blond hair short under that hat. "I'm not sure even my uncle would ride this one."

CJ's Uncle Rafe, multi-PBR champion, now a high-faultin' bull-riding trainer. "I doubt that, kid."

"No seriously—he had this bull that tried to kill him—"

CJ stopped talking when Reuben shot him a look.

He breathed out, centering himself. Then, just before lifting his hand, he looked out into the crowd.

The bleachers were full for tonight's semifinals. Just local entertainment, but if he landed enough points here, he could move on to something bigger—like a junior PBR event.

Reuben scanned the crowd—usually some of the team showed up to the events. Conner, maybe. Or Jed.

Or—his heart slammed into his sternum, full halt.

Gilly. Wearing a—*no.* That couldn't be.

A dress. Cut above her knees, girly and sweet and pretty.

She was standing up, her hand over her eyes against the setting sun, her hair turning to a dark sizzle under the twilight, scanning the cowboys in the gate.

For a second he was standing on the shore, watching her land in her broken airplane. Watching her as she stared out the window like she might actually be looking...for him.

It took the breath from his chest.

Below him, Custer shifted, his muscles bunched.

Reuben ripped his gaze off Gilly, to CJ.

"Ready, Rube?"

He breathed in, tried to right himself, found his center.

*This one, Gilly, is for you.*

He lifted his arm.

"Pull!"

CJ yanked open the chute and the crowd erupted.

First move out of the chute, Custer reared—and Rube expected it. He pushed himself up over the bull's shoulders, gripping the length of the bull's body with his legs.

Custer landed hard, and Reuben jerked onto the backbone, glued to the animal.

He was a big man, yes, but he had nothing on fifteen hundred pounds. Custer threw himself up, rearing again, then landed in a spin.

For Reuben, time slowed, narrowed, focused, one thrilling, terrifying millisecond after the next. Holding on, breathing, anticipating, doing.

That's what he loved about bull riding. As dangerous and jarring as smokejumping, bull riding pared every action down to one.

Stay on the bull.

No thinking, no choices. Everything by instinct, ground in by training. He didn't have to rely on chance, on favor. Just his strength against the bull's.

He heard the roar of the crowd, thunderous in his ears, then the horn blared.

Eight seconds.

Eight seconds to lose the fire inside, to break free of the fist of regrets. Failures.

Grief.

Eight seconds to remind himself of who he was, who he'd become. Maybe even be proud of himself.

He released his hand.

Launched himself off the bull.

He took a breath, cauterized, even cleansed as he landed, then scrambled through the dirt while the clowns caught the bull.

Then he jumped onto the rail and raised his hat to the crowd, breathing hard.

He spotted Gilly. She was on her feet, cheering, whistling.

For him.

He couldn't swallow, his heart hammering as he hopped over the rail into the corral area, waiting for his score.

Pete met him there. "Are you kidding me? That was fantastic!" Pete, with his long surfer blond hair and charmer blue eyes hadn't a smidgen of cowboy in him. He spent his off days in epic sports that were probably every bit as dangerous as bull riding. BASE jumping, free-climbing, even white-water rafting.

Still, Pete understood the rush of adrenaline after a challenge. Probably had his own residual hum to work off after this week.

They announced Reuben's score, and it landed him at the top of the leaderboard. He hopped the rail, waving his hat again.

He wanted to look for Gilly, but didn't know what he'd do if she were looking back at him, so he simply scanned the crowd.

He must have worn a sort of dazed expression because Pete gave him a strange look as Reuben took off his hat, rubbed the inside sweat rim.

"You okay, dude?"

"Did you see Gilly?"

He didn't know why he asked that—wanted to take it back when Pete glanced over his shoulder, scanned the crowd. Gave a whistle of appreciation.

"You mean Legs McGee over there in a blue dress? As Conner, our former green beret would say, *hooah* and it's about time."

"Okay, Romeo, that's enough," Reuben said, but found her too, now that the crowd was focused on the next rider.

She wore her hair in a soft, messy bun, sipped a fountain drink from the Hotline, cheered for the rider who went down in the dirt.

"Reuben—when are you going to ask her out?" Pete moved over to the rail, one foot on the bottom rung.

"What—no. I can't...she wouldn't..."

And now Pete was looking at him, a quick glance of confusion.

"Listen," Reuben said. "I've known Gilly since, well since I moved here seven years ago, when I was a greenie hotshot. She's not interested in firefighters—and especially not me. We're just coworkers. Trust me, there's no spark there on her side. Besides, her dad's a preacher, for cryin' out loud. And I'm not exactly a saint."

"Aw, c'mon, Rube. When's the last time you went out with a girl—seriously. The dawn of time?"

Reuben watched as the next bull rider settled into the chute. "What are you, my matchmaker? I promise, I'm no monk. I'm just not—it wouldn't work. We're all over the place in the summer. It's not the right time to start a relationship."

"Dude—you don't need to *start a relationship*. Just take a girl for a whirl on the dance floor."

Reuben's mouth closed, tightened. He looked away. "I'm not you, Pete. I don't know how to... I'm no Casanova."

Pete laughed, shook his head. "I'm not either. I'm just not afraid to ask a woman to dance. Go—talk to her. What could it hurt?"

What could it hurt? How about him doing something stupid? He wasn't like the other guys, especially Pete, or Jed. He couldn't make a girl fall into his arms with a smile. More often, Reuben turned into a monosyllabic oaf next to the cute ones.

Cute *one*.

*Small* and cute, and for a second he had an image of trying to pull Gilly into his arms, inadvertently crushing her. She stood a good eight inches shorter than he was, and he felt like a buffalo next to her. Worse, with those big blue eyes and beautiful dark auburn hair, he sort of forgot his own name when she walked into the room. Which meant he was bound to do something stupid, trip over himself, say something idiotic.

Hurt her.

Besides, even their meager teammate friendship meant enough to him to not want to screw it up.

They *were* friends—proven by the fact that she often let him sit copilot just to soothe the angry bear of his temperamental gut. She didn't betray him to Jed, or even Miles.

Not to mention that she held his life in her hands every time they went out on a jump—and most recently saved his hide from being barbecued.

So, yeah, someday he *might* scrape up the courage to say something to her. But he wasn't crazy enough to ask her to dance.

Which meant that, after he'd gotten his score, unbuckled his chaps, and headed into the Hotline for a cool drink, words left him when Gilly came sauntering into the saloon and grill with her sister, the way too vivacious Juliet.

Juliet could drive a man crazy with her cheery flirting. But for some reason, half the guys on the crew every summer fell for her smile, lining up to buy her a basket of O-rings, or even some filling the church pew on Sundays so they could walk her home later.

Nope. Reuben preferred a woman like Gilly, who didn't need to flirt to have a man appreciate her smile, and—*whoa*, she had legs. Pete was right—Legs McGee.

Tan, muscular, beautiful legs shifting under that dress, tucked into cowboy boots.

And there went his brain, turning to mush.

He tore his gaze off her form as she walked in, down to the bar and stared into his half-empty beer.

The Hotline, the local hangout, buzzed with the stories of the season. Jude County hotshots released from shift were filtering in, settling in at the yellow picnic tables in the center of the room, waitresses delivering craft beers, baskets of curly fries, fresh grilled burgers. Pictures of past teams were rearranged to make room for this year's crews.

On the dance floor, a band was setting up.

"Hey—can I ask you a favor?" The voice turned him and he smiled at Conner, sauntering over to him, holding his own frothy beer. "I'm going to head down to Kalispell this weekend, and I was hoping we could switch shifts. You could cover my shift coming up, I could take yours next week." The former Green Beret wore a smile, wiping the froth from his upper lip.

His girlfriend, Liza, had survived a bear mauling only two weeks earlier and was still in rehab in Kalispell hospital.

"Of course," Reuben said. "Except I was counting on my shift getting me out of having to go down to the ranch for Labor Day weekend. My mom is hounding me."

"I love your mom," Jed said from where he shot darts with Kate. "She makes the best chocolate chip cookies."

"That's what happens when you have five sons and two daughters," Reuben said, wishing he could avoid the twinge of grief every time he thought of his family working the ranch without him.

But there was no room for him there, not anymore. His father had made that clear even before his sudden death.

Besides, Reuben had been born to jump fire, not herd cattle.

Maybe.

"To a season without a casualty."

He looked up, and even Conner turned at the voice.

Juliet leaned on the bar, holding up a lemonade. "This is the kind of summer we all like to see."

Reuben raised his glass, saw Gilly glance at him, give him a wry smile.

Heat filled his chest, his face, and he looked away.

"I think we should probably raise the glass to Gilly," said CJ, holding a pool stick. His fellow rookie, Tucker, appeared beside him, clearly his opponent.

"To Gilly," Jed said, and out of the corner of his eye, Reuben saw a blush press her face.

"I didn't do—"

"You nearly lost a wing and crashed into the lake. So, yeah, you did something."

The room quieted, and Reuben couldn't believe he'd spoken up, let alone the tone of his own voice. Almost, what—angry? But he wasn't angry—just so immensely relieved—and yes, there it was again, the frustration, along with a fresh realization that she had nearly gotten killed while saving his backside.

Because he'd let them run the wrong way.

So much for breaking free of his regrets.

"Yeah, okay, so again, to Gilly," said CJ.

CJ and Tucker returned to their game, Jed and Kate to

laughing over their darts. Conner pulled out his cell phone, moved away, thumbing a text.

Which left Juliet to sidle up to him.

Up close—or even far away and squinting—she cut a form a man might take a long, second look at. Another man. A different man. One who didn't mind the way she giggled, pressed her hand on his arm. "You were magnificent on that bull, Reuben. I couldn't believe it when you stayed on. And then just *jumped* off and waved to the crowd!"

She smiled at him, standing so close he could smell her perfume—which made him need to sneeze.

"And you should have seen the bull. Meanest one in the lot. Nearly took apart the chute." CJ, clearly lured over by Juliet's presence and, thank you, because Juliet turned to him.

"Juliet Priest," she said, holding out her hand. "And you are?"

Right then, as if on cue, the band started up with a song.

"CJ St. John." He took her hand, and Reuben rolled his eyes when the kid pressed a kiss on it. "Wanna dance?"

Of course she did.

Then it was just Gilly and Reuben at the bar , watching the couple work their way onto the dance floor.

For a second, she looked at Reuben.

Blue eyes, so beautiful that he just swallowed.

"Hey," he said, a sound that confirmed that, indeed, he was some throwback Neanderthal. He wanted to cut and run right then.

"Juliet was right. You were pretty amazing. Congratulations on winning."

"Thanks." More brilliance, but it was all he had. Worse, even sitting, he still loomed over her. Funny, she didn't seem that petite on the radio or in her NIFC uniform or her jumpsuit.

He ran a thumb down his glass, parting the condensation there. Thought of something. "You want a drink?"

"I can get it."

She began to raise her hand, but he held up his.

"Please—Gilly. You... Thanks for what you did. It was a big deal." He offered a smile, mostly because these words came easily, honestly. "What are you drinking?"

"Root beer. Preacher's kid and all that." She offered a smile, and he felt like the chiefest of sinners with his half-drunk beer.

He ordered her drink, and she slid onto a high-top chair next to him. At least he wasn't looking down at her.

She pulled the basket of popcorn toward herself, began to pick at it.

On the dance floor, the band played a Brad Paisley cover.

"They grounded you," Reuben said, almost a grunt.

The bartender brought her drink. She took a sip, and it left foam on her lip. She grabbed a napkin, wiped it off. Nodded.

"I'm sorry."

"It's okay. Miles will forgive me by next season."

"He competes in the rodeo circuit during the winter months. I'll talk to him—"

"No!" She held up her hand then made a fist, put it back into her lap. "I can take care of myself."

"I know, but—"

But what? He glanced out at the dance floor, seeing CJ with his arms around Juliet, slow dancing.

"It was my fault."

"What? Rube—you can't control the fire—"

"We should have run the other way. I knew it in my gut. Same as..." He winced. Shook his head. "Nothing."

She was staring at him. "You kept them all alive. I know. Hannah told me how you picked her up, practically carried her to safety."

"That's what I do—carry things." He meant it as a joke, but a frown crossed her face.

Then, however, she sighed, looked away. Gave a small chuckle. "Me too."

He didn't know what to say, and a silence filled in between them.

*You look pretty tonight.* The words crossed through him, hung on, and suddenly he couldn't think of anything else but that. Pretty. Tiny. Sweet.

He stared at his beer, hating that the words glued in his chest, clogging everything else.

This was why he didn't talk to women. Didn't talk to, well, Gilly.

"Reuben, man, get out here!"

CJ, calling him from the dance floor. Reuben looked at him, wanting to incinerate him where he stood. But the rookie wore a grin, two-stepping, of course, with Juliet. He twirled her in and out and back, dipping her.

Reuben glanced at Gilly, wishing he could read the expression on her face.

Shoot. What if she wanted to dance? And he just sat here, and...

"Gilly, ask *him* to dance!"

Now Juliet was in on it, waving at Gilly, who was turning white. She swallowed, clearly embarrassed.

He couldn't take it. Seeing Gilly sit there, waiting for him to actually cowboy up. "Gilly, do you wanna—"

"No, I'm fine." But it was the funny, half smile that appeared, then disappeared, that made his gut clench.

Did she want to...

And then she glanced at CJ and Juliet on the dance floor.

That's all it took. He was tired of standing in the middle, not following his gut.

And his gut said Gilly wanted to dance.

Tonight, regret wouldn't chase him home.

And they thought bull riding was tough. He took a breath. "Let's dance, Gilly. I promise not to step on your toes." He held out his hand, and when she only hesitated a moment before taking it, he congratulated himself on the best epic victory of the night.

She had a strong hand, despite her size, and she followed him around the tables to the dance floor.

The band had picked up a Josh Turner song, appropriately *Why Don't We Just Dance*, and he looked down at Gilly. "It's been a while, but my mama taught me how to two-step."

She nodded, a smile curving up her face. "I'm not much of a dancer."

"Just follow me." He took his first step.

Right onto her foot. "Sorry. Right foot, left foot, quick, quick, slow."

She came to about his chest, and so he held her back a little, just so he could find her eyes, and tried again. They sputtered around the sides of the dance floor, halting, starting again. His hands began to sweat.

She kept that pretty smile but glanced a couple times at Juliet twirling with CJ.

Oh, this was a bad idea.

*My two left feet, our two hearts beating...*

Reuben took a breath and tried to twirl her out. She bumped into another couple, and he pulled her back fast. "Sorry."

"We don't have to— "

"I can do better." He nearly barked it.

*Nice, Rube.* He glanced again at CJ and realized—the kid had no rhythm. Just a crazy desire to wiggle his body and twirl his girl.

Yes, Reuben could do *much* better. He moved them to the center of the floor, found the beat, and led them in a circle, landing the steps, quick, quick, slow. Quick, quick, slow.

Then he took her hand and twirled her out. Back in again.

She giggled—wow, really?—and he felt it in his chest, warmth, the slow unwinding of the coil of tension.

He led her out in a turn under his other arm then caught her in a cuddle hold.

She might be tiny, but she had moves, and she followed his lead as if anticipating him. Even looked up at him and grinned, her eyes shining.

And that's what did it. His heart skipped, his brain stopped, and he missed a step.

The next moment, he'd tripped over his own oxen feet, and in a flash of horror, felt his momentum shift.

The floor came up at him, Gilly trapped in his arms, and all he could think was to twist, to turn his back to the floor and hold onto her.

Cushion her as he crashed onto the dance floor.

Sort of.

He landed with his body curled around her, one leg under her, one on top of her, his arms crushing her to his chest. The dancers parted, gasps echoing into the chorus of the song.

Gilly lay tangled, her arms pinned against him, her leg under his, her face buried in his chest.

Struggling.

"Let me go."

He didn't hear her the first time—the chorus muffling her cries.

But he definitely heard her when she slammed her fist into his chest. "Reuben. Let. Me. *Go*!"

The music still played, but with her near shout, hands came down, lifted her away from him.

Rescuing her from his embrace.

He scooted back, trying to free her.

And then, he was just sitting alone on the floor. She had scrambled to her feet and now stared down at him.

He expected embarrassment, maybe anger.

Not the wide-eyed horror, the almost terrified expression that flushed her face.

Nor the sense that she wasn't staring at him, but *through* him, to a fixed point of pain that he'd managed to stir to the surface.

"Gilly—"

She turned and fled.

His only saving grace was that the music covered his sharp epitaph of frustration, freshly lit, a live coal in his chest.

# CHAPTER 3

GILLY NEEDED A FIRE to put out, and pronto.

And not the kind issuing from the industrial stainless steel oven in the Hot Cakes commercial kitchen, smoke a fine acrid wisp curling out as she tugged open the door.

"Are you kidding me?" Juliet nudged the back door closed with her hip, dropped her empty delivery tray on the stainless steel counter, and rushed over to survey the crispy, blackened chocolate-fudge-and-peanut-butter cupcakes. "Please tell me you haven't burned the shop to the ground!"

Gilly had grabbed a couple of industrial oven mitts and pulled the sizzling cakes from their tomb, searching for a place to set the sacrificial offering.

"Here—" Juliet made room on the counter, pushing aside a bowl of banana-nut muffin mix, another of lemon poppy seed.

Gilly set the muffin tin on the counter, shook off the gloves, and stepped back, fighting the very present urge to flee.

"What happened? I leave you for five minutes—"

"Fifteen. You were gone for *fifteen* at least, and—"

"Didn't you set the timer?"

Hmm. Maybe not. Gilly made a face at her sister. "I was

reading weather reports..."

"I don't want to hear it." Juliet shook her head. "Okay, I get that you don't want to help out today—"

"That's not it. I'm glad to help. Sweep. Do dishes. Even deliver. I just don't cook."

"Bake. This is *baking*. And all you had to do was put the batter in the tins, set the buzzer, and wait."

"There's a fire in Idaho and they've pulled in the Lolo and Sawtooth teams—"

"Stop talking!" Juliet held up her hand. "Listen—Belle will be back from setting up the cake in a couple hours, and then I don't care what you do. But I really needed you this morning. We don't have weddings very often, but with all the teams in town waiting for the next big flare-up, we can be sold out of muffins by nine."

Juliet walked over to the charred muffins, grabbed a hot pad, and dumped the lot into the garbage.

Sighed.

And Gilly wished, just for a second, for the fun Juliet, the one from last night who'd roped her into—well, even that had ended up a disaster, hadn't it?

"I'm sorry, Juliet."

Her sister wore a pink Hot Cakes Bakery apron, matching pink T-shirt, a pair of jeans, her brown hair up in a bun and hairnet—the same type of apron and hairnet she'd made Gilly wear.

Although Gilly's apron looked like a piece of modern art, smeared with flour, banana batter, and chocolate frosting.

Five hours was not enough sleep on her day off. *Someone* should have mentioned last night as Gilly drove them home in her Mustang the fact that spending the night reliving the debacle on the dance floor might interfere with today's mission.

Namely the mixing, baking, and decorating of twelve dozen designer cupcakes.

"I'm sorry, Juliet. I'm not cut out for this job." Gilly reached behind to untie her apron, but Juliet caught her arms.

She wore what Gilly might call desperation in her expression. "I need you. Just for a couple of hours. I'll finish mixing and baking—"

"And decorating."

"For sure." Juliet's smile tweaked up one side. "You load the cases."

"Done," Gilly said, glancing again at the fire report, a screen on her cell phone.

"For cryin' in the sink, Gilly. You don't have to put out every fire."

Gilly moved the tray of fresh peanut-butter-and-chocolate-fudge muffins to the front room.

Painted a faded pink, the room glowed with a princess touch, from the gold-leafed antique cash register to the hanging chandelier lights, to the old-fashioned cupcake case, the ornate scrollwork painted a crisp white. With white-painted metal French tables and chairs, and the words Hot Cakes Bakery stenciled into the wall in decadent chocolate brown, her sisters had clearly snubbed the prevalent fire theme that swept through the town of Ember: the Hotline Saloon and Grill, the Spotfire Diner. Even the local football team named, appropriately, the Flames.

Although occasionally, Gilly had the urge to point out the word Hot in their name.

Still, Juliet and Belle managed to create a business that now included mail-order desserts. Probably because they rose at four a.m. and worked like dogs. Or, perhaps, like firefighters.

Gilly returned to the back room. Juliet was filling a fresh tin with banana-nut batter. A smile quirked up her face, some private thought.

"What?"

"I was just thinking about the fire you so adeptly doused last night."

Gilly reached for the cherry-vanilla cupcakes, topped with red frosting and a white-chocolate heart. "What fire?"

Juliet slipped the tin into the oven, set the timer.

Oops, maybe Gilly *had* skipped that part...

Juliet turned, grinning. "The one sparking between you and that dark-haired hunk of a cowboy."

"Reuben?" Heat flushed Gilly's chest. Oh, she'd embarrassed him—evident by his expression as she screamed.

Why had she screamed?

It wasn't Reuben's fault he had resurrected her demons. That being trapped, even a little, beneath him had scoured up the nightmares. That she could think of nothing else but running from the Hotline in a full sprint. She knew how it looked—pitiful. Weak. And it only confirmed that dating—and especially *dancing* with—any of her teammates was not only awkward but turned her into someone in need of protection.

Which was exactly what she told Juliet after her sister had tracked her down, sitting in her Mustang, the engine revving.

"That was the stupidest move ever," she'd muttered, mostly to herself, but also to Juliet, referring to her bright idea of the blue dress. And, of course, the dancing part.

"No it wasn't. You two were cute." Juliet had slid into the passenger seat, glowing, it seemed, from her twirl around the floor with CJ. He had come out and waved at her, leaning against the door jamb as Gilly pulled away.

"I can't afford to be cute. The last thing I need is for Reuben—or any of the team, really—seeing me as some sort of, well, a *hot cake*, in need of rescue. They need to depend on me."

Juliet rolled her eyes. "Stop trying so hard to prove yourself. In fact, you could let someone rescue you once in a while." She'd looked at Gilly and winked.

No, no she couldn't. Wouldn't.

Even the memory of the fall turned her a little sick. Gilly escaped with the cupcakes to the front.

"Reuben?" Juliet mimicked loudly from the kitchen as she frosted cupcakes. "Oh, him?"

"Stop."

"Gills. I *know* you've had a little thing for him going on, oh—five years?"

Longer. Try seven, from the first time he'd shown up at fire camp, young and strong, refusing to quit. And frankly, the way he'd spoken up for her last night had made her feel, for a second, brave and invincible. Then he'd somehow turned her brain to oatmeal with those brown-as-dark-chocolate eyes, so much that she'd ended up on the dance floor...

And clearly the frosting was going to her head.

"I just admire him, that's all. He's a hard worker. And yeah, he has a tough side—"

Tough was an understatement. She couldn't breathe, watching him fight the bull last night, his thick, ropy arms straining to hang on, his torso lean and strong. The way he had leaped from the bull as if ready for another go-round.

She swallowed, found her voice. "Reuben is the man most likely to not give up, and I respect him for that."

"Respect. Right." Juliet looked up at her through the kitchen door, her eyes full of mischief.

"Stop. Listen. Here's what you don't know—and if you tell anyone, I'll personally drop you from a high altitude. Reuben suffers from just about the worst case of airsickness than anyone I've ever met. I discovered his secret after we aborted a jump—he nearly didn't wait until we landed, practically sprinted to a nearby trash can."

Poor guy had looked green and a few shades of yellow before he finished.

"Are you serious?" Juliet came to the door, leaned on it, arms folded.

Gilly continued to load cupcakes into the case. "Yeah. I let him sit in the copilot seat whenever it's empty. Less turbulence than the seat in back."

And admittedly, she kept doing it because of the quiet thank-you, the soft gaze in his eyes, the tiny tweak of a smile under his dark beard. The kind she wouldn't mind brushing her fingers—

"Gilly? Hello, talk about turbulence. I hope you're dreaming about Reuben and what might have happened if you hadn't gotten tangled up on the dance floor."

"Huh?" Gilly looked up. "No. I'm not—"

"I have ways of making you admit the truth." Juliet held up her frosting gun.

"No—I mean it. He isn't interested in me."

"Are you *kidding* me? Did you see the way he looked at you when you walked in? Poor guy had to scrape his chin off the floor."

Gilly froze, a red velvet cupcake in her hand. And see, that was why she didn't date. Because, while Juliet might like that reaction, Gilly knew how fast that could go south.

Get a girl hurt.

But Juliet seemed not to notice. "And you weren't exactly suffering in his arms. I even heard you giggle."

Giggle? Had she? For a moment there—a long moment—yeah, she'd actually relaxed in his arms.

If she were honest, she might admit she'd had the same feeling back at the fire when he'd turned and looked at her.

Peace. Hope.

And definitely the slow burn inside her. Oh no…no… She turned to Juliet. "Listen. I'm not going to get swept away by Reuben. He was just being nice, and let's remember, I'm not the swooning type."

"You mean you don't *let* yourself swoon." Juliet's smile faded. "And that's because you don't let a guy within arm's length." She touched Gilly's arm, her voice soft. "There's no reason to be afraid anymore, Gills. You're not the girl you were—"

Gilly returned with her empty tray to the kitchen, brushing past Juliet.

"You *can* be tough and tender. Brave and beautiful. Sweet and strong. You don't have to turn off the sweet girl inside to be a firebomber."

Gilly couldn't look at her. "You're not in my world. These guys depend on me—they nearly died last week." She picked up a try of freshly frosted white chocolate cupcakes.

"And you nearly died saving them," Juliet said as Gilly returned to the front. Juliet walked over to the door, unlocked it, and turned the Open sign over.

The sun gilded the sidewalk, and across the street the diner, too, opened.

Gilly set the tray of cupcakes on a case shelf.

Juliet turned to her. "Being afraid isn't a weakness. And neither is being pretty, or even letting someone sweep you off your feet. Especially if he looks like Reuben."

Out front, a truck pulled up.

"Listen—it's just easier for you, Juliet. You don't look like you need defending."

"You don't either. Not with that permanent chip on your shoulder, the dare-me aura practically radiating off you. I can guarantee that the last thing the guys around you think is that they have to protect you."

Yeah, well, that wasn't the feeling she'd gotten from Reuben as he'd fallen—as he'd wrapped his arms around her, twisted his body as if to cushion her.

And yeah, she'd ended up half under his body, but even then he was pushing himself off of her.

Not to mention the look of horror on his face.

Except that could have been from the way she'd completely freaked out. She sighed, the echo of the past crashing over her. Raising gooseflesh.

Juliet put her hand on Gilly's arm, jarring her free from her thoughts. "You're safe, Gilly."

Gilly found her eyes, her worried expression. "Yeah. I know."

"No, really. I'm armed." Juliet held up her chocolate frosting gun again. "But in truth, don't let your fears—or your failures—tell you who you are or who you can't be. Or who you can't be with."

"You sound like Dad."

"Casualty of a lifetime in the second pew."

Gilly grinned. Shook her head as she returned to the kitchen. "Listen, Jules, I'm happy being single. Just me, my plane, the teams, and fire. Except I won't even have that if Miles doesn't take me off the restricted list."

Juliet rolled her eyes. "I do not understand you. You are surrounded by cute firefighters and all you can think about is dropping them out of the sky."

"Spoken like a girl in a pink T-shirt, the words Hot Cake written on the front. *Pul*-eeze."

The buzzer went off, and Juliet retrieved the banana-nut muffins, set them on the counter. "What, you don't like working here?"

"It's not that—it's just, well, as I've said, I'm just not a hot cake."

A throat cleared behind her and she froze.

Turned.

And of course, there stood the man who'd swept her off her feet—and right onto the floor.

He'd clearly heard her, too, because a blush pressed his whiskered cheeks. He wore a black T-shirt stretched across his muscled chest, a pair of desperately faded jeans, boots, and a Stetson pulled low over his eyes.

"Hey," he said quietly.

"Hey," she said.

"I'll take six carrot-cake muffins," he said in a voice barely above a whisper.

She pulled them out, boxed them, then put them in a bag. Rang them up.

He handed her a twenty, and she found change, dumped it into his hand.

Expected him to turn, leave. But he didn't, just stood there. Then, "You okay, Gilly?"

And it was the soft drawl, the way he looked up, glancing

fast to meet her eyes, his brown, dark and sweet that had her suddenly realizing...

Maybe she *did* swoon.

Oh, boy. She managed a tight nod, however, and he turned, walked out the door.

"That's a hot cake if I've ever seen one," her sister said, holding a tray of the still-warm banana muffins.

"Oh, please," Gilly said. But she watched as Reuben climbed into his truck, slid on a pair of aviators, and pulled out from the curb. He hung his arm out the window, his biceps thickening against the frame.

Yeah, she needed to put out a fire, and pronto.

He'd hurt her.

Reuben pulled away from the Hot Cakes Bakery, Gilly's words like a boulder in his chest. *I'm not a hot cake.*

It wasn't so much her words as the way she'd looked at him. Her blue eyes wide in shock, and then a shadow across her face, their disaster on the dance floor evident in the way she glanced away, couldn't meet his eyes after that.

Embarrassed. Probably even a little afraid of him, if not repulsed by his bull-in-a-china-shop moves after his spectacular landing, trapping her on the dance floor.

Then there were her words—*Let. Me. Go*! Which would have been enough if not for the lick of panic, the flare of fear deep behind her eyes.

She'd practically run from the Hotline, her sister hot on her tail, and they hadn't returned.

He'd wrecked their evening out, and worse, he'd trampled all over their fragile relationship with his impulsive decision.

There was no going back. And certainly no way to fix it.

Now, at best, things would be awkward between them.

He braked at the light then turned toward the campground that bordered the Ember Fire Base. Conner had called an ad hoc meeting to unravel the ongoing mystery of who had stolen Conner's experimental firefighting drones and dropped them in the forest like matches. The working theory was that the arsonist was igniting the northern forest in hopes of taking out the smokejumper team.

That had Reuben pounding his fist against the steering wheel, another layer of frustration.

He'd like to find their arsonist as much as he'd like to go back in time and fix last night's bumble.

On the seat beside him his cell phone rang. He glanced at the caller ID then picked up the call, turning on the speaker phone. "Mom."

He could picture her standing in their lodge kitchen, staring out the window to the vast pastureland that made up the Triple M Ranch, some ninety miles southeast of Ember. The herd often liked to mosey toward the house in the morning, Black Angus clumping together, grazing in the pasture closest to the house. Hondo, their Australian sheepdog, would be barking, anxious to get to work.

Knox and his other brothers would already be outside, saddling their horses. His sisters, too, probably—they worked the ranch as well as his brothers.

On a day like today, the blue sky stretched from the ends of the earth, cloudless and bright. Reuben could almost smell the piney, fresh wind through the towering lodgepole pines that bordered their house, cresting down from Black Mountain, across the Geraldine River, and through their nine thousand acres of legacy ranchland.

Mom would have been up early with his sisters, Ruby Jane and Coco fixing a mountain of eggs and sausage. He could almost hear Wyatt and Ford fighting Tate for the last helping. Knox would be outlining their projects for the day—probably haying, if he read the calendar right.

"I'm so glad I caught you, Rube. I thought you might be out fighting a fire somewhere."

He sort of was—a fire of his own making, the kind that burned in his gut and never seemed to die.

"We've been home for a few days. But we might deploy to Idaho—Miles has us on standby."

"I wanted to see if you were coming home for Labor Day. You haven't been back to the ranch in ages, and your siblings would like to see you."

No, probably they wouldn't, but his mother would, he guessed. But Gerri Marshall would never admit to being needy. She'd been a rancher her entire life—grown up on the neighboring Grady G, and the word *clingy* was not in her vocabulary.

Even after his father died.

"I dunno, Mom."

A pause, then, "Actually, Knox could use some help. Our new hired man, Uriah, has to have hernia surgery, and he'll be out for a few weeks. You were always so good at hay bucking—"

"Knox is still haying the old fashioned way? Mom, seriously—"

"It's the way your father taught him."

*Them.* The way their father had taught *them.*

Reuben tried to ignore the omission, the way it felt like a stab in his side. He'd walked away from his birthright voluntarily—probably he should remember that.

"We're having a few other families out for a barbeque. I think Chelsea moved back last fall. She's joined her father's practice—"

"Mom. Chelsea and I are old news. Besides, you should be talking to Knox, not me."

"I never understood what happened between you two."

"It's done, Mom." Because he'd never tell her how he'd found his kid brother tangled up in the barn with Chelsea only a few months after Reuben and she had started dating.

He should have gotten the hint, then, that Knox would take whatever belonged to him. But he'd stood there, dumbfounded.

Because no one should have to stand on the sidelines watching their future, everything they thought they wanted, being ripped away.

Especially by his own brother.

"I just worry about you, Reuben."

"You don't need to, Mom. I can take care of myself."

"You can always come home, you know."

No, actually, he couldn't, but he didn't want to break his mother's heart. "I'll try, Mom."

"Your father was proud of you. And so am I."

Oh. He had no words suddenly, his chest tight.

"Please be careful," she said quietly. He wasn't so dense that he couldn't recognize her way of saying she loved him.

"I will." *I love you, too, Mom.*

He hung up. He probably hadn't needed that reminder of his bad decisions. And his inability to fix them.

He pulled up to Conner's fifth-wheel camper at the far edge of the permanent campground. Jed's motorcycle was parked next to Conner's truck.

As he opened the camper door, holding the box of cupcakes, Reuben caught the tail end of Jed's voice.

"It seems the arsonist has either stopped targeting us or vanished."

Jed looked up at Reuben, and Reuben nodded. With no new fires in the last couple of weeks and Conner's last drone lost somewhere in the Cabinet Mountains, maybe the arsonist had given up.

Or—and this thought had Reuben's gut in a knot—he was regrouping.

Jed had a map spread out on Conner's table, the locations of the arson fires marked in red, and all others—natural and man-made—fires in blue. He stood over it, drinking a cup of coffee, his face grim, his expression that of a leader. The kind who planned on keeping his team safe and out of trouble.

So far, so good. They'd all lived through a summer the arson inspector from the National Interagency Fire Center said might be the hottest in decades.

Jed put down his coffee. Looked over at Reuben, now seated at the U-table bench. "So, are we going to talk about it or pretty much forget it ever happened?"

Reuben stilled, glanced at Pete, who sat across from him and played some video game on his phone that required him to tilt it back and forth.

"Forget what?" Pete asked, looking up at them.

Conner was in the kitchen area, opening the box of cupcakes. "The fact Reuben asked Gilly to dance last night at the Hotline."

Reuben frowned at him. He'd clearly left out the most important part of that event. Still. "I choose option B. Forget it ever happened."

Pete looked up, grinned at him. "My idea. Good job."

Oh for crying— "It was a disaster, okay? Let's move on."

Kate, who had opened the door, stepped inside. "Are we talking about Gilly?" She wore her auburn hair caught back in a ponytail tugged through a baseball cap, jeans, and a Montana Griz T-shirt. She walked over to the coffeepot and helped herself. "They were cute together. Reuben has some crazy-hot dance moves."

Seriously? "Oh good grief. Were you there? Did anyone see—"

"I can't believe she said yes," Kate said, buffaloing over him. "I mean, of course she said yes to you, Rube. It's just that she hasn't—doesn't date."

Ho-kay. If they weren't going to bring up the debacle, then he wasn't going to chase it around. Except, "Of course she said yes to me? Am I the team pity case or something?" Reuben reached for a carrot muffin.

Kate shook her head, drank her coffee. "No. You're trustworthy. Dependable. And not, well, whatever *he* is." She gestured loosely to Pete, whose mouth fell open.

"What am I?"

Jed's mouth drifted up one side. "I'm not sure of the word—a charmer?"

"Pete gives them just enough to stay interested but not enough for them to show up on his doorstep the next day," Kate said.

Pete set his game down, folded his arms over his chest. "I like to keep 'em guessing."

"Exactly my point. Reuben is a straight-up, you-get-what-you-see guy," Kate said. "And Gilly needs a guy like that." She took another sip of her coffee. "She'll be okay. Your fall just sort of…well, brought up some old memories. It had nothing to do with you."

Shoot. So they *were* going to talk about it. But he focused on the last part of that sentence. "What kind of memories?"

Kate ran a finger along the top of her cup. "It's not my story. But let's just say that Gilly used to be very girly. She was a lead ballerina in the Northwest Ballet Company."

*Lead ballerina?* And now he really felt like an ox as he remembered stomping all over her feet, knocking her over. "Can we talk about something else?"

"Listen, Rube. It wasn't as bad—" Kate started.

"I am not a dancer, okay? I'm a sawyer. And a bull rider. I totally embarrassed her, and I have no clue how to make it up to her."

"You don't have to make it up to her," Kate said, but the grins on Jed and Conner's faces were enough to make him want to hit something.

"Let's just talk about the fires," Reuben said. He pushed his way off the bench. His head nearly hit the ceiling of Conner's trailer as he headed for the coffeepot.

Conner's camper screamed bachelor pad with his maps of the Kootenai National Forest, the Cabinet Mountains, Glacier National Park, and the Bob Wilderness area papering the walls. Most were marked up with previous fire jumps, rescues, and x's where his drones had crashed. He had bigger x's where the fire service determined his drones caused fires. All except the last one, which had crashed while Conner was searching for a lost camper.

"The last confirmed drone fire was Whiskey Creek. Are there any more that were ruled arson or at least not ruled weather related?" Reuben asked.

"No. But I did notice a pattern to the fires." Jed traced the maps. "Conner says his drones have a one-mile radio-control radius. All the drone fires were located within ten miles of logging roads, hiking trails, or highways out of Ember but in areas where the hotshots couldn't access via their vehicles. As if the arsonist hiked to the farthest place out, then sent the drone into an inaccessible area."

"But all within our territory," Pete said. "So we'd answer the call."

"Right."

"So we were being targeted," Reuben said. "Why?"

Jed reached for a muffin. "I don't know. Who would want to hurt smokejumpers—especially after the casualties last fall?"

"The entire community felt that loss. It's hard to believe it would be someone connected to the Jude County Wildland Firefighters," Kate said, her voice solemn, probably thinking of her father, Jock, their former jump boss.

Last time Reuben had seen him, Jock had told him to keep running and had turned back to the fire himself to save the other half of his crew.

Reuben met eyes with Pete, probably reliving the moment a second later when Reuben dropped his saw and turned to run after Jock.

To stop him.

The hesitation still woke Reuben with a start, a slick sweat in the middle of the night.

"I don't think our arsonist is a hotshot," Jed said, referring to the arson case a few years ago where a firefighter had set fires in order to find more work. "The hotshots weren't called out to three of these fires."

"What about someone who doesn't want us to fight fires—wants to let them run?" Kate asked

"The suspected arson fires were in dense forests deep in the north, not near Ember. The kind the team jumps into.

Looking at the map, this feels personal." Jed took a sip of coffee. Paused, then, "What about someone who lost someone? Maybe a family member who blamed Jock or—" He looked at Pete, Reuben, then Conner. "Or the survivors."

And there it was. The fact that they all could have died on that mountain. But three had survived—Pete, Conner, Reuben.

"You should have let me go after Jock," Reuben said quietly to Pete. It just slipped out.

"We're not doing this again," Pete said, clearly tracking with him. "If you'd gone, you would have died, too."

Instead, Reuben had just stood there, feeling the yank in his gut to run after Jock. And doing nothing—*nothing* about it.

Now Reuben turned to the opposite window. Sheesh, this trailer was small. "If someone is after our team, I'm going to find him," he said.

That turned everyone quiet.

A squawk came over the scanner on Conner's workbench in the corner, where an entertainment unit might have stood.

Conner walked over and turned up the volume. "Dispatch, receiving a call about smoke sighted." He leaned in, listening. "It's from a pilot—he's calling in coordinates."

Conner walked over to the map, studied it as dispatch confirmed, then pointed to the spot. "It's north of Yaak about forty clicks. I don't see a fire road, but that doesn't mean there isn't one."

Jed grabbed his handheld radio, stepped outside to call in.

Conner had served for years as a Green Beret, knew maps and terrain like the own grain of his hand. Probably knew radio communications, too, given the array of electronics amassed on his workbench. Reuben recognized a ham radio and walked over to it.

"My dad had one of these. Used it to talk to his brothers on it. They lived all over—Maine, Minnesota, California, Alaska, Colorado—even one in Hawaii. They had their own frequency. He even made me learn all the ham codes. The one thing I could get right that didn't involve letters jumping off the page."

Silence behind him, and he looked over at his team staring at him. "Aw, c'mon guys. It should come as no surprise to you that I'm not a great reader. Remember, I saw down trees and ride bulls. Not a rocket scientist."

"Rube, just because you're not a great reader doesn't mean—" Kate started, but he held up his hand.

"It's okay—listen, do we need to head over to HQ?"

Jed was just stepping inside to Reuben's words. "Looks like we're going to get deployed—at least a handful of us." He dropped the walkie into his belt.

Kate had gotten up, drained her coffee cup in the sink.

Conner reached for his keys, but Reuben stopped him. "I'm taking your shift, remember?"

"Right."

Reuben followed Pete out, and they climbed in Reuben's truck. They followed Kate and Jed out of the RV park, toward Ember HQ.

"What if Gilly's there?" Pete asked.

Reuben threw him a look. "What if you get out and walk?"

Pete looked out the window. "You know I'm going to have to start calling you Twinkle Toes."

Reuben tapped the brakes.

Pete held up his hands. "Chill, bro. I'm just saying, I'm trustworthy. I'm not sure what that was all about. Charmer? Really?"

Reuben grinned as he pulled in, but his smile faded as he spotted Gilly through the big windows inside the main area of HQ, toeing up to Miles, all five-foot-two of her, gesticulating her fury.

"Still grounded, I think," Pete said as he got out.

"Which is totally unfair, since she saved our lives, and Jared would have let us fry down there." Reuben slammed the door, pocketed his keys, and headed for the office.

"Dude! What are you—" Pete started but Reuben stiff-armed his words and yanked open the door.

"You know I wouldn't put anyone in real danger—" Gilly was saying.

"You nearly crashed an eighty-thousand-dollar air-plane—" Miles talked over her.

Reuben didn't know why he suddenly had a singularity of purpose. Or what, exactly possessed him to march right up to Miles, to interject himself in between them.

"But she didn't," Reuben said into the fray. "And she didn't get anyone killed—on the contrary, she saved at least five lives."

Reuben knew he had a low, even dangerous rumble to his voice. His father's voice, the kind that could command atten-tion in a room. But he'd never seen it shut down a room—even for a split second. But suddenly everyone stopped—the dispatcher, the weather guys, the air traffic controllers, the air tactical group supervisor—the one Jared had probably com-plained to—and even Hero, the agency chocolate lab.

Only the blip of the radar and the static of the radio to confirm that yep, he'd stomped all over Gilly again. At least her business.

And how. exactly did he find himself here?

The question loomed as Gilly turned, stared at him.

With the stunning power of her blue eyes. Deep-indigo blue, the kind a guy could get lost in. Which, of course, was exactly what happened.

Miles turned to him. "This isn't your business, Rube. I know she saved your team but—"

"No buts," Reuben said, coming back to himself, although he cut his voice lower. "Sure, she might have taken a risk, but Miles, don't get me started on how many times you—"

Miles held up his hand. Narrowed his eyes. It paid to hang around the boss during the off season. A fellow bull rider, Miles had a few vices he didn't want the rest of the team knowing about.

And then there was Gilly, who actually deserved to fly, no extortion needed.

But in case Miles needed a push— "I'm not flying if Gilly's not the pilot."

The words came out on their own, but as he stood there, watching Miles size him up, yep, he parked himself in his ultimatum and didn't move.

Met Miles's gaze with his own.

Miles clenched his jaw. Looked at Gilly, who was still staring at Reuben, eyes big.

"Fine. It's probably the last drop of the season, anyway." He turned to Gilly. "Get out of here."

Reuben took the hint and headed down the hall to the locker room, where his team was suiting up.

A tug on his arm, halfway down the hall, however,

stopped him.

He expected a smile. Or a thank you.

Not the dark-eyed glare of an angry woman. "What was that?"

"Um—"

"I can take care of myself. I don't need you coming to my rescue."

"I didn't—I mean—"

"You don't have to protect me, Reuben. Really. Okay?"

He didn't know why, but standing in front of her, he felt a little stripped. Raw.

And simmering with the primal urge to do just that—protect her.

Shoot. Just when he thought he'd done something right.

"Okay."

Her posture softened. "Good. See you onboard."

Then she walked past him.

So much for escaping awkward, for fixing things. Thank the heavens he had a fire to jump into.

So maybe she didn't need to be quite so defensive.

It was simply in Reuben's gene's to protect his team.

If she hadn't figured that out before, she sensed it last night when he'd taken her in his arms, stared down at her with a gaze that could reach right through her, steady her.

And when they'd fallen, he'd secured his strong arms around her.

It could happen to anyone—getting their feet tangled. She'd fallen plenty of times on the dance floor. And it wasn't his fault that he had resurrected her demons.

But now, as she stood at the entrance to the team locker room watching him suit up, it occurred to her that Reuben might be the kind of man who could, well, keep those demons from haunting her.

Strong enough to chase them away, if she let him.

She turned away, but not before she took in his wide shoulders, muscled arms, a sculpted chest that tapered down to a trim waist, strong legs. He wore a dark, coffee-brown beard, his hair tousled and behind his ears, now tied back with a dark-red bandanna.

When he suited up, Reuben appeared raw, rough edged.

The kind of guy to look at fire and not flinch.

The kind of guy who couldn't help but stand up for the people he cared about.

Yeah, she'd *definitely* been too defensive.

*Don't let your fears—or your failures—tell you who you are or who you can't be. Or who you can't be with.* Juliet in her head.

Oh, she was reading *way* too much into how he'd toed up to Miles on her behalf. After all, who else knew about his airsickness? Maybe he really *wouldn't* get into a plane without her at the controls.

Her gaze fell on Kate now pulling on her Kevlar jump pants and jacket. She turned up the collar, then checked for her 150-foot rappelling letdown rope in the leg of her pants, padded by motocross-style shin guards. She'd drastically cut down on her jumps this summer, but with the teams fresh off a fire, maybe she'd volunteered.

Kate also fitted a small tent and sleeping bag in her suit, something Jed had taught her years ago, during her training in Alaska.

Her helmet with the mesh grid sat on the bench beside

her. She laced up her boots—heavy duty with the thick sole for trekking through ash and cinder.

In her hundred-pound personal gear bag, she'd have water, her fire shelter, a GPS, her radio, an extra pair of socks, toothbrush and paste, a first aid kit, headlamp, a few energy bars, tent stakes, bear spray, and her favorite spoon.

Another tip from Jed.

And all these hints Kate had passed onto Gilly. Right before Gilly went to jump camp, hoping she could someday join Kate on the fire line.

Kate looked up and gave her a wry smile. Gilly returned it.

If she couldn't be an official smokejumper, she could at least get the team to their drop zone safely.

The other female smokejumper, Hannah, closed her locker, gathered her dark hair into a pony tail and waddled toward the briefing room carrying her gear. Brave and tough, despite her short, curvy frame, Hannah had surprised them all with her grit. She'd spent an hour under her fire shelter earlier this summer—earning a few burns that had landed her in the hospital. Gilly and the entire team would have understood if she'd decided to hang it up.

But so few women made it as smokejumpers. Hannah had a tight fist on her accomplishment and wasn't going to let a few burns keep her from being among the elite.

Gilly tried not to envy her. Or taste the old bite of failure, acrid and thick in her throat.

She hated how her fears kept her from—well, the life she wanted. Smokejumping. Even, maybe, Reuben—or more accurately, romance. A man in her life. *Not necessarily Reuben.* She had no doubt he wouldn't ask her to dance again, anyway.

Frankly, she wasn't sure how she felt about dating a guy

she'd have to climb onto a chair to kiss.

Her face heated at the thought, and the one behind it that had his arms curled around her, her own over those magnificent shoulders, her fingers twined in his unruly hair.

Feeling all that strength and power channeled, focused, on her.

She shook herself out of the image, almost trembling.

No, no that couldn't happen. Ever.

Because despite her sister's teasing, there was no room for anything between teammates but getting the job done. Sure, Jed and Kate had something special—but that had started years ago.

She should probably just erase last night from her brain. Poor Reuben probably wanted to forget it, too.

Gilly walked past the lounge and into the ready room, equipped with four long parachute-folding tables and older, heavy duty Singer sewing machines. Near the front, chairs were set in a semicircle to face a whiteboard with the roster list and call-out activity sheet hanging next to a large map of the entire Kootenai range—their main territory.

She knew the national forest from memory, every peak, ridge, canyon and river—from the air.

"Gilly," Jed had come up behind her. "Did you get a flight map from air control?"

"Yep. We're all set. I finished up my preflight, plotted our route, and now I'm headed out for my preflight check. Wheels up in fifteen."

She sat in the back, however, as Jed briefed them on the fire. Just a little flicker, probably not big enough to cause a problem, but the area around Yaak was as dry as Egypt, and with the little camp town only a few miles away and populated by summer and hunting cabins, they needed to get in and snuff it out before it grew into something the fire service couldn't extinguish.

"It's just west of Davis Creek, in the canyon, between Black Top and Mushroom Peak in the Cabinet Mountains. There's an old hunting road that we can use to flank it. We'll do a burnout along the edge, contain it on this side of the ridge. If it jumps the ridge, we'll have to call in the tankers. The NIFC would like to get it under control asap, see if we can keep costs down on this fire."

From Jed's calm explanation, it sounded like something they could do in their sleep.

"We'll get on the ground, and if we need to call for reinforcements, Gilly will bring them in. Pete, I know you're on the jump list, but I want you to stay back with the second crew."

She liked hearing her name in the game plan. See, she was a vital part of the team.

Gilly got up, noticed Reuben didn't even glance her direction, and headed outside to her beautiful Twin Otter, just back from a one-hundred-hour inspection.

She ran her hand along the smooth white surface and along the red stripe. She stood back, gave the plane a once-over, checking the tire pressure and wings before diving into her checklist.

Then she ducked into the cockpit, grabbing the ARROW documents—airworthiness certificate, registration, radio station license, operating limitation documents, and weight and balance information—all attached to the plastic pouch on the cockpit wall.

She opened the aircraft log and noted the signer on the inspection. Patrick Browning. She hoped he'd checked the transponder—it had been replaced in the winter and had its own inspection schedule.

Yes. He'd made a notation in the margins. Patrick was thorough, if not an old hand at the game of patching up aircraft.

Gilly did her cockpit check, making sure all the valves and switches worked, leaving them in the correct position. She turned on the battery switch and noted the fuel quantities for later recollection, then made sure the magnetos were off.

She grabbed the de Havilland checklist and did the manufacture preflight check, looking for "smoking"—or loose—rivets, checking all the nuts and bolts.

The first jump team exited the building and headed toward the plane, geared up like soldiers going to battle. Jed, Kate, CJ, Hannah, and Reuben.

Gilly bent down to check the tires, moved the plane forward, then back, looking for oil in the oleo struts. Then she moved the flight controls, making sure the yoke worked in tandem.

She looked over and saw Reuben helping load the gear into the back of the plane. He didn't look at her, and the swill of regret lined her throat.

He'd just been watching her back. Why did she have to be so defensive?

Well, he didn't know what it felt like to always feel like you didn't measure up. That if you let down your guard, life would sneak up on you, devour you.

She checked the prop, making sure she didn't move it—yes, the magneto was off, but you never knew. And she'd seen a pilot nearly killed when he'd started the plane by accidentally moving his prop.

No dripping oil and the fuel looked good. She checked the level with a dipstick, just to confirm, then checked the vents.

Finally, she grabbed ammonia and a rag and climbed up on the outside of the plane to clean the windshield.

*Leave the problems on the ground.* Advice from her teacher, the one who'd told her she didn't have to jump from planes to be a part of the team. Dwayne would be delighted to see her today, not only a jumper pilot but also flying tankers.

Well, formerly flying tankers. But at least contributing.

Not letting her failures completely derail her.

She saw their spotter for today's run, Cliff O'Dell, come out of HQ. An older man and former jumper out of Missoula, he knew exactly where to send the jumpers to make sure they didn't land in the middle of a fire.

By the time she finished cleaning the windshield, the team had already climbed in, strapped themselves into the seats positioned along the walls. The gear boxes were strapped down in the middle.

Cliff climbed in beside her in the copilot seat.

"Last run of the season," he said and picked up the pre-takeoff checklist.

"Hopefully. Parking brake."

"Set."

"Fire T-handles."

"In."

"Emergency fuel switches."

"Off."

She tuned out the chatter in the back as she read through the list.

Finally, "Everyone buckled up?"

She glanced back for a second. Kate shot her a thumbs-up. Nodded at her.

No, she might not be a smokejumper, but she kept them safe and alive, at least until they left her plane.

Gilly turned the beacon light on, tested the brakes, glanced at the circuit breakers, and confirmed the transponder was on. Then she turned the mixture on rich, moved the carb heat to cold, flicked on the master switch, pumped the primer, locked it, and inserted the key.

"Clear prop!" She touched the brakes, put her hand on the throttle, and turned the engine over. It fired to life, and she taxied out to the strip.

"We have a blue-skied day, with few clouds and a bump-free ride to the jump site," she said over the intercom. "Strap in and enjoy the ride."

She trimmed the tabs for takeoff, set the flaps up, the carburetor heater back to the full position, then checked her heading.

She confirmed with the tower, waited for the go-ahead, and then throttled back to about 2000 rpm. She checked the directional gyro against the runway heading, then released the brake.

"Let's go."

The plane lurched ahead.

Gilly knew it seemed an anomaly to her parents—that she felt so comfortable at the yoke of a plane. Maybe it was simply the power of the airplane, the dichotomy of her smallness inside the powerful bird.

Or maybe she simply liked to think her fears hadn't completely won.

Regardless, she loved the power of a plane as it hurtled down the runway. Her airspeed indicator registered fifty-five knots, and she eased back on the yoke, urging the plane into the air, pushing the plane up to seventy-five knots for the climb.

The plane tried to shimmy and she held it steady, her arms vibrating with the shudder of the crosswind.

Gilly kept the horizon even with the cowling until she reached a thousand feet, then turned into their heading, finishing the climb to five thousand.

Below, the Kootenai Mountains spread out in a glorious, rumpled, jagged array of gray rocky peaks, pine-green valleys, pockets of late-season snow, and falls that cascaded down to turquoise-blue glacial lakes. Rivers cut through canyons, over ledge rock, sometimes white-frothed, other times lazy.

And she soared above it all.

They cut northwest on a heading of three-three-eight, and she called it in to the tower.

Static, then their response. "Delta-Four-Three, please recycle your responder."

She glanced at Cliff. "Check the transponder is set to Alt."

"Roger."

She toggled the radio. "Delta-Four-Three to ATC. Do you have my primary target?"

"That's a negative, Delta-Four-Three."

She glanced at Cliff. "Do you see me at all? Do you have a Mode C Readout?"

"Again, negative, Delta-Four-Three."

"Recycling." She retyped in her 1200 Squawk digits, then reached over, turned her Mode C to Standby, then back to ALT.

"I checked the antenna," she said, mostly to herself.

"We're over Yaak," Cliff said. "Population two hundred forty-eight. Best fishing and hunting in the northwest." He pointed to a peak maybe twenty miles away, and she could just make out a fire tower. "That's the Garver Mountain Fire Tower."

She buzzed by it to her right and caught sight of a thin trickle of smoke past the far ridge, a wispy column of gray that indicated the fire—which her team would neatly extinguish—was still fighting for life.

She'd find a nice flat, open area, drop them down below the flames.

"Delta-Four-Three, recycle your responder."

"They still can't see us," Cliff said.

"Call in our position," Gilly said as she angled over the ridge, toward the fire.

Flames spit up in a fifty-acre area—the call in must have come in just after the lightning strike or whatever caused the fire.

"I'll go in back and start looking for a jump spot," Cliff said. He took his map with him as he climbed into the back.

Gilly banked then came back to circle the area.

A good jump spot had to be within walking distance of the fire but not so close as to allow the wind to blow them into the turmoil.

She felt movement and looked over to see Reuben land in the seat next to her.

He looked green.

She hid a smile. Poor guy. It had to be cosmically unfair to get airsick every time you went to work. He glanced at her, gave her a wan smile.

See, maybe they had a chance of being friends. Someday.

She heard Cliff in her headset. "We need another pass. It's pretty dense down there."

She banked the plane again, and the left wing fuel indicator light flashed on. Reuben noticed it, tapped it. She frowned. The fuel pump must have malfunctioned.

She flicked it off, transferring all the fuel to the right wing. Then she glanced at Reuben. "Don't worry. The plane can fly on one engine."

It seemed she'd had a similar conversation before—too recently.

Still, "We're down an engine here, Cliff. We either dump these guys off asap, or we need to turn around and head back." She'd done the fuel math before she left—she could get home on the remaining gas in the right tank.

But just barely.

"I'm not seeing a good jump spot, Gilly," Cliff said.

Reuben was looking at her, shaking his head.

"What?" She pulled away one ear of her headset.

"I don't have a good feeling about this!"

She shook her head, put the headset back on. "Anything, Cliff?"

"I see something down canyon, south of the fire. If you climb over the ridge, we can come around and approach from the south."

She affirmed and banked, climbing toward the ridge.

Admittedly, the plane felt sluggish, the left prop spinning wildly, useless in the wind. But like she said, she could fly on one—

The right wing fuel indicator light flickered on.

She glanced at Reuben, who had straightened in his seat.

"I see it."

Just a warning—and it had to be faulty. She'd checked the fuel compartment manually, dipped a stick in, and it'd come back full.

But if the indicator was correct, they'd soon be gliding. Over jagged mountains, spires of lodgepole pine, and on their way into the dense forests of the Kootenai range.

Gilly kept her voice steady. "Forget the drop, Cliff. We have another indicator light on. I'm headed back to Yaak or even that service road we saw west off Black Top. If we have to, we can put down—"

The right engine sputtered out.

The sudden rush of silence whooshed through the cabin, alerting everyone to the fact they were falling from the sky.

Gilly drew in a long breath, her heart banging in her chest. *Don't. Panic.* She'd landed dead stick dozens of times. Well, in practice.

A twin-engine plane could glide for—at this altitude—at least ten miles.

Except, a glance at the altimeter said they were dropping fast.

They wouldn't make Yaak.

Reuben pressed his hand on his gut, looking white.

Gilly whipped off her headset, her heart thundering. She turned to him, to all of them. "We'll have to glide it down."

To a person, they stared at her as if they didn't comprehend.

"We've lost both engines—"

"So we jump." Reuben unstrapped from his chair. Got up.

What? No—

Cliff wrestled with the door, opened it. The cool air of the slipstream thundered into the plane, and she had to grab the yoke to keep it from unseating, sending them all out in a tumble.

"Close the door! We're too low! We're only at twelve hundred. You won't have time to deploy."

She turned to look at them again—Jed peering out to the ground, as if to confirm.

She was right, and they knew it. "Sit down—strap in. I'll get us down, I promise."

Reuben flopped into the copilot seat. "What can I do?" His voice was calm, albeit dark.

She turned to him. "Have you ever flown before?"

"Yeah. We had a Cessna on the ranch."

"We need to get to that road." She pointed toward a forest service road, a trail through the arching, dark pine.

Reuben shook his head. "We're not going to make that."

"We are—"

"Do the math, Gilly!"

"Shut up! I've got this!"

Reuben's jaw hardened.

But yeah, she looked at the altimeter. "Okay, change of plan. We'll put down there, in that creek bed." After a season without rain, the bed was cracked and rutted, only in use in the spring when the mountains filled it with glacial runoff. Flat and wide, maybe forty feet across, it was littered with gravel and rock, but still, a wide path.

The wind shrilled, whistling as the plane descended, gliding.

She would make it. She had to. The team was her responsibility.

More math, and she realized they were coming in too hot. She'd have to do a forward slip, try to slow them down, get them lower.

"I have to bank into the wind, try and slow us down. I'll apply the opposite rudder to keep us flying straight."

"You need help with the yoke?"

Gilly's arms burned with the effort of holding it straight, the wind wanting to jostle it from her hands. But she shook her head.

"You got this," Reuben said, and it wasn't a question. Maybe an indictment—she couldn't read his tone.

She banked hard, fought for control with the foot pedals.

They'd hit a crosswind, the air gusting across the nose, pushing them east.

"I see the creek," Reuben said.

She noticed then his hand on the yoke. It might have been there for a while.

They were still coming in too fast. She angled her flaps up, hoping to slow them more.

The air thundered, shook the plane as they dropped below tree level.

Fifty feet, twenty.

*Oh, God, please let them live through this.*

She fought to maneuver them into the center of the creek.

Or *not* a creek—more like a dry riverbed filled with boulders and rocks. And not too far ahead, a drop-off—who knew how far—into a gorge below.

A terrible crunch shook the plane as she landed, bounced hard, and hurtled back in the air.

"Hold on!"

And then the plane hit the ground again. She slammed the brakes, fighting as the wheels shuddered over rocks, the rutted creek bed. It ricocheted against a boulder, slamming the plane around. It skidded backwards, then jerked up again, and crashed over onto its side, the wing splintering off.

Metal screamed—or maybe that was Gilly—as the plane rolled over and over, like a ball.

Down the riverbed, toward the gorge.

And then her stomach ripped up through her as the plane dropped over the edge, falling… falling…

# Chapter 4

IF REUBEN NEVER STEPPED foot in an airplane again, it would be too soon. At least that was his second thought after waking up, still strapped in his seat, hanging upside down in the cockpit.

The first had something to do with the fact that he was alive amidst a tangle of sheered metal. The air reeked of oil, hydraulic fluid hissed out of broken hoses, the avionics panel sizzled with sparks.

They needed to get out of the plane before it went up in flames.

Except, no, they'd crashed because they'd run *out* of fuel.

And just because his father had pulled him from a flaming airplane once didn't mean that rescue would happen again.

*Again.* What kind of rotten luck was it for a guy to crash-land in an airplane twice in his life?

His head throbbed. He reached up and touched his forehead. It came back wet and slick.

His helmet had flown off in the crash—he must have forgotten to click his chin strap. He'd been too busy trying to figure out how to help Gilly.

He applied pressure to his wound and fought for his bearings.

The plane had landed not just upside down but with the nose up. He looked straight out at the creek bed some ten feet below.

"Gilly?" He looked for her, but her seat was empty, the buckle undone.

"I'm out here."

He strained to follow her voice and spotted her through a massive tear in the hull behind him. Sitting on one side of the aircraft, the seats running parallel to the hull, Jed and Kate had stayed buckled in. But the impact had knocked CJ, sitting in the opposite seats, through the gaping tear of the plane.

Reuben didn't see Hannah or Cliff.

He unbuckled, bracing himself on the ceiling, let himself fall, and crawled back to Kate, who was working her buckle, her hands shaking.

The gear had mostly been thrown from the plane, but dislodged seats lay crumbled, tumbled on top of each other, equipment spilled—Pulaskis, the saws—and parachute gear tangled through the opening.

"Shh, I got ya," Reuben said to Kate. "Your buckle is caught on your jumpsuit." He was shaking too, deep inside, maybe from relief, but he caught her in one arm, held her up, and with the other hand, released the buckle.

She fell into his embrace with a gasp.

"How badly are you hurt?"

She rolled over to her knees, shook her head. She'd been wearing her helmet, good girl, and now worked it off. "I'm fine."

But next to her, Jed hung, his arms dangling, blood running down one arm, pooling.

"Jed—"

"Let's get him down," Reuben said, his voice steady.

Outside, he could hear wailing—maybe some wildlife creature. He braced Jed in his arms as Kate unbuckled him, and Jed fell into the cradle of Reuben's embrace. Kate grabbed Jed's legs and she and Reuben maneuvered him out of the body of the plane.

Reuben was about to set Jed on the ground when Kate stopped him. "He's got a piece of metal sticking out right below his ribs. It might have hit a kidney. Lay him on his side."

He set Jed down while Kate surveyed the damage—took his pulse, checked his breathing. Jed wasn't moving, his pallor dusky, and the sight of him shook Reuben.

Jed, the one who knew how to stay alive—and keep them alive.

Kate took a deep breath, started to probe around the wounds. "It went deep and sharp for it to saturate his jumpsuit."

"We should take off the suit," he said.

"No. He'll go into shock if we don't keep him warm. We'll try and stop the bleeding. Do you have a knife?"

Reuben reached into his pant leg, found his camp knife there, and handed it to Kate. "I'll check the others."

She nodded as she began to attack the layers of padding, running her arm over her eyes, taking another deep breath.

If anyone knew how to stay calm in disaster, it was Kate.

He got up, searching for Gilly, Hannah, CJ, and Cliff.

He spotted Hannah sitting at the edge of the forest, her knees drawn up, staring at him. She appeared white, shaken, her lip fattened. "Hannah?"

She didn't move, and he was about to go to her when—"Rube, I need you!"

He found the voice—Gilly—and she was leaning over CJ. He lay with his arm under him, his legs at odd angles, unconscious. Reuben knelt beside CJ, took his pulse.

Alive. And his breathing seemed okay—but what did he know?

"His arm looks broken, his shoulder might be dislocated. And I wouldn't be surprised if he has a hip fracture along with broken legs. But I'm most worried about his neck—" She pointed to a hematoma on his forehead. "I don't know how hard he hit, and I'm afraid to move him."

Gilly looked over at him, and he startled at the expression on her face. She, too, had hit something because she sported her own hematoma. But the set of her jaw, the darkness in her eyes…

She was angry.

"Maybe we can find a piece of airplane to stabilize him—"

"We need help," she said, rising. Only then did he see her sway, just a little. "I'm going to check on the radio."

He didn't want to tell her that the entire avionics board looked destroyed.

Instead, he stood up, watching her take a step, one eye closing in a wince. "Are you okay?" He reached out his hand to steady her.

Gilly pushed it away. "I'm fine. Find Cliff."

Cliff. But Reuben watched as she picked her way back to the plane, the slightest hesitation on one side.

She *was* hurt.

But yeah, not as bad as CJ or Jed. Reuben shot a glance at Hannah, who had gotten up now, still just staring at him. "Are you okay?"

Overhead, the sky looked unblemished by their disaster,

blue and bright, just the finest cloud of smoke past the ridge of mountains. On either side of their crash site, scrub brush gave way to forest, towering spruce, pine. Along the edges of the creek, downed, stripped trees, and massive boulders suggested a once-abundant flow.

Looking back at the plane, Reuben realized they'd fallen on a boulder the size of a Fiat, almost like an albatross landing on its back, the front end propped up, tail section splintered in two.

He guesstimated they'd fallen maybe twenty feet off the side of the dry waterfall into the ravine. Bounced into the shallow pool below, skidded, and landed on the boulder.

A flight overhead should be able to spot them, if Gilly could raise HQ on the radio.

"Cliff?" He raised his voice, heard it echo, but no voice answered. He started for the far edge of the plane, scrambling over rocks, trying not to turn his foot in pockets of rock and debris.

Another glance at Hannah, and this time she was pointing. He followed her gaze.

His heart about stopped.

Cliff had clearly fallen out of the plane mid-tumble, because his body lay cast from the plane half-way down the falls, his bones broken by a bed of jagged granite. Even from here, Reuben couldn't make out how he might have lived. And as he grew closer, he saw the man's ribs protruding from his jacket—no smokejumper padding for him.

He worked his way up to Cliff, where he lay on the rocks, a pool of blood under his skull, his eyes still open. "Aw, Cliff, I'm sorry." Reuben checked Cliff's pulse, then gently closed his eyes.

He paused, not sure what to do. Then he took off his

bandanna and placed it over the man's face.

He climbed down, shot a look at Hannah, but she'd turned her back to him, pacing now at the edge of the forest.

Reuben spotted Gilly in the plane, seated on the floor, working the radio. His fleeting hope disintegrated when she threw off the headset with an accompanying epitaph of disgust.

Reuben scrambled back to CJ, knelt beside him. He still hadn't moved, but his breathing seemed steady.

Reuben needed to find a cold pack for CJ's head. And a blanket—yes. He stumbled back to the plane, feeling strangely woozy, as if—yep, he was going to lose it.

He held it together long enough to get to the edge of the forest, lean against a tree as he lost the muffin from Hot Cakes.

Nice.

He drew a hand across his mouth, though, feeling better, and guessed he might have a concussion.

"Here."

He turned, found Hannah holding out her water bottle and a bandanna.

He cleaned out his mouth. Then he tied the bandanna around his wound.

He glanced at Hannah.

Hannah was one of the tough ones. Feisty, determined to finish the summer despite already living through a flashover, landing in the hospital with second-degree burns, and now surviving a plane crash. Or maybe not quite so feisty, because her expression seemed close to unraveling. She bit her lip. Swallowed.

"Is he dead?"

Reuben glanced at Cliff, back to Hannah.

"No—I meant CJ."

Reuben shook his head. "I don't think so—"

And as if in answer, he heard a yell, something feral, that rent the air.

He whirled around and saw Gilly racing over to CJ, who had woken up and begun to thrash around.

"He's in pain!" This from Hannah, who stood rooted as Reuben ran to CJ.

Indeed. His face white, CJ clutched his waist with one arm, groaning, breathing hard. He let out another wail.

Gilly gripped his arms, trying to keep him from moving. "What hurts?"

CJ let out a growl, something of a curse in it, and Reuben didn't blame him. "My shoulder—ah, crap—and my hip—" He tried to move his leg and let out a scream.

And when he looked at Reuben, so much pain in his eyes, Reuben wanted to glance away.

"Just breathe, CJ," Gilly said.

"It's hard—I can't—" He reached up with his good hand, pressed on his chest. "I can't breathe!"

"You're hyperventilating," Gilly said. "I know it hurts. Just breathe with me." She leaned up, put her hand on his belly. "In through the nose, out through the mouth, breathe from your belly. Slowly."

"I can't—"

"Do it," Reuben said, nothing of a bedside manner in his tone.

CJ's eyes widened, but he glanced back at Gilly, began to mimic her.

Hannah had come closer, though still standing ten feet

away.

Reuben headed back to Jed and Kate.

Jed lay on his side. Kate had gotten his jumpsuit opened up, cut it apart, and wrapped the material around the protruding metal.

"If we remove it, he might bleed out—I just don't know." She checked Jed's pulse again. Then she kissed his cheek, pressed her forehead to his. "Hang in there, we'll get you some help. Don't die on me, Jed."

Then Kate sat down, her hand on Jed's body, as if assessing his breathing, in and out.

She held up her radio, fished out of her jump pants. "I can't get hold of anyone—my guess is the mountain is causing interference."

Reuben took out his radio, confirmed the static reception.

"We're in trouble here, Rube. Jed's too hurt to move and CJ—who knows how injured he is. Gilly said something about the radio being out and the transponder down before we crashed… They don't know we're down." Kate looked up at him. "You gotta go for help."

He took in her words. Yes, of course. He was the least hurt—

"Rube!"

He turned to Gilly's voice and spied her beckoning him over.

CJ seemed to be calmer, breathing in rhythm now. Gilly got up, walked away from him.

Reuben met her.

And for the first time since the crash, he took a good look at her. A goose egg lifted right above her brow line. She'd scraped her arm—a thin line of blood traced her skin. And she'd ripped her pants, her knee bloody and a little swollen. He guessed that might be why she was limping.

But he saw none of that on her face, her jaw tight, her mouth a bud of frustration.

"CJ's still in a lot of pain. He might have internal bleeding How's Jed?"

"He's got a piece of metal in his back. Kate's wrapped something around it to keep it from moving, but...I don't know."

"Hannah seems okay—in shock, maybe. And Kate—well, we know Kate." Gilly's glance landed on her best friend, and for a second—*only* a second—weariness flashed across her face. Then she looked back at Reuben. "I saw you found Cliff."

"Yeah. He's—"

"I know." She put her hands on her hips, closed her eyes, her jaw tightening even more. Then she sighed and looked up at him. "I guess I'd better get going."

"Huh?"

He knew he sounded a little like an oaf, but, "What do you mean?"

"I mean somebody needs to hike out, and since I'm the pilot, that means me."

"In what world? Listen—yeah, you're right. Someone needs to hike out. But you're in no shape—"

"What are you talking about? I'm fine?"

"You're limping."

If looks could kill, he'd be a pile of ash in the creek bed floor. "I'm fine. I just banged my knee a little."

"You'll never make a hike out. Yaak is thirty miles from

here!"

"I can get to the road—it's probably—"

"About nine miles is my guess. And between here and the road, there's a river and at least one ridge of mountains, and you'll never make it on that knee."

"Watch me!"

He held up his hand. "Stop. Someone needs to stay here and take care of everyone—"

"They have Kate—"

"Kate has her hands full with Jed!"

"How about me?"

The voice jerked him out of the flood of frustration that threatened to drown him. He turned, saw Hannah standing there, nodding.

"I'm fine. I'll stay. I can monitor CJ and make sure everyone has water—really. I can do this." She looked at Gilly, back to Reuben. "We'll be okay until you get back with help."

Reuben's mouth tightened. He looked at Gilly. "You sure the radio's out?"

She gave him a look.

"Okay." He looked up at the sky, checked his watch. "I'd say we have about eight hours of daylight. If we get moving, we can reach the road in about four or five hours. It's due east…" He took a second, then pointed. "That way."

"For crying out loud—how do you know that?"

"The same way I know that I can do this alone. You're just going to slow me down—"

"I'm going with you, okay? I told everyone I'd get them home safely, and I will." Then her voice dropped, and she swallowed, her eyes bright. "Especially since it's my fault."

"It's not—"

She held up her hand. Shook her head, her eyes wet.

Her wretched expression silenced him. He knew what it felt like to feel to blame—whether justified or not—and the excruciating need to find a way to fix it.

"Fine. But once we hit the road, I'm headed to the Grover fire lookout, not Yaak. It's only a few miles from here, and yeah, it's a climb, but they'll have radio equipment. If we push hard, we can make it before dark."

She hesitated only a moment before walking back to the plane. She climbed in then emerged with one of their equipment packs. He recognized it as his and reached for it, but she slung it around her shoulder.

Ho-kay. He'd just let that ride for a minute or two. It weighed nearly a hundred pounds, so probably she'd let it drop sooner than later.

He retrieved the equipment box, undamaged in the crash, opened it, and found water, MREs, and a first aid kit. He brought the supplies over to Kate. Looked at Hannah. "You sure?"

"I'm sure." And indeed, she looked better, less white and, despite the fattened lip, her eyes had cleared, brightened with determination. She grabbed a bottle of water from the box and headed back to CJ.

"If we get going now, we can bring help back by tonight," Gilly said, a *hurry up* in her voice.

But Reuben hesitated. He couldn't help but crouch before Kate, take her hands in his, hold them. Meet her eyes.

"We'll be back. I promise."

She refused to slow him down.

Still, Gilly couldn't tell if Reuben was favoring her or if this was simply his normal pace. Because to her mind, they should have reached the river by now. With the sun past the apex—she could at least figure that out—daylight had a countdown not in their favor.

"You can go faster," she said, catching a tree branch Reuben held for her. "And you don't have to wait for me—I can keep up."

He hadn't said much the first couple of hours. Could be that he was more injured than he let on…or maybe it took all his energy to climb the first ridge and descend. She ached to her core, her knee screaming as they slipped and spilled their way down the ridge. The man seemed to possess an inner Magellan that pointed due east.

Except, maybe he did, or at least understood how the forest worked, because he stopped every once in a while to sniff the air, check the trees, orient himself to the sun. Listen.

Apparently, she'd trekked into the woods with Daniel Boone. Or maybe this was Lewis…which left her as Clark? Or Sacajawea.

Whatever the case, she wasn't here as a tagalong.

But it had taken all her energy

A slight frown creased his face as he glanced over his shoulder, catching another tree branch out of his way. "I'm moving as fast as is prudent," he said. "We don't want to get off course. Besides, the ground is rutted, and if we turn an ankle or get hurt, that won't help Jed or CJ."

He waited until she grabbed the branch then turned back to bushwhacking.

What he left out, of course, was the fact that she'd started limping—even she could admit it—over the last hour. Her knee burned, and she thought it might be swelling.

She didn't remember hitting the yoke, but anything could have happened during the blinding seconds they'd careened and tumbled through the rocky creek bed and out over the cliff.

It still felt surreal—everything from the tanks sputtering out to the glide into the trees, to crashing, and even CJ and Jed fighting for their lives.

Cliff, dead where he fell.

The deep breathing she'd done to help CJ get out of his hyperventilation hadn't just been for him. She'd had to gather her bearings, let the truth sink in.

Somehow she'd screwed up. Despite her extensive pre-flight check, she'd missed something. How could she have left the base with only half-full tanks of fuel?

She'd killed Cliff, put the rest of her team in jeopardy.

Reuben stood on a balding boulder in a tiny clearing and Gilly climbed up to join him. The forest fell around them, with shaggy, thin black spruce, peeling white paper birch, lush cedar and hemlock, and towering high above, black cottonwood. Despite the heat of the day, the forest shade had cooled her skin, now simmering under the eye of the sun.

"The river, according to my memory, should be about a half mile from here. Listen for it," he said.

"How do you know that?"

Gilly shaded her eyes, searched for the spiral of smoke, and found it to the west, a thin wisp. The air didn't quite smell like fire yet, heady instead with the redolence of pine, cedar, and the loam of decaying needles.

"I have a photographic memory."

"Really?"

He pointed to a tiny blip on the horizon to the northeast. "There's the lookout tower."

She nodded as if eager, as if her leg didn't scream in protest. But she refused to be the weak link here.

To admit that Reuben had been right, that she should have stayed behind.

"It's time for me to carry that," he said, blindsiding her as he reached for the pack.

"No. I got this."

But he put his big, strong, tan, capable hand around the strap, his mouth a tight, thin line. "I am sure you do, Gilly, but I'm done arguing with you. I'm carrying this pack—it's not only what I'm good at, but plainly, it's my turn. Let me carry it or I'll just have to carry you."

Her eyes widened for a second. "Over my dead body."

"No, I'd carry that, too. But let's hope it doesn't come to that."

She wasn't sure if he might be kidding. But when no smile emerged, she tightened her mouth into a thin line of frustration and released the pack.

He swung it up onto his thick shoulder like it weighed nothing.

She felt like she'd released half her body weight. For a moment she thought she might be able to take flight.

She wanted to when she followed Reuben off the rock, again through the forest, her knee on fire.

And shoot, she couldn't help the slightest shard of disappointment in herself when she realized she'd hoped to impress him.

Now she was simply dead weight, limping along behind him.

"The answer is, yes. I really do have a photographic memory. It was the only thing that got me through school."

"So, you can see something—"

"And I memorize it instantly, remember exactly what it looks like. It started in second grade when I couldn't seem to learn to read. I memorized what the words looked like and simply read from that memory."

"You didn't sound the words out?"

"I couldn't…they wouldn't stay in one place." He held a white pine branch out of the way for her. And, for the first time on their trek, met her eyes. "I'm dyslexic."

She caught the branch. "I'm sorry."

"It's no big deal." He charted them around a grouping of birch and along a bouldered area. "When I looked out the window of the plane, I did a mental calculation of the road to the river and then to the lookout tower—it's something I do every time we fly. It helps keep my mind off… Well—"

"Your stomach? Motion sickness? That's why you like to sit in the cockpit."

He glanced at her. Gave her a one-sided smile. "Actually, not really. This is my second plane crash. The thought of going down literally makes me ill. I have a well-founded fear of flying."

"Your *second* crash?"

She used the trees to brace herself as they climbed down a tumble of rocks. And, for a second, caught up to him.

He still wore the bandanna Hannah had given him around his head, his dark hair spiking out from it. The nearly black, dried blood caked the edge, saturated one area. He hadn't shaved lately—maybe for a few days—and his whiskers lay rich and thick on his chin, dirt and a little blood scrubbed in, maybe from when he'd pulled Jed from the plane.

He didn't look like a man who would let his fears manhandle him. But then, she'd done a superb job of fleeing her fears for the past decade or more, so…

"I know. Rotten luck, huh? Except last time, it was just me and Dad, out in the cold for a few hours waiting for my brothers to find us." He turned and for a second acted like he was going to offer her his hand as she climbed up a rather large boulder, then thought again.

But he watched, as if a sentry, as she scrabbled up, hoisting herself onto the boulder, then scooting up behind him the rest of the way.

See. She was just fine, thank you.

"Where did you crash?" They stood on another overlook, and yes, in the air, she smelled water, although she heard nothing of the rushing she'd expect with a river.

He pointed—indicating she should keep moving—down into the dark forest, and she headed toward it, down the rock, sliding on her backside.

Her knee burned, and water edged her eyes. She landed on her good leg, bracing herself on boulders, then started down the trail ahead of him.

He said nothing, and she couldn't tell if he was debating intervention, or the answer to her question. Then, "We crashed on the ranch, in one of the far pastures. We were flying low, counting cattle, and we got caught in the crosswind of an approaching blizzard. We tried to land, and I did a ground loop."

"I nearly did that once—my wing caught the ground and spun the plane."

"In my case, it cartwheeled."

The way he said it… "Rube, were you the one *flying* the plane?"

Silence and she glanced back at him. He walked, head down, thumbs hooked into the strap of his utility bag.

"Wow. Was anyone hurt?"

"I broke both my legs."

"Oh no."

"Yeah. I was in a cast to my waist for about six months. Missed my senior prom, didn't graduate with my class. Didn't play college football."

He was so matter of fact about it, no emotion, but she had this strange urge to stop, to maybe put her arms around him.

Except that would be as awkward as their little trip on the dance floor.

She still hadn't quite figured out how to get past that.

"So, if you're so afraid of flying, why are you a smoke-jumper?"

"Because fear's not going to win. I love being a smoke-jumper and yeah, I'm not keen on flying, but I so rarely crash…"

She looked back at him again, and he was grinning.

And her heart did this strange little flip in her chest. Her entire body turned warm.

Juliet's words thrummed in her mind. *That's a hot cake if I've ever seen one.*

She looked away, nearly stumbled, caught herself on a tree.

"Okay, really—how bad is your knee?"

Shoot. She righted herself, kept walking. Up ahead, the forest seemed to clear out, and now she could hear water. "Not bad," she snapped. "I'll be fine."

So much for their little spark—her tone put them back where they should be. Two teammates trying to find help.

Reuben said nothing for too long as they walked, and his

silence drove into her, settled into her bones.

Maybe she should have tempered her tone.

Juliet was right—she should stop trying so hard to prove herself.

Gilly pushed through a knot of bushy pines and stopped, Reuben nearly banging into her. She stood on the edge of a gorge, a drop of sixty or so feet into a gently running river.

"Pete Creek, if I remember my map," he said, looking down.

She had a feeling he did.

What he'd left out was the fact that they'd have to rappel.

"So, now what?" she asked, already scrutinizing the cliff. As she looked over the edge, her hands began to sweat.

"We'll have to climb down," Reuben said.

Oh no.

She rubbed her sweaty palms on her pants. She could do this. Really.

"My letdown rope and descender are in my bag," he said. "You go first, and I'll belay you."

"You don't have to belay me." Her voice contained more confidence than it should.

"It's a far drop."

She glanced up at him and affected a frown, ignoring the silent scream of terror inside. "I can descend without help, Rube."

He raised a hand. "Down, girl. I'm just...are you a rock climber?"

And there it was—the noose that she'd stuck her head into. She shook her head. "I...I trained to be a smokejumper."

He just blinked at her.

"A few years ago—about a year after Kate spent the summer in Alaska. I was a hotshot and wanted more." She shrugged. "It didn't work out."

Understatement of the decade, but he didn't have to know the details.

Like her irrational, insane fear of heights.

A fear that didn't seem to touch her behind the controls of a plane. But get her in a parachute, about to jump out… Or on a sixty-foot ledge.

For the team. She could do this. Would do this.

She reached for the rope he'd pulled out of his bag. "I'll find a tree.

His hand on hers stopped her. "I didn't know you wanted to be a smokejumper," he said quietly.

"Yeah, well, it's not—"

"Easy. If I hadn't just seen you do it, I wouldn't have imagined someone your size could pass the requisite 90 minute, 110-pound pack test. That's tough."

She glanced at him. "I made it through the pack test just fine. It just...wasn't for me."

Her throat burned with the lie, and she turned away, hating that she'd nearly let him see—well, too much.

She rooted through the gear bag, found webbing, and secured it around a nearby, sturdy cottonwood. Then she connected the carabiner and fitted the rope through it.

He came over to her. "Throw down enough line to hit the bottom. I'll set up a retrievable system."

She threaded out enough line to touch the river, then handed him the slack. He clipped it into the carabiner and set up the belay system so they could retrieve their rope once they reached the bottom.

He tucked the rope slack into the letdown bag. "We'll throw this down, and when we reach the bottom, we'll simply tug on it and the knot will release."

"Nifty," she said, still eyeing the drop. She wiped her palms on her pants again.

Reuben made a loop, fitted the descender into it, tested the tension.

Then he handed her the harness. "You go first."

"No." She shook her head, trying to keep her voice cool. "I got this. You go first."

He frowned but seemed to consider it. "Okay, maybe that's best. Then I can catch you should—"

"You will not catch me! I can rappel just fine."

She might have put too much *oomph* into her words, because he recoiled, tilted his head as if surprised.

"Ho-kay." He climbed into his jump harness and clipped himself into the rope. Re-shouldered the pack and walked to the edge of the cliff. "Are you sure you shouldn't go first?"

"Just go."

He made a face and put on his gloves. He backed out and leaned over the edge, letting his feet find position.

Then he looked up and met her eyes.

Smiled.

It was the smile that drew her to the edge of the cliff to watch him descend.

As if he might be a billy goat, born to scale the rocks. He flew down the rope, letting it slide through his braking hand, barely slowing until he hit the river.

He stepped into water up to his shins.

She'd always known Reuben was a strong man, the kind who knew his way around the wilderness. Seeing it in action stirred up a new feeling.

They just might make it out, save the rest of their crew.

*If* she could get over the edge and down the cliff.

He unstrapped his harness, stepped out of it, took off his gloves, and shoved them into the elastic straps on the harness. Then he knotted the rope around the figure eight rappeller, gave the rope a tug, and let it go. Gilly brought it up hand over hand.

He was a big man—when she stepped into the harness, it could wrap around her twice. She had to cinch down the legs and waist almost to nothing to make it fit. But she removed the slack from the rope, donned the gloves, and then reached for the excess rope.

"Coming down!"

She threw the pouch containing the excess rope over the side, watching to make sure it landed. He caught it, but let it dangle.

If he pulled on the rope in the pouch, the knot would give, releasing the tension, and she'd plummet to the bottom.

She swallowed down the swirl in her gut—

"Just take it nice and slow. One step at a time!"

Gilly wanted to ignore him, to shout down that she could handle this, but the words glued inside.

*Don't look down.* She remembered her training—those first few days in the letdown area, learning how to get out of a tree. Kate was such a master, she'd taught that part of the course this summer when she took over the new recruits.

Maybe Gilly could have done with a refresher. She leaned back, her hands slick inside the gloves, trying not to let her stomach rebel. She let the rope hold her, her entire weight sinking into the harness, burning her legs, her waist, with the pull. She shuffled her feet down the side of the cliff, her backside out.

Reuben had made it look so easy.

Her feet scraped against the rock, one foothold slipping.

"Just go slow—"

"I am going slow!"

"Fine. Well, if you fall, I'll catch you."

He wasn't serious, was he? Because the last thing—

Her feet slipped again, and pebbles washed down the face of the cliff.

"Rock!"

"Thanks for that," he said.

And now she was sweating. Rivulets of heat ran down her back, her arms shook with the strain of holding herself, and her knee decided to stop working. To top it off, her braking hand was shoved up too tight behind her, almost in a submissive position.

"I'm coming up to get you—"

"Stay where you are! I'm fine!"

"Pull yourself up with your guide hand, just a little. It will release your brake— Whoa!"

She'd been following his instructions and suddenly her brake hand gave way, and she slid down the cliff face, falling forwards, slamming her face against the rock.

She bounced off and put up her knees as she fell another five feet. Her brake hand lodged at her waist, barely holding her, wrenched and burning.

Her knees dug into the side of the rock, the jagged granite tearing through her pants.

She could admit it—maybe she should have let him belay her.

*Don't scream.* Because then, yeah, Reuben would probably start climbing up the forty-some feet...

She tried to breathe as she glanced below, but her lungs were closing up—

"Gilly! Listen to me!"

Reuben stood below her, his arms out as if he really might try and catch her, his feet braced, his expression calm. But his eyes held just enough worry to betray him.

"There are a couple of footholds just below you. Put your feet down, get yourself settled."

His low voice held no edge of panic, and she leaned into it, taking long, even breaths as she lowered one foot, found the ledge, then the other. She let her weight settle on her feet.

"Now, steady yourself with your guide hand and move your brake hand down."

He waited as she moved her right hand down.

"Tuck it just below your hip, but don't get your hand too far back."

Like before? But she listened and repositioned.

"Now, let out slack, slowly, and lean back. Remember, use your hip as a brake, a lever."

She let out rope, leaned back, and found herself resting again on the harness.

"Let it out slowly. Walk down the face of the cliff."

One foot, then another. She began to descend, her heart in her throat.

*Don't look down.*

Her foot slipped again, but she caught herself and for a second dangled free of the rock—

"Lean back, not forward!"

But she was too far back and—

Her guide hand broke free, almost on reflex, to grab something—anything. It found purchase again on the rope, and she yanked hard to right herself.

"No, Gilly, not that one!"

And then she was falling.

Her scream rent the air, her arms flailing as the entire rappelling assembly released.

No—*no*—!

She hit hard, something—not rock but an unyielding force that grabbed her, pulled her in, cushioned her as he fell back into the water with a cold, shocking splash.

And heaven help her, for a second she simply curled into Reuben, holding on, breathing hard.

"Gotcha," he said softly.

# CHAPTER 5

"ARE YOU OKAY?"

Reuben simply lay there, clutching Gilly to his chest, his heart somewhere on the outside of his body, trying to catch his breath.

She, too, seemed shocked, or dazed, or—

He pushed himself up, still holding her. "Gilly?"

"Yeah. I'm okay." But she was shaking, and for a second he had a replay of their incident on the dance floor.

But when she looked at him, something akin to disbelief filled her eyes. "You caught me."

"You didn't think I'd just let you land on your head, did you?"

She frowned. Then, "Thanks."

And that's when he reverted back to his stupid self, something idiotic emerging from his mouth. "That's what teammates are for."

*Really, Reuben?* Because he'd pretty much stopped thinking of her as a teammate, well, honestly, years ago, but it suddenly became a crashing reality maybe five seconds ago. Especially since he had no desire to pull Conner, Pete, or even Kate into his arms.

And that forbidden thought kept going through his head as he helped Gilly up, coiled the rope, and headed downstream. He'd spotted a place where they might get out, a tumble of boulders that made climbing easy. Something that might not injure her knee any further. She was trying to hide it, but by the way she babied it, it had to be hurting.

But she didn't mention it—didn't even grunt—as she climbed up the boulders onto the other side.

He didn't want to think that she was out to prove something—especially to him—but he couldn't shake it.

He knew that kind of bullheaded stubbornness, the kind that could get a person hurt, could damage relationships. Could keep a man from going home.

From his estimation, they had about a mile to the road, maybe less. Overhead the sky had begun to turn a deep umber, the shadows waxing the mountains in lavender and magenta.

They needed to reach the forest service road by twilight, make some progress toward finding the path to the tower. If he had to, he could leave Gilly at the service road to maybe flag down a passerby.

She tripped, and he reached out to grab her elbow.

"I'm fine." She yanked away, but offered a smile. "Really."

"I know," he said, lying, not sure what to do with her determination to press on.

Half of him wanted to pick her up, throw her over his shoulder. He should have listened to his gut and demanded she stay behind. With the sun dipping and Jed and CJ in serious danger, they needed to move faster. He didn't want to mention it, but frankly, he could have made twice the time without her.

The other half understood how regret had teeth, how it

bit down, wouldn't shake loose.

Her foot kicked a log and she grunted, something that suggested she'd wrenched her knee.

"Do you want to stop?" He said it, but—

"No. Of course not." She leaned on a tree, then another as she made her way forward. But at the third tree, she did stop.

Let out a long sigh. "I'm sorry." She turned to him, her expression angry, fierce. "I should have stayed back."

He didn't want to agree, so he pinched his mouth shut in a tight line.

"I'll be okay—it flares up when I put a lot of pressure on it. I just need a second here."

He glanced at the sun, hazy over the mountains. The line of smoke, bigger than before, tufted the horizon. The Davis Canyon fire was growing. They'd probably need a full team of jumpers to put it out now.

She straightened up from the tree. "I probably wouldn't have made a very good smokejumper, limping all over the place."

She started walking again, but her words had reached out, nudged him.

"We have plenty of turned ankles, wrenched knees, and pulled groins when we land—we're often hobbling all over out here," Reuben said.

She looked back then. "Really?"

He startled at the surprise that lit her eyes at his words. "Yeah. Of course."

She nodded, then worked her way over a downed log. "I think I told myself my knee would have held me back. Used it as a justification."

He had to ask—it was drilling a hole through him. "What happened, Gilly? If you passed the pack test—what did you fail?"

She sighed then. "Guess. And you can use the rappel as a hint."

He traced the quick and easy memory of her abysmal descent down the cliff. Her lack of balance, the way the rope slipped too fast through her hand, her scream as she pulled the wrong rope, releasing the rappel. "Did you fail the letdown portion?"

"Nope. But *that* was only from twenty feet up."

Hmm.

And then—wait. Her expression when he'd told her they'd have to rappel.

"You're not afraid of heights, are you?"

"That's the one." She shook her head. "I froze—not just once, but three times—right in the door of the plane, and that's the deal. Three strikes you're out, no matter if you've passed every test, scored better in every other category, and outlasted every man. And especially no matter if you've spent years dreaming about being a smokejumper. If you can't get out of the plane…"

She raised a shoulder, and he had the strangest urge to reach out, to turn her around, look her in the eyes, and tell her that if he could, he'd figure out a way to get her out of a plane and onto their team.

Because no one should have to watch everything they thought they wanted slide by, out of reach.

"So you decided to become a *pilot*?"

She laughed, the sound of it sweet, stirring. "I know, right? But my dad had this missionary friend, Dwayne King, who flew planes in Alaska, and he was visiting our church, found out about my failure, and said he'd teach me to fly. I spent the summer at his base, Kingdom Air, in Alaska and came back with my pilot's license." She held a branch for him. "The thing is, I'm not afraid in the cockpit. Just when I step out into thin air."

"That's when I *stop* being afraid," he said, emitting his own low chuckle. "When I know I can disembark the canister in the sky, spread my wings, and fly."

She made a little sound, one he didn't know how to interpret.

"What?"

"It's just—yeah. I'd love to do it. Just once. Jump out of a plane."

Again, that crazy urge welled in his chest. And the words nearly emerged—*I'll take you jumping*. "So why smokejumping, though?"

Now leaning on a tree, Gilly glanced back at him.

Or maybe she was just resting. He paused, dug out a water bottle, and offered it to her.

Reuben thought through his response and found one that didn't dig out his regrets, his bitterness with it. "Remember how I told you that I broke both legs when the plane crashed?"

She wiped her mouth, nodded.

"Well, I was doing most of the work on the ranch at the time, with Dad. I had a few colleges lined up to play ball at, but I was thinking I'd stick around, help run the ranch, maybe take it over someday. But that winter, because I was confined to a bed or a wheelchair, my brother Knox stepped in. He's only fourteen months younger than I am and has a good head for numbers, was a straight-A student." He took back the water bottle, took a chug.

"I wasn't. I played football. And I was pretty good at roping cattle, herding, branding, and generally the grunt stuff any hand could manage. It was that winter that I realized, as I saw Knox and Dad spend more and more time together, as Dad explained the working of the ranch books, holdings, and finances to Knox, that he wanted Knox to take over."

He put the water bottle back into the pack, took a breath to shake out the acid forming in his chest. Affected a smile. "It didn't really sink in until later, but when it did, I realized there was no room for me at the ranch—at least not at the helm. And I didn't want to play second fiddle to my younger brother. So—I did the next best thing."

"Smokejumping?"

"Bull riding."

She frowned at him, but then she pushed off the tree, started out again.

He looked away, not able to bear the way she shuffled along.

"The thing is, my dad didn't stop me from leaving. I sort of hoped he would—that he'd tell me we'd run the ranch together, all three of us, that I might not be as smart as Knox, but I had what it took to get it done. But he didn't. He stayed silent, walked me out to the truck, told me to keep in touch. Let me drive away without a word."

He couldn't voice the rest, but clearly the success of the ranch had meant more to his dad than working with his eldest son.

He shook the thought away lest it burn a hole through him.

"I started hiring myself out as a cowhand, bull riding on the weekends, and that's where I met Miles. He was also a rodeoer, but he said during the summer he worked with the Jude County Hotshots. It sounded like good, hard work, something I could do, so I came up to Ember, met Jock, and signed on. Two summers later, I tried out to be a smokejumper."

He nearly reached out again when she tripped, but he held back.

She steadied herself on a tree.

Okay, that was enough. "Really, Gilly, let me—"

"I can do this! I'm fine. I just need to rest. I—" She stopped, hung her head. "I'm sorry."

He stood there, nonplussed. "For what?"

"For being weak!" She rounded, her eyes flashing. "For demanding I go along—I'm just slowing us down, and CJ and Jed need us to go faster!"

He couldn't argue with that. But he wanted to, seeing the agony in her expression.

"I just—I hate it when women can't keep up. Or act—"

"Like the weaker sex?"

"Yes! My sisters run a cupcake shop, for Pete's sake. Can you get any more…sweet?"

"What's wrong with sweet? I love Hot Cakes," he said.

She looked up at him, her jaw tight. "Of course you do. You can't see the…embarrassment."

"I see hard work. And two businesswomen who are getting it done."

She stared at him, frowning. Then shook her head, starting off again. This time she didn't bother to hold back her grunts as she walked.

A part of him turned to agony with every little sound she made.

She kept talking, and he didn't miss the strain in her

voice. "They want me to join them." She shook her head. "Can you imagine me—baking? I nearly burned the place down this morning."

He couldn't help a smile. "I doubt that."

"Have you ever eaten my baking?"

"No, but I'd like to."

Or—shoot, had he really said that? He wanted to gulp it back the minute she stopped, looked at him, her mouth open.

Because to his ears, it sorta sounded like...

"No. You wouldn't. Trust me. I'm not a girly-girl, and I can't cook."

Huh. "What does cooking—or baking—have to do with being a girly-girl? Some of the world's best chefs are men."

She started moving again. "You don't get it."

"Enlighten me."

"I don't want people to look at me like that—"

"Like what?"

"Like…I'm a hot cake."

She stopped, turned and stood there, her hands on her hips, looking up at him, so much ferocity in her gaze that he just wanted to burst out laughing.

Because that was exactly what she was. Sweet and hot. So she didn't have the traditional curves. She was strong and lithe, even hidden under her pilot jumpsuit, and could too easily resurrect the way, however briefly, she'd moved with him on the dance floor. Graceful. She embodied all sorts of hotness.

And that package came with a giant-sized allotment of kindness and determination to save his hide.

Yeah, she had *hot cake* written all over her.

Oh shoot, his humor must have shown on his face, because her expression changed from ferocious to incredulous.

"You—what you are you thinking, Reuben Marshall?"

"Nothing."

He strode out ahead of her.

"I don't believe you."

He was grinning, but slowed his pace, not wanting to aggravate her knee more.

"It's just—" No. *No.* He couldn't actually say the word.

And then, abruptly, he stopped. Through the thinning trees, under the waning of the sun, he made it out—the forest road. A gravelly strip of salvation.

She caught up to him, and before she could launch into another barrage, he pointed to the road. "We follow that, and we'll find the trail to the lookout tower. We'll have a chopper in here by midnight."

She seemed relieved enough to let him off the hook as they came out to the road. Asphalt and gravel, it cut north from Yaak. One could follow it all the way to Canada.

"If we follow this about a mile or two, we'll be about a half mile from the Garver lookout tower road. We'll have to do more bushwhacking and maybe cross Pete Creek again—"

"No—"

"Sorry. The road intersects it just north of here. But…" He turned to her. "Are you sure you don't want to hunker down here and wait? I'm sure someone will come by—"

"No. I can make it."

And by the way her jaw clenched, he knew she meant it.

"But your knee—"

"I'm fine. Don't leave me here, Reuben. I'll keep up."

"Hey, hey—calm down. I know you will. You're a real trooper…" And then the nickname just slipped out, unintended, but it sat right there, on the forefront of his tongue, his brain, and he couldn't help it. "Hot Cake."

Her mouth opened. "No, you *did not* just say that."

He made a face, wincing. "Sorry, I just—but you are. Totally a hot cake. Feisty and tough, and—I'm sorry, Gilly, but you are hot. You about knocked me over in that dress, and I know we probably shouldn't ever talk about it again, but I loved dancing with you, even if I embarrassed us. I'm so sorry about that. But you're also really sweet and kind and—"

"I am not." Her mouth closed in a tight, thin line.

"You saved my life. And could have died doing it. So, yeah, I'm calling it. Sweet. Kind."

And that shut her down. She folded her arms over her chest. Looked away.

"Not so good at taking compliments, though. C'mon." He started down the road, north, listening to her shuffle after him.

"Fine," she said finally, quietly. "Just…don't tell anyone."

He waited for her to catch up. "It'll be our secret."

She glanced up at him then, the barest of smiles on her face.

No, he wouldn't mind so much carrying her if it came to that.

The road had turned into a dusky ribbon, the gravel shiny under the glow of the fading sun. They walked along in silence, and he noticed her gait had picked up on the smoother surface.

Common sense said that he should leave her—he had no idea how she'd climb the route to the tower. But the expression on her face when he'd suggested it…

If they didn't get help soon, well, he had no idea how long

Jed had before he turned septic with his injury. As for CJ...

Gravel crunching, a motor—the sound of an approaching vehicle—made Reuben reach out for Gilly, draw her to the side of the road.

He could hardly believe it when he turned and spotted an ancient station wagon—it looked like a 1970s Ford Pinto Cruising Wagon, with the round safari windows—heading toward them, kicking up dust on the dirt road.

It slowed and strangely, Gilly reached out, touched his arm. Slid her hand down to his.

Held on.

Huh.

The driver leaned over, rolled down the window. In his early seventies, good looking, with short gray hair, white at the temples, the man wore a graying scuff of whiskers, a blue denim shirt rolled up at the elbows, and a fishing vest, the pockets empty.

Reuben startled, recognizing the man. "Hey, Brownie, what are you doing out here?"

Jim Browning—Brownie—owned the buffalo ranch just outside town. His son, Patrick, fixed planes for the base. And of course Reuben had known the grandson, Tom, the best—he'd been on his team, had died in the flare-up last fall.

Brownie squinted at them. "Reuben? Is that you?"

"And Gilly Priest." Weird that she wasn't more excited. Even more strange was the solid grip on his hand. "Our jump plane went down about ten miles due west."

"Oh no. Anyone hurt?"

"Yeah, actually. We could use a lift to get to a radio. Call in help."

Strange, now that he thought about it, that he hadn't

heard one flight overhead all day. Didn't anyone know they were down? After Gilly hadn't returned, the folks at headquarters should have started getting suspicious. The thought niggled at him, but he tucked it into the back of his brain as Brownie opened the passenger door.

"Get in. I have a radio at the cabin."

Reuben started toward the door, but a tug on his hand stopped him. He shot a look at Gilly. She was frowning, her lips tight.

"What—"

"I don't...maybe we should just hike to the tower."

He touched her shoulders, leaned down to meet her eyes. "What's the matter? We're running out of time, Brownie has a radio, and your knee is about to give out."

She swallowed, glanced at Brownie. Back to Reuben. "I…" Then she sighed. "You're probably right. I'm fine."

He didn't believe her. Still, their options were fading with the sunlight. "Gilly—everything is going to be okay. I promise."

She offered a smile, but it felt fake, everything about it forced.

What—?

"Now or never, kids," Brownie said. "But I'll be glad to call it in for you if you decide to stay."

"No, we're coming," Gilly said and let go of Reuben's hand.

But as she got into the backseat and shut the door, he felt that same niggle in his gut, the one he'd had when he'd seen Jock run back into the flames. When he'd followed Pete to the black.

They should be running the other direction.

*Run.*

Gilly slid into the backseat, refusing to acknowledge the word booming in the back of her brain. But something about the car, everything from the color, an orange-red, to the interior—aged with layers of dirt, fishing tackle, and the scent of dead animal—all conspired to weave through her, constrict her heart, her throat.

She knew this car. Or at least something similar to it. The memory raised the fine hairs on the back of her neck.

"Are you okay?" This from Reuben, who'd climbed into the front seat then turned around to look at her.

She looked away. Nodded.

She didn't know why she couldn't look at him. Why a second ago she'd been holding his hand—yes, for nearly dear life. A reflex she couldn't explain—and the next she felt like he'd sold her into slavery.

Her heart thundered in her throat, her palms dappled with sweat, she couldn't breathe.

Yeah, she was *just* fine.

"Okay," Reuben said, frowning. He turned back around to look at Brownie. "Thanks for the ride."

"I'm going up to the cabin to do some fly fishing," Brownie said as they headed north up the road.

Away from the lookout tower. But if Brownie had a radio, then they wouldn't need the tower.

Gilly curled her arms around her waist, fought the tremor that snaked up her spine. Her knee ached—she desperately needed ice—and her head throbbed from the crash. She put her hand to her forehead. It was hot. Maybe she had a concussion—that could attribute for the pitching of her stomach.

But not the way the smells of the backseat racked up the shudder or the quiet, building urge to throw herself from the car.

This *couldn't* be the same car.

She shook her head, tried to pay attention to what Reuben was saying, his explanation of the plane crash.

"So she put us down in this creek bed, but it was a harder landing than we'd expected, and a few of us are pretty hurt."

She noticed how he avoided putting the blame on her, but, well—

If CJ and Jed died, she'd know exactly whom to blame.

Then Reuben flashed another look at her, a half smile that fell into concern again when she couldn't return it. Then, suddenly, he draped his hand over the seat, touching her good knee, as if hoping to reassure her.

Oddly, the gesture soothed the roil in her stomach, settled it. She reached out for his big hand and slid hers into it. Squeezed, just for a second. His hand enveloped hers, warm, scarred, a little roughened, but strong.

Yes, she was with Reuben. She'd be fine—they'd all be fine.

Hadn't he caught her from crashing into the river?

She let his hand go as a new heat started in her stomach, worked its way out to her body, into her heart. *You about knocked me over in that dress.*

That silly, too-girly dress that had her feeling half naked all over again.

They hadn't driven very far when they pulled off the main road, turning east, cutting through a hunting path in the woods, the wagon slowing to bump over roots and under low-hanging branches. Brownie had flicked on his lights, and they cast a pale swath through the lurking purple and green shadows of the woolly forest.

"If we can raise our team on the radio, we can get a chopper to our location."

"I can drive you folks back to town, if that helps," Brownie said. "Or Patrick can. He should be back from fishing by now."

Her ears perked up. "Patrick is here?"

"Our annual trip at the end of every summer for Tom's birthday." He was silent for a moment, then added, "It's a hard day, and Patrick needed some time alone, so…"

Gilly looked out the window, rubbing her arms against the strangest rush of chill.

They emerged to the dark cabin, nestled in a small clearing. She guessed it couldn't be more than two rooms, tiny as it was. It sat under a ruff of towering cottonwood, tucked into the embrace of a stand of white pine. A small porch led up to the front door.

Brownie parked. "Looks like Patrick isn't back yet. Go on in. I'll turn on the gas to the cabin, and we'll stir together some grub while we wait for him."

"We just need to use the radio," Reuben said, getting out and grabbing his pack. Gilly followed him, climbing up the steps into the tiny cabin.

Brownie disappeared for a bit, then came around the side of the cabin, where he'd probably turned on the gas, and unlocked the door, flicking on a flashlight to illuminate the interior. The light skidded across a linoleum table and metal chairs circa 1950 in a tiny kitchen area with dishes drying in a rack over the sink. A separate propane tank powered the stove and refrigerator from the same era.

"I think there are some eggs in the refrigerator, Gilly," Brownie said. "Reuben, I'll power up the ham."

She glanced at Reuben, who was suppressing a smile at Brownie's immediate assignment of her to the kitchen.

Brownie lit a lamp on the table, the wick saturated in oil, and a warm glow puddled around the cabin. It illuminated the small room, a doorway to what Gilly guessed was a bedroom. A ratty tweed sofa lined one wall, anchored by an old desk. A chipped coffee table that showed boot scuff marks sat in front of the sofa.

On the desk sat a small square silver box, a large dial in the middle surrounded by smaller dials. A speaker sat beside the radio, an old silver microphone connected with a wire to the assembly.

"My parents had one of these on the ranch," Reuben said, picking up the microphone. "An old HR0-500 ham."

Brownie lit the gas lamp over the desk. "We use it for making calls back to the ranch in Ember. Patrick must have taken the mobile device."

Reuben pulled out a chair. "Hopefully I can pick up someone—I remember Conner's frequency, but he might not be listening."

"Better to use the emergency frequency," Brownie said.

Gilly went to the fridge, opened it. No light, but a cool breath cascaded over her, and her stomach immediately emitted a growl.

Inside, a carton of eggs, a piece of salami, and a shelf of beer suggested a fishing weekend rife with hope. She pulled out the eggs. Set the gear pack on the counter while she found the cast-iron pan.

A layer of bacon grease coated the bottom.

Maybe she wasn't so hungry.

She glanced at Reuben, watched as he worked the radio.

"It doesn't seem to want to power on," Brownie said. He was fiddling with the connection to the battery, a large 12-volt.

Brownie got up, made a face. "We might have to use the battery from the car. It'll drain it, but if we only use it for a short burst, the radio'll power up." He turned to Gilly. "Did you find everything?"

She managed a nod, not sure what to say.

"I'll be right back. Make yourselves at home," Brownie said and headed outside.

The door shut behind him with a click, and she looked at Reuben.

He stood up, watching Brownie go, then turned to Gilly.

"What is it?" He walked over to her. "You're freaking me out a little. Why didn't you want to get into the car with him?"

She ran her hands over her arms, suddenly aware of the chill that had gathered in the cabin. "It's nothing—I was being…it doesn't matter. The important thing is that we get help."

He must have seen her shiver, because he reached out and touched her shoulders. Ran his hands over them, down her arms.

He had warm, big hands, a solid grip, and she had an insane urge to lean into him, to let him enfold her in his embrace.

She was just tired. And hurting. And— "The fact is, the car reminded me of something that happened. Years ago—it's not a big deal, but…"

And then she swallowed, because it *was* a big deal and her lie would lodge there, right in the center of her chest.

Her throat suddenly thickened and she shook her head and stepped out of his grip. "I'm sorry. I shouldn't have brought it up. Really, it's not important."

She headed for the kitchen, but Reuben's voice stopped her.

"Gilly."

He came up behind her, and she could feel his solid presence. "What happened?"

She shook her head, crazy tears burrowing behind her eyes. Now? Really? But maybe if she could get it out, he could tell her she was just overreacting, letting the past manhandle her. She could break free, find her footing, not let her fears turn her weak.

"I was attacked when I was sixteen by a man in a station wagon."

She said it plain out, hoping that by voicing it, it might dispel the silent hold the secret had on her.

She felt his hand on her shoulder, turning her. And when she looked up at him, Reuben wore horror in his eyes. "Did you say you were…*attacked*?"

She made a face, trying to shake away the rush of emotion. "He didn't really hurt me—someone came along and scared him off. But, yeah. I was walking alone late at night, going home from the fire base. It was summer, and nothing ever happens in Ember—we all know each other, right? And I only live about a mile away. It was late, though, and dark. I reached the gravel road and heard a car behind me, slowing, pulling up. I turned, and I saw it—this station wagon. Just like Brownie's—with the round window in the back.

"I freaked out a little, started to run, and that's when I heard footsteps. It was dark and I tripped, otherwise I would have outrun him. That's when I hurt my knee—I landed hard on a boulder, and it hurt so bad. I didn't realize I'd broken my kneecap. I couldn't get away."

He swallowed, looked stricken.

"I don't know what he looked like. And it was dark. He came over, picked me up, threw his hand over my mouth, and I was just—helpless. I kicked and tore at him, but he wrestled me back to the car. Opened the back door and threw me in. And it smelled…" She pressed her hand to her mouth, the bile rising. "Dirty. Old. Feral. He was ripping at my shorts, and I was kicking him, but he was big—*really big*—and strong, and I was no match for him."

"Oh no." Reuben's jaw hardened, and he shook his head, something fierce in his eyes. "Tell me he didn't—"

"No, that's the thing. Jock, Kate's dad, came driving up the road—I could hear his motorcycle from a distance, and I started screaming. I think maybe the man realized that he couldn't, well…so he let me go. Just threw me out of the car, into the ditch, and drove off. Jock found me there and took me home."

"And you never saw him? Never pressed charges?"

She shook her head. "I didn't know who it was—I could never have recognized him. I didn't tell my parents for years. And they were so worried about my knee, and I felt so angry and…weak. And helpless. And stupid for walking home in the dark." She looked away, not able to tell him the rest, the real reason she was walking home so late, so she cut to the important part. "I vowed that I'd never let anything like that happen again. Ever." Tough, not tender. Brave, not beautiful.

Reuben took a long breath, nodding. "I'm so sorry, Gilly." For a big, tough man, he wore a surprising amount of emotion in his eyes, and she had to look away. "I need to know, right now—do you think it was Brownie?"

She shook her head. "No. It was just the memory…"

She felt his hand on her arm, and then, suddenly, he tugged her into his embrace.

Holding on, protecting her.

And, strangely, she sank into him. Just let the past shudder out against him.

Yes, maybe Reuben was exactly the man to keep her safe, help her finally break free of her fears.

The door creaked open then, and she took a breath, started to untangle herself from Reuben's embrace.

But oddly, he didn't let her go. Instead, he put her behind him, stepping out in front of her.

"Hey, Patrick," Reuben said calmly. "Why don't you put that gun down, huh?"

# CHAPTER 6

T O REUBEN'S EYES, PATRICK looked a little like old Custer the bull, blood in his eyes. He'd come in while Gilly was tucked in his arms, holding on, and it took Reuben a full second to realize that Patrick wasn't fooling around.

Patrick wore his hair high and tight in a military shave, a goatee, a dirty green flannel shirt, and jeans. And a dark-edged anger in his expression.

If he had the power, Reuben would, in these moments, rewind time and choose differently.

Like not letting Jock run into a fire that could kill him. Or not giving into Gilly's demand to hike out with him. And especially the moment when he should have listened to her silent pleading not to get in the station wagon.

Because even if Patrick was just protecting his land— which Reuben completely doubted—Reuben had somehow put Gilly in danger.

Again.

Reuben had dredged up all her nightmares of being attacked.

*I vowed that I'd never let anything like that happen again.*

"Don't move, Gilly," Reuben said quietly.

"Reuben, don't be silly—it's Patrick."

Gilly tried to come out from behind him, but he had hold of her arm, held her securely in place.

Patrick had kicked the door shut behind him, his hands full with a lever-action .22 rifle.

The kind of rifle used for shooting the wolves which came after their cattle.

At this range, the bullet might go through both of them.

Reuben raised one hand. "I'm not sure what you think is happening here, Patrick, but your father picked us up on the road, and we're just here to use the radio. The jump plane crashed and—"

"I know." His tone said more than that, however, and the words settled into Reuben.

He knew. Because—?

"Oh good—I wasn't sure anyone caught our transmission before we crashed." Gilly slipped out of Reuben's grip, grabbing the pack from the counter. "We need to get back to the team."

She took a step toward the door.

"Stop, Gilly. Now," Patrick snapped.

That's exactly what Reuben was going to say. Because even he could see that Patrick's words weren't meant to convey that help might be on the way.

On the contrary, Reuben suddenly had a dark, gut feeling that Patrick had something to do with the fact that half his team was scared and dying in the woods.

"We just want to use the radio, and we'll be out of here," Reuben said. He kept his voice calm, centering himself, just like he would before settling upon a bull. He needed to think. Still his breathing. And an eye on Patrick's gun told him to approach softly, with no recrimination in his tone.

"It doesn't work. Hasn't worked for years. And you're not going anywhere."

Gilly frowned at him.

"And no, Gilly, HQ has no idea where you are." Patrick didn't even glance at Gilly when he spoke, his gaze only on Reuben. Reuben itched for a distraction, the chance to put Patrick on the floor.

As it was, Gilly froze. And Reuben ached for her when she said slowly, "I don't understand."

A beat, and Reuben met Patrick's eyes. *Please, don't hurt her.*

Patrick's voice fell, dark and steely. "I think you do."

Gilly looked at Reuben, but Patrick took a step toward Reuben. "Sit down, Reuben. Over there."

He motioned to the sofa, and Reuben held up his hands, glanced at Gilly.

"Let Gilly go. She has nothing to do with this."

"Nothing to do with what?" Gilly said.

"I'm not angry at Gilly," Patrick said, ignoring her. "She's just a casualty of firefighting." His eyes hardened. "Like my son, Tom."

Yes. Reuben had put the puzzle together, and connected this moment to last fall's tragedy.

And what did Brownie say about this being a hard day?

A hard summer. His mind went back to Conner's lost drone, the one that found its way from the Browning property to the Whiskey Creek fire.

"You blame us for Tom's death," Reuben said quietly. "And I understand. I do, too."

"What?" Gilly said. "Wait—you're blaming Reuben for the fire? Patrick—!"

"Stay put, Gilly!"

"I know you miss Tom—we all do," Reuben said, his hands still raised. He was using his very best mental telepathy to tell Gilly to sneak out, that he'd keep Patrick's attention on himself. Or die trying. "But we can't change it—"

"Shut up! This *is* all your fault—all of you. Conner, Pete, and you. Tommy trusted his team. I trusted the team. And you all left him to burn to death on the mountain."

Reuben had no words. Because Patrick was right.

His jaw tight, Reuben glanced at Gilly, who was staring at Patrick with a white-faced horror.

"Wait—Patrick, you haven't been—trying to *kill the team*, have you? Are you the one behind the arson?" Her voice pitched to a low-toned of disbelief. "Did you have something to do with the plane going down? The low fuel tanks?"

"You don't understand, Gilly." Patrick had the shotgun leveled at Reuben and looked a millisecond from coming unglued.

Where was Brownie? The question niggled at the back of Reuben's brain.

"They left Tom there to die. A terrible, horrific death!"

"I know, Patrick," Gilly pleaded. "I know, but this isn't—"

"And they deserve to die in the same way!"

Reuben didn't like the way Patrick's hands shook. He just needed a second—a moment when Patrick might not be looking at him.

"Please, Patrick, don't hurt him!" Gilly held up her hands, Reuben's pack swinging nearly off her shoulder. "He isn't to blame—"

"He is completely to blame! All of them!"

"Not Hannah. Not CJ. Not Kate or Jed or—"

"Listen, Patrick," Reuben said quietly. "We both know that Gilly isn't a part of this. If you need justice, do what you have to, to me, but let Gilly go—"

"I don't think so, Reuben."

Patrick started backing toward the door, and Reuben inched forward.

"Get back!" Patrick swung the gun at Gilly. "Both of you. Or I shoot her."

Reuben went completely still, everything shutting down to a cold halt. He looked at Gilly, the way she paled, the shaking of her hands.

Why hadn't he listened to Gilly's warning on the road?

Reuben fought for a breath through his constricting chest, only finding it when Patrick turned the gun back on him.

Gilly, however, was shaking her head in a sort of crazy disbelief. "No!" She took another step toward Patrick. "Please, Pat—"

And that's when Patrick took his eyes off Reuben.

It was all Reuben needed. He lunged at Patrick, intending to slap the gun away.

The carpet caught him, and he tripped. Patrick turned back, brought the barrel up—

The shot exploded nearly in Reuben's ear.

Something shattered behind him, heat and searing pain burning in his skull.

Gilly screamed as he fell. Fire lacerated his head, and he slapped his hand to the heat, seeing shades of gray. He landed hard on the floor, dizzy. When he pulled away his hand, it came back slick and hot.

Bloody.

"You shot him! Oh my gosh—you shot him!"

But even as the world tilted, he saw—what? Gilly leaping at Patrick, the bear spray out, full throttle. Patrick threw his hand up to protect his face against the blast, screaming.

Then before Reuben could get up and tackle him—before he could even find his feet—Patrick twisted the gun around and clipped Gilly against the head.

She dropped like a cannonball, the spray canister flying out of her grip.

Patrick stumbled back, coughing, spitting, words issuing from his mouth about Gilly, the lot of them. He made it to the door. "It's better this way, anyway. Burn both of you—all of you—like they did."

Then he slammed the door behind him. Locked it from the outside.

"Gilly!" Reuben wanted to get up, but his legs wouldn't move right—and the entire room was spinning.

He held the floor as it swayed, and tried to make his way to Gilly.

But she'd come to life, pushing herself up, crawling to him.

Patrick had cut her, bloodied her cheek. But she seemed to ignore it, catching Reuben as he tumbled forward.

He closed his eyes, felt like half his skin had peeled from his head, heard ringing in his ears behind her voice and the sound of a zipper.

Then something soft pressed the wound.

He yelped.

"Sorry."

He butterflied his eyes open and found her peering down at him.

"First aid kit. Good thinking," he said, his eyes longing to close again. Except her face crumpled, and she looked away, shaking her head.

"Sorry. I won't cry. I just… won't." She closed her eyes, made a noise, as if holding back a wail, then took a deep breath.

"Okay. You're going to be okay." She leaned over him, and he was vaguely aware now that his head had landed in her lap, cradled there. She pulled the cotton away and examined his wound.

"It's deep and long—the bullet grazed your head. Your ear is cut, and I can see your scalp."

"In other words, it's just a flesh wound. I've had worse."

She frowned at him, and he agreed it might be the wrong time to pull out his Monty Python quotes.

Instead, he groaned again as she replaced the cotton pad.

And the room started to darken around the edges.

That's when he smelled it—something rancid, like a skunk had broken loose in the cabin, sprayed the air.

"What's that smell?"

Gilly seemed bewildered, but looked around, catching on fast. "The bullet hit the wall, destroyed a lamp—"

"It's propane. It's flooding the room with gas—and with the lamps lit, the room could ignite. We have to stop the leak."

"I'll do it." But as she got up, he saw her stiffen, her breath catching.

And only then did he see the flicker of flame in the window.

"It's too late. The front porch is on fire," she said in a voice he didn't quite recognize.

That's where Brownie went. Setting them up, locking them in, and burning them alive. Like his grandson.

"Brownie is our arsonist."

"And Patrick rigged the plane," Gilly said, crouching beside him. "He might have even been the one who crashed and stole the drones—he would have certainly known how to refit them for his use. But it doesn't matter because right now, we have to get out of here."

He agreed. Only problem was, his legs didn't want to move. His entire body turned to slush as the room tilted, spun, and made him want to hug the floor.

She tried the door. "It's locked."

"Try the back bedroom, see if there's an escape."

He lay there like a drunk as she left him. She returned in moments, dropping to her knees, shaking her head.

"No good. The front door is the only one." She got up then and started for the window, working the latch to open it. "If we can open the window, the gas might evaporate—"

Glass shattered as a shot decimated the window. Gilly screamed, jerked back, grabbed her hand. Blood dripped from it.

"He shot me!"

Reuben pushed himself up, felt like he might vomit on the spot, but grabbed her, pulled her down.

Another shot chipped at the wall in the kitchen.

"They're not going to let us leave!" Gilly said.

He said nothing, just took her hand, found the glass embedded there. "You're not shot—just cut." He eased out the glass then reached for the roll of cotton gauze in the pack. But his hands shook, so she took it and wrapped it around her hand.

The rancid smell had dissipated with the night air, but smoke from the fire began to filter in, hover around the ceiling. And, with the gas lines alive and thick with gas, the place could torch any moment.

"Reuben—I'm..."

He thought she might say scared, but the word that came out was "sorry."

"You're sorry? For what?"

"For not having better aim. I thought I got his eyes, but I should have ducked or grabbed the gun or—"

"Gilly. Stop." He touched her arm. "No. You were awesome. But we have to get out of here—"

"How about the bathroom?"

"Yes!"

He levered himself to all fours, fighting his way across the floor.

The flames crackled into the window, licking the frame, igniting the grimy curtains.

Gilly had a hold on his collar and pulled, directing him through a door toward the blackness of a bedroom. He hit his head on the jamb to the bathroom.

"There's no window!" he said.

"No. And no toilet. But there's washbasin and a tin tub— we could get in it."

"We'll never fit, not both of us. But this place has a porch which means—"

"There's a crawl space under the house!" Gilly said.

He sat on the floor, holding onto the tub as it swayed.

"What now?" she said.

"We gotta…move…this…" He couldn't think clearly.

"I'll help you. We'll do it together." She got up, wedged her body against the wall, her feet against the tub.

He managed to get to his knees. "I can only do this once, I think."

And then, with a roar, he ripped the tub from the floor.

Black filled his eyes, the room pitched, and he felt himself falling.

"No! Reuben, stay with me!"

But the floor came too fast, too hard. He crashed onto it, woozy.

When he pushed himself up, he knew he was going to faint.

"Reuben, don't leave me—"

Gilly climbed over him, kicking at a drainage pipe in the floor. He opened his eyes enough to see it rip free, and with it, a chunk of board. She had her feet braced on either side of him, sawing the pipe back and forth to open a gap.

Then suddenly, he heard a splintering, and she threw the pipe out of the room.

A gap opened up, about the size of his thigh.

But, of course, just about big enough for Gilly.

"Go," he said, his voice echoing in his head. He added oomph to it when he smelled smoke. "Get out of here!"

"No!" She kicked at the boards.

They didn't move.

"Please, Gilly, go."

"I'm not leaving without you!" She was frantic now, jumping on the boards. "Please, please—"

He couldn't take it. He pushed himself up, grabbed her hand. Pulled her down to meet his face. "I can't fit through there. The house is going to explode. Go. Now. *Save our team*."

Something in his words must have clicked, because she stopped fighting and just stared at him.

Oh, she had gorgeous eyes—many of them—but all of them were a shade of blue, with flecks of green and gold.

He traced her face, memorizing it, and then, because he couldn't stop himself, he closed the gap and kissed her. Quick and over before she could respond, but mostly because he'd lost his mind on the crawl to the bathroom, and he didn't know what else to do to say good-bye.

Then he shoved her through the hole, a hand on her shoulder, all the way down, until she crouched in the blackness under the house. He tossed the gear pack down after her. Then he stuck his head down through the hole.

And sure enough, light dented the far edge, a crawl space under the length of the building.

"Go, Gilly!"

And thank God, she did, scrambling toward the light.

He closed his eyes, and breathed in the cool air, letting the oblivion take him.

*Our team.* Reuben's words hung in her mind, burning as Gilly scrabbled out from under the back of the house, crouching in the shadows to search for Patrick. Or Brownie.

Her brain still couldn't wrap around the fact that they'd been—were—trying to kill her.

Them.

Her team.

She wasn't going to let any more of them die. Starting with Reuben.

No. The sound of Patrick screaming stirred inside of her.

She couldn't believe she'd bear-sprayed him. Or that her crazy idea *worked*. She'd watched him talk to Reuben, all the while rooting in the pack for the bear spray. Waited for the moment when he turned to her.

Except it hadn't quite turned out like she'd hoped—Reuben shot, bleeding, passed out with his head stuck in a drainage hole while the cabin burned around him.

The death Patrick hoped he'd have.

The death the Brownings had planned for all of them—first by arson and then by the crashing of her plane. She thought of the ripped chutes from earlier in the season, the ones Kate had found and fixed. She would bet that Patrick had had a hand in damaging them during the off-season.

Gilly gritted her jaw against a rise of fury and scuttled out into the yard, dragging the pack behind her, not sure what to do, but sure of one thing.

Reuben was not going to die.

Halfway to the forest's edge, she spotted the woodpile. A beaver dam of split firewood, a chopping block, and embedded in it, an ax.

She ran toward it, keeping low, aware of the glow illuminating the night, the flames curling up around the roof.

Dropping the pack, she put her hands on the ax and pulled.

It refused to move, like Excalibur in the rock. She glanced again at the house, then stood up straight and wiggled the ax, fighting for leverage. The ax barely budged.

She could use some of Reuben's epic strength.

*Please , God!*

The cry came from inside, but she let it ring out, fill her chest as she heaved upward.

The ax tore free of the wood and landed with a clunk on the wood-chip-covered ground.

She picked it up, ducked, and huddled in the darkness.

Patrick came striding around the house, patrolling for escapees, his gun held loosely in his grip. She suppressed the crazy urge to run out, ax raised, but…

She wasn't the kind of person who could embed an ax in a person's body, even if they had just tried to burn her alive.

She hunkered down, barely breathing as he walked past. Waited until he rounded the side of the house—

Then she dashed across the grass, shimmied under the crawl space, dragging the ax with her.

Reuben lay where she'd left him, his head positioned in the hole, breathing in the sweet, albeit dirty, air.

"Rube—wake up." She patted his cheek. He didn't twitch.

"Rube!" She patted him again—nothing, and she got desperate.

If he could do it, so could she. After all, his quick peck had shocked her enough for her to freeze, for him to wrestle her through the floorboards and shove her out of danger.

Hers could do the same.

She leaned forward, but instead of a quick kiss, she pressed her lips to his, added passion.

And, just for a second, she lost herself in the fact that for the first time well, ever, she actually *wanted* to kiss someone. No, not just someone, but Reuben. Strong, capable…sweet Reuben.

It lasted only a second or two, but long enough to stir inside her something she hadn't realized she possessed…

Sparks. A desire to get free and maybe give him another chance to ask her to dance.

She broke away, her hand on his cheek, and he roused, opened his eyes.

Blinked at her. "Um…"

"Yeah, I know. Now, let's get you out of here." She pushed on his shoulders and he groaned, but pulled his head out of the hole.

She shoved her way up and found him sitting on the floor.

Smoke filled the room, and the fact the cabin had yet to blow seemed a miracle from God.

"Look out," she said, climbing up through the hole. The room was so tiny she had to stand outside the door, but after he moved his feet she managed to bring the ax down on the wood.

It bounced off, barely leaving a dent.

"Oh, boy," Reuben said. "That's really pitiful."

"Hey!"

But he was climbing to his knees, bracing himself on the wall with one hand. With the other he reached out for the ax.

She surrendered it. And in one quick, chilling move, he brought the ax down on the floor, cracking it. Another one-handed swing and he'd doubled the hole.

"C'mon!" She jumped through the hole to the dirt floor and backed up to accommodate Reuben's girth.

He slid down beside her, so big he had to back his way through the hole. Once in the dirt, his head hit the floorboards as he groped for purchase, pulling himself along on his stomach.

She scrambled to the edge and put a hand on his shoulder. "Shh."

They stilled, waiting as Patrick looped once again around

the outside. Gilly watched him pass then slid out, checking. "We're clear."

Reuben wasn't a quick man. Strong, yes, solid—but not quick. He lumbered out of the crawl space so slowly she thought he might still be half in by the time Patrick returned.

She grabbed his arm to help, and it slipped out of her grip. So she settled on the scruff of his shirt, pulling him along.

He seemed woozy, his head a bloody mess now, and when he got to his feet, he nearly fell over.

She looped his arm around her shoulder. "Run with me."

She couldn't look behind her, just started off in a staggered sprint towards the woods, but she refused to crumble under his weight, gritting her teeth.

They reached the forest line, and she half pushed him into a thicket of brush, falling down beside him. He lay on his back, groaning and she clamped a hand over his mouth, as Patrick circled the house again.

Patrick stopped just feet away from their hiding place, watching the flames lick out through the windows, curl the roof shingles, a dark outline of bitterness against the glow of the fire.

He'd torched his own family cabin with the hope of killing them. She couldn't imagine a pain, an anger that burrowed that deep.

The house exploded—a massive burst of yellow, white, and orange, ripping through the night, blowing off the roof, turning the house to an inferno. Splinters of wood, glass, and debris rained down into the yard, spilling into the forest.

Gilly ducked her head, and then suddenly, Reuben rolled over, covering her body with his, his arm over her shoulders, his leg across hers, his face next to her own.

He smelled of dirt and blood, sweat and strength, his body a blanket, long and powerful, protecting her.

She searched for the fear, the revulsion that should be radiating out from her core, that should push him away, but felt nothing.

No—she felt something. A lot of something—the crazy urge to roll over, tuck herself in his arms with the hope that she'd stop shaking. Maybe even curl her hands into his shirt, lift her face, let him kiss her again.

This time, a kiss they both might participate in.

Heat emanated off the blaze, even from thirty feet away.

"What happened?" Reuben asked in her ear. "I think I might have blanked out for a bit there."

Which meant his protection of her—him rolling over to throw his body between her and danger—emanated from pure instinct.

She didn't know why a shard of disappointment sliced through her. "The house blew up," she said quietly.

"And we're not in it," he said. He finally lifted his head, rolled onto his back. He found her eyes in the dim light. "You saved my life, again."

She lifted a shoulder. "It's what I do."

But she didn't know what to say when he reached up, touched her cheek. A soft, kind gesture that had her turning away.

"He cut your cheek," Reuben said.

"And he shot you," she countered.

Reuben's voice hardened. "And now that he knows the team is out there…"

Patrick's outline had disappeared. "I wonder if Patrick was killed in the explosion." Despite all he'd done, she couldn't deny a twinge of sadness.

"But what about Brownie?"

She shook her head, glanced out at the flames, now two stories high, curling around the cabin roof. Sparks ignited the night sky and cinders fell into the nearby forest.

"We need to get out of here," Reuben said. He pushed himself up, then groaned, leaned forward, holding his head. "The world is still spinning. I think I have a concussion."

"You probably do." She'd dropped his jump pack near the woodpile. "I need to get the pack—stay here."

"Be careful."

Crouching, she skirted the edge of the forest, keeping an eye out for Brownie against the illumination of the blaze. When she reached the edge of the woodpile, she darted out.

The pack lay on the ground, protected from the flames by the stump. She grabbed it, shouldered it—

And that's when she saw the figure moving around the house, watching the flames. No—not one, but two, the firelight revealing their faces, grim, angry. She crouched behind the stump, her heart in her throat.

The pair got into the station wagon, leaving the house to burn. Cinders cascaded around her, lit scrub around the house aflame.

It occurred to her that this blaze could turn into a raging forest fire.

The car drove away, down the trail, and her heart fell. She had no doubt of their destination.

She waited until the vehicle disappeared in the woods, then she stumbled back to Reuben. "We gotta go," she said as she rustled through the pack for a headlamp.

Reuben was on his hands and knees, his head to the

ground.

"Can you walk?"

He lifted his head, tried a nod, winced.

"Okay, I'll help you." She fitted on the headlamp then stood and helped him up. He immediately leaned over, breathing hard.

"Just give me a minute here—"

She put her hand on his shoulder, aching for him. But this forest was tinder dry, and—

A bush nearby had trapped flying embers and now flamed to life.

Reuben looked up, the fire glowing against his eyes. "This entire forest could go up!"

What she was thinking, exactly.

She wrapped an arm around his waist. "Let's go."

Funny, she'd forgotten about her knee in the adrenaline of the fire. Now it burned as she put weight on it. And Reuben swayed against her, balancing against trees as they limped away.

"I might have to crawl to the Garver lookout tower," he said.

"No. We'll get someplace safe—"

"Pete Creek should be not far from here, to the east." He stopped, looked up at the stars, the moon now risen in the east. He pointed at it. "Follow the moonlight."

Romantic words in a different time and place. Now, simply practical. She kept an eye on the moon, centered herself on it, and picked her way through the forest, leaving behind the crackle and heat of the fire.

The forest closed in against their wan light from the headlamp. Reuben grunted, moaned as he leaned on her, bracing himself on trees, stumbling now and again.

And every time he did, her knee threatened to buckle. Tears welled in her eyes as she dragged herself over downed logs and boulders.

"I'm sorry," Reuben said after a while.

"For what?"

"For not listening to you when you didn't want to get into the car with Brownie. I should have—"

"What are you talking about? We needed help—and why wouldn't we trust Brownie? We didn't know he'd turn on us, that they were behind the arson. I can't believe it—the crash. I'm still in shock."

"But—if I'd listened—"

"And what if they hadn't tried to kill us?" Even now, as she said it, the words sounded insane. Patrick Browning, arsonist? Murderer? She'd known him—well, her entire life, really. She'd grown up with Tom. "We'd have called in for help by now. You just don't know."

Reuben said nothing, his big hand holding onto her shoulder as if glued there.

She wondered if he might be holding on because he didn't want to let her go.

"I do know I wish I'd kept you safe. I never want you to feel scared or helpless again."

Her throat thickened with his soft words. Funny, with him around, she felt the opposite of helpless. Triumphant. Bold. Brave.

She held his hand, her other arm around his waist as they came to a clearing. Bushy black pine and spruce edged the tiny space as if reaching out to urge them on. A breeze lifted, shuddering the poplar, the birch, and stirring into the air the redolence of smoke.

And water.

"I smell it—Pete Creek," she said.

He pointed to a black dip in the horizon where the trees thinned out. "There."

She followed his direction, worked them through the forest, and they bushwhacked their way to the edge of the creek.

Reuben collapsed at the edge, leaning against a tree, his head back. She studied the cliff, where the edge dropped into darkness.

A fist formed in her gut.

Reuben crawled away, and she heard retching in the woods.

When she found him, he sat holding his head, pain lining his face, his eyes closed. "Just give me a second here."

"Let's find a place to rest." Her headlamp fell on a giant boulder, a pocket of protection beckoning from an indentation at its base. She grabbed his arm, urging him over to it.

He groaned but relented. She propped him up on the boulder, dug out water, and handed it to him.

"Toothpaste," he said, and she found his brush, his paste, and he cleaned his mouth, spat on the ground away from them.

"Let me take a look at that wound."

She'd tucked gauze pads under his bandanna, now soaked with blood, so she untied it and peeled back the cotton. Still bleeding, but barely.

"I keep a small collection of bandanna's in my pack," he said, offering a smile. "One cannot have too many bandannas."

She rummaged through the backpack and unearthed his last fresh bandanna.

She affixed a fresh pad to his head, made to wrap the fresh bandanna around it but he took it, wet it and cleaned her cheek.

The gesture curled warmth around her, stilled the trembling inside. "I still can't believe Patrick was trying to kill our team."

"We need to get to the lookout," Reuben said. "I gotta shake this off." Only then did he affix the new bandanna over his head.

"I can't see the bottom of the gorge." And she didn't want to mention how her knee had decided to stop working, swelling against her pant leg.

She rubbed it, however.

"You need ice for that," he said.

"It'll be okay. What we need to do is get back to the team." She closed her eyes. "I hope CJ is holding on. And Jed—he looked pretty bad. I can't believe we crashed. I can't help but feel like I could have landed us better."

"You weren't to blame for that crash—clearly. And you just saved my life—again."

She looked away, her eyes pricking at his words.

She didn't know what to do when he reached out, put his arm around her, pulled her against himself, as if it might be completely normal.

He leaned his head back on the rock. She let herself sink against him, staring up at the sky.

"In different circumstances, this is my favorite part about being a smokejumper," Reuben said softly. "Sleeping under the stars in a strike camp, the fire out, or mostly out, my body aching, knowing I put everything I had into the day. Doing what I could to fight the fire with everything inside me knowing that I left nothing on the fire line except my sweat."

She smiled at that. "I felt that way when I dropped that load of water on you guys. Peace—knowing I did everything I could to save you."

His arm tightened around her. "I think I learned it from my father. We'd work hard all day, roping, branding—everything that has to do with roundup—and then at night we'd camp out under the stars, bone tired but satisfied. I loved those days with my dad. I longed to be like him when I graduated. He wanted me to go on and play college ball, but I just wanted to be a rancher. When I walked away from it, I never thought I'd love something as much as I loved ranching until I became a smokejumper."

"If you loved it so much, why did you leave?"

He stilled. Sighed. "I told you how I broke my legs, right? And how Knox stepped in to fill the gap? Well, he also sort of stepped in with my girlfriend."

"What—?"

"I don't know what happened—it was probably nothing—but it was right after the prom I didn't go to, and I found Knox and Chelsea making out in the barn and…I'm not proud of what happened next. Pride. Anger. It wasn't pretty. Knox got the brains, but I got the brawn, and I don't go down easy."

"I know."

She didn't know why she said that, but it eked out a smile from him. It vanished fast, however, as he continued his story. "My other brothers jumped in when they found me beating the stuffing out of Knox, and then my dad intervened. He was furious, and that's when I woke up and realized that my dad had chosen sides. He'd picked Knox and kicked me off the ranch."

"Oh, Reuben. You don't think he really picked Knox, do you?"

"It felt like it, but I was pretty angry and wasn't thinking right. Truth is, it wasn't as much about Knox as feeling like there wasn't a place for me anymore."

She was quiet, her heart breaking for him, the teenager driving away from the world he wanted to belong in.

"The worst part is the next time I went back was for Dad's funeral. He had a heart attack one Saturday while riding fence. Alone. Which, if I had been there, he might not have been."

"You don't know that, Rube."

"Maybe not. But it feels that way. My pride cost me my dad. And now it's too late. Dad is dead, Knox is running the ranch. I can't go back."

She winced at the hurt in his voice, thankful for the padding of night that hid the tears in her eyes.

"Since then, no matter what I do, I feel like I'm going to screw it up. Or make the wrong decision. Like…" His voice dropped. "Like I did with Jock and the boys."

He looked away, closed his eyes as if the memory elicited pain. It probably did.

"That day on the mountain, I didn't like how spread out we were. But sometimes it works out that way, and who was I to say anything? Jock was in charge. I just followed orders. But when we got word of the fire out of control, Jock told Conner, me, and Pete where to go—and then ran back for the rest of team. I stood there, Gilly, watching him leave, and for a split second felt like I was supposed to run after him. I even dropped my saw, ready to get him when Pete stopped me. Or maybe just stopped me long enough to second guess myself." He shook his head. "I still wonder if I should have gone after him."

"And what—put him over your shoulder and drag him away? You know Jock—he was like you. He wouldn't give up."

"Bullheaded is the term, I think."

"Or just the guy you can depend on."

He drew in a long breath, glanced down at her. "But not the guy who makes the right decisions."

"And how can you? You can't see the full picture. You just have to go with your instinct. But...God has an aerial view. He knows where to guide us. We just have to trust Him."

"Even when it doesn't turn out the way we hope—even when people die?"

She wished she could reach inside Reuben's heart, put a hand around his grief, work it free. "I know I sound like a preacher's kid right now, but my dad says that the only way we can have peace with our decisions and choices is if we trust God."

"And if we don't think God is on our side? What then? Because, really, Gilly, why would God help a guy like me?"

Oh, Rube. She knew what it was like to feel like you weren't enough, that somehow you were destined to fail despite your best efforts.

She went quiet then, blinked. "Or a girl like me."

"Huh?"

She took a breath, not sure how to explain the burning to tell him... "I didn't tell you why I was walking home so late that night I was attacked."

His gaze was on her now, so much compassion in his eyes and she had to look away.

"I was making out with a hotshot from the Jude County base."

He said nothing, just steady breathing as he listened. His barrel chest rising and falling as he probably imagined the scenario.

"It was a stupid summer fling, and I knew I wasn't behaving like a preacher's kid should. But he made me feel pretty and told me that he was in love with me…"

Reuben stiffened, sitting up. Gave her an expression that looked very much like the one she'd seen at Brownie's when he'd asked her if Brownie was the one who'd attacked her.

As if he would like, very much, to tunnel back through time and revisit the moment.

Her voice quickened. "I didn't let it go all the way, but far enough, and I was feeling pretty guilty. I didn't let him drive me home like he offered, and then…that's when it happened." She looked up at him. "So, you see, I sort of deserved—"

"Are you *kidding* me?" The power of Reuben's voice thundered under her skin, jarred something loose. "You actually think that you *deserved* to get attacked?"

Even as he said it, she knew it sounded stupid. "I know. My brain says it doesn't make sense, but in my heart, I feel it."

His countenance softened then. "Oh, Gilly."

She lifted a shoulder, but tears filmed her eyes.

"That's why you're always trying to act like you don't need help, right? Because you're afraid if you do, God won't show up, because deep down inside you fear you're not worthy of help."

And see, she knew he could look at her, see through her. She bit her lip, nodded.

He searched her face. "We're a pair, aren't we? It's a miracle we survived a plane crash and a burning building with God not on our side."

She frowned then, his words settling into her bones.

"God *is* on our side, Reuben. At least I want to believe

that, even if my heart tells me I'm not worth it."

He nodded, as if her words might be making sense.

"My dad always preaches that we have to believe God when He says He loves us and has a good plan for our lives. That's how we get peace for today and bright hope for tomorrow, like the hymn says. But only if we trust in Him."

"Because if we try and fight our own battles, then how do we know God is saving us—or it's in our own strength?" Reuben said softly.

She looked at him. "Right."

"My dad used to tell us Bible stories, and I remember this one he loved about a battle Jehoshaphat fought. This huge Moabite army is invading Israel, and Jehoshaphat pleads with God for deliverance, and God says to him, basically, don't be afraid, because the battle is not yours but God's. Dad used to say that to me. 'Reuben, just stand, do your part, and see the salvation of the Lord on your behalf.' I remember once being frustrated that I'd missed a tackle and let the runner score. I was trying to anticipate the runner, and he juked me out."

"Which means?"

"He fooled me. Left me on my face in the middle of the field. My dad told me afterward to just get up, don't panic, and keep playing my position, just like Jehoshaphat."

"So did God save Jehoshaphat?"

"Yep. The Moabites actually ended up killing each other. Israel did nothing to win, and in fact, just went down the battlefield and picked up all the spoils of war. And they hadn't fought at all."

"Now *you* sound like a preacher's kid," Gilly said.

Reuben leaned back, settled his arm around her.

Silence fell around them, the smell of smoke drifting in the air or perhaps off their clothes, the sounds of the forest around them, a chirrup, the far-off howl of a wolf.

She turned to him. "God is on your side, Reuben, and I'll prove it."

He glanced at her. "How?"

She swallowed, thrumming up the courage to believe the words she'd just spoken. "When we get back, you should ask me to dance with you again at the Hotline."

He blinked at her, a half frown, half smile on his face. "Oh, you don't want to do that."

"Try me."

It was the texture of her words, the softness of them that startled her.

Because not only had she just invited Reuben into her life but maybe, at the moment, into her arms.

And, by the way he was looking at her, he had read her meaning clearly.

She swallowed, and he searched her face a long moment.

"I really have to kiss you," he said softly.

She nodded, and he brought his hand up, cupped it around her neck, drew her close.

And then he was kissing her. Sweetly, with enough passion to suggest he might be thirsty for her, but gentle enough not to spook her. He smelled of fire, yes, and sweat, and tasted salty, but she couldn't help but reach up and finally, *finally* run her fingers through that tempting thatch of whiskers. He made a sound of approval, and she felt something inside her release.

Reuben. Here, right here, yes, she could believe that she didn't have to be tough, didn't have to be brave. Could let go, let him hold her.

Protect her.

She curled her hand around his neck and sank into him, kissing him back with a hunger she didn't expect. Didn't understand.

But for the first time—*ever*—she felt totally safe.

In fact, as he settled his arms around her, she realized… Gone was the shudder of revulsion, the rise of panic, the tumult of horror.

Just Reuben and his arms around her, kissing her with such tenderness it made her ache. She opened her mouth, deepened her kiss, and it wasn't long before he pulled away, his eyes wide, trembling a little.

"You know how to keep a man awake," he said.

"I feel it's my duty as your teammate to do everything I can to help you stay alive."

"You're the best smokejumper I've ever met," he said with a smile.

# CHAPTER 7

T HE EARLY DAWN PRESSED away the shadow from the creek bank, back into the folds of the trees, the smell of pine thick in the morning dew. The faintest hint of smoke hung in the air—Reuben guessed the Davis Canyon fire must be growing. Which meant that his team was even closer to trouble. And although he and Gilly still sat in a pocket of shadow, he could see enough to realize the truth.

She wasn't going anywhere on that knee.

Gilly sat with her back to the boulder, her mouth in a grim line of pain. He'd had to widen the rip in her pants to get a good look at her knee. How she'd walked on it, how she'd half dragged him through the forest, he couldn't imagine.

She was a toughie.

The morning light revealed their battle from last night. Gilly wore the scrapes and bruises of their flight through the forest, grime on her face, her jumpsuit so grubby she might have rolled in the dirt. She had, actually, as she'd fled the cabin. Her dark auburn hair had come undone from her ponytail, but determination lit her beautiful blue eyes.

Yeah, she would have made a fantastic smokejumper. He wished he'd known her back when she was trying out. He would've figured out a way to tap into that fighter inside, get her out the door and into the sky.

Now, at his touch on her knee, she winced, one eye closing.

"You should have told me it was this bad. You were holding me up for hours—"

"I was fine."

"You were *not* fine. I should have been carrying you."

Although in his condition, no, he couldn't have carried anyone. His head still throbbed, but at least the roaring headache had lessened, and he no longer had the urge to retch, the world no longer a whirl.

He could confess that it'd helped that she'd curled against him all night—maybe for warmth, but he considered it medicinal. A way for him to stay awake, his entire being ultra-aware of holding her in his arms.

He couldn't believe how far twenty-four hours had taken them. Just throw in a plane crash, being held at gunpoint, and nearly being burned alive to take the awkward out of their, um—relationship?

He wasn't sure what to call what had happened between them. Survival-induced kissing? Moral support? One heck of a fantastic teammate?

He knew what he wanted to call it, but he'd been halfway to true love before they got on the plane, thanks to the Fountain Lake fire, and especially since that little blue dress.

Even if he hadn't been trying to stay alert long after she'd fallen asleep in his arms, he would have sat there watching the moon trace her face, glide over the petite nose, the high, graceful cheekbones, the tiny perfect, kissable mouth. And *wow* that mouth could kiss. At that thought a tiny ball of rage formed in his gut. Simmered. Turned to live coals.

The story of her attack had kept him awake as the night turned to grays, then rose-golds, and finally enough light for him to stir them to action.

If he ever caught the man who'd…well, he wouldn't have any trouble figuring out what to do, and he wouldn't spend one moment letting regret stare at him in the mirror.

In fact, the entire story and everything she'd done to keep him alive made what he was about to say stick in his throat, a burning snag lodged there.

He couldn't leave her behind. But with her knee the size of a prize-winning cantaloupe, she couldn't walk, either.

"I need to carry you."

She looked up at him, then back at his hands cupping her enormous, whitened knee, and shook her head. "No, I can walk."

He didn't want to, but frankly, Gilly had girl-who-won't-quit written all over her, so, although it put a fist in his gut, he leaned back, stood up, and held out his hand. "Get up and prove it."

Her jaw ground tight, and she reached out, grabbed his hand. Used her other leg to stand up on. Then he let go and backed away.

And felt like a class-A jerk when she tried a step, cried out, and started to fall.

He caught her easily, hoisted her up in his arms. "Babe, I think we both know the truth here."

"You're not carrying me." She pressed her hands to his chest. "You're still recovering from a concussion, and we're running out of time. Don't tell me you're not a little worried about Patrick and Brownie finding the team."

"I'm out of my mind with worry."

"Me too. Which is why you have to put me down."

He drew in a breath.

"And leave me here."

He stilled, his body going cold. "No. Absolutely not."

"Yes, absolutely." She was wriggling now, pushing against him, and well, she already had issues with being held against her will, so he set her down. Gently. Knelt next to her.

She might be a little right, because the world could still spin on its axis if he moved too fast. But for now, he was upright, could think clearly—or *mostly* clearly.

Because a part of him was seriously considering her words.

"No—"

"Shh. I'm fine here. We're what—a couple miles at least from the cabin? And yeah, we probably made a trail like a bulldozer through the woods, but I doubt Patrick is looking for us. He thinks we're dead, remember?"

He remembered most of it. Nodded.

"So, see, we're the last things on their minds right now. Whereas the team is in jeopardy every minute we sit here arguing." She reached into the pack, pulled out a canister of water, a power bar, and her silver fire tent.

"I'll spread this out—it'll be a reflector, and when you call in for help, tell them to look for me. The PEAK Rescue chopper can swing by and pick me up."

"I'm not leaving you here—"

She pressed her hands against his face, her pretty blue eyes staring up at him, and, yes, deep inside he saw a flickering fear. But along with that, a determination and a jaw-tightening courage that reached out to him, wrapped a hand around his heart.

"Yes. You are. I'll be fine. Go up the mountain, Frodo,

find the lookout tower, call for help, and…" Her mouth edged up in a wry smile. "I'll be waiting for you when you get back."

He started to reply, but she pulled him toward her and silenced him with a kiss.

Something solid and resolute, and thank goodness he wasn't dreaming last night. Because although he hadn't thought he'd fallen asleep, the memory of kissing Gilly, of this woman kissing him back, surrendering herself into his embrace, seemed like some kind of delicious dream.

But here she was again, kissing him like she meant it. Like she didn't have a crazy amount of baggage.

And like she did fully expect him to come back to her. She pulled away and met his eyes. "I know that disaster lends itself to powerful emotions, but Reuben, you're exactly the man I thought you were. So, please, go up that mountain and bring our team home."

And what, really, could he say to that?

He kissed her again, put his crazy rush of emotions into it, then released her, and got up. "I'll be back as soon as I can."

"I know."

*I know.* So much in those two words. He held onto them as he rappelled down the fifty feet into the ravine. Unlike the other ravine into the creek, this edge jutted out, and he free-rappelled down.

She *might* have made it, but with her climbing skills, more likely she would have ended upside down.

Back in his arms.

Reuben hit the creek bottom, regret like a fist in his throat. *The only way we can have peace with our decisions and choices is if we trust God.*

He started down the creek, hearing her voice.

*Okay, God. You're on point.*

Reuben found a scalable cliff on the opposite side and climbed up. Casting a look at the over the gulf he couldn't see Gilly—now tucked away in the forest—and it gave him some measure of peace.

Then, in the hope that she could see him, he lifted his hand in a wave before he started through the trees.

He settled his bearings first thing—found the Garver Mountain Lookout Tower and headed southeast, affixing its location to the sun, calibrating it as he headed east.

He moved three times as quickly without Gilly, something he reluctantly admitted as he stopped for a drink. An hour later, he hit a forest road.

The sun arched overhead, still early morning, and a breeze caught the sounds of blackbirds and chickadees calling, the stir of the wind through the busy white pine, their long needles cradling thick pine cones. It always amazed him, the rebirth of a forest after a fire, the release of seeds into the ground from the cones under heat.

As if creation was made to flourish even under suffering. Start anew, despite the ashes.

His words to Gilly hung in his head as he spotted the lookout tower some five hundred yards ahead. *Now it's too late. Dad is dead, Knox is running the ranch. I can't go back.*

But what if he could?

Except, where would that leave him and—well, what he'd discovered with Gilly?

Which was…?

He could still feel her kiss on his mouth, her small compact body nestled against his.

Yes, he would definitely take her up on that dance when they got off this mountain.

The trail had turned nearly vertical, and his breath razored in his chest as he climbed from one boulder to the next, up the trail dissected by lean, towering spruce, mossy boulders, and tufts of red paintbrush.

It led to a log cabin, the original lookout now squatty and dilapidated, the front porch sagging in on itself. A few yards away, the lookout tower, a square building with a 360-degree view of the Cabinet Mountains, sat on stilts at the apex of the mountain. A set of stairs zig-zagged up to the top, and Reuben stopped for a moment, breathing hard, his head pounding, the rush of blood in his brain thumping with his heartbeat.

He looked around, getting his bearings. To the east was the ripple of mountains in Glacier National Park, hazy purple along a cloudless blue sky.

To the north and west, the forested hills dropped off, fell hundreds of feet to the creek, a view filled with thick Fraser fir, white pine, and rolling foothills.

And above it all, a roiling cloud of gray smoke, filled the sky. He tried to calculate Gilly's position.

He'd thought the smoke was from the Davis Canyon fire. But if he read the sky and the terrain correctly, smoke scarred the sky from two wildfires.

One in the distance, due west.

And one closer, larger, straight down Garver Mountain, over the creek, and headed right for Gilly.

The Brownings' cabin had ignited the entire forest.

And Gilly, sitting in the grove of pine trees, facing east toward the creek, had no idea an inferno bore down on her.

Reuben's hands slicked with sweat as he opened the door to the lookout.

*Get help. Get back down the mountain.*

Over the years, the place had turned into a bivouac for

campers, an overnight nest for rental. Still, the old fire-look-out equipment remained, including the old Osborne Fire Finder, a type of turning board over a map that helped pin-point the fires, along with a table, chairs, and a bunk large enough for two. Someone had stocked the shelves with toilet paper, kindling for the wood stove, and water.

*Please, God, let there be a radio.*

The prayer felt wrenched from deep inside and left him hollow a long moment.

He searched the cupboards, the desk, and the square table under the fire finder. Nothing. He tore apart the bed, searched through the meager supplies, a keen eye on the blackening cloud.

No radio. He sat on the bed, breathing out hard, his head in his hands. How could the lookout tower not have a radio?

He picked up the lantern, threw it across the room where it shattered and gripped his knees, the world spinning.

He fell and landed on all fours, nearly banging his head on the fire finder table. Sat back against the bed, breathing hard.

So much for trusting God.

Because guess what—Gilly was down there by herself in the middle of a firestorm, and he'd hiked up the mountain for nothing. Reuben should have known that he was on his own here.

He couldn't breathe as he pushed himself to his feet, one thought carrying him.

Get back to Gilly.

Voices. Laughter. They trickled up to him, carried on the breeze. He stepped out onto the balcony and looked over the balcony. Down below, two bicyclers, their mountain bikes perched on their shoulders, stared at the black smoke.

He wanted to weep with relief. Or at least hope.

"Hello!" It hurt to yell, but he pulled himself to the edge. "Hello!"

A man and a woman, early thirties, they wore biking clothing, helmets and backpacks.

The man looked up at him. Waved.

"Do you have a cell phone?" Reuben yelled.

"It doesn't work up here. But we have a short wave, hand held."

"I'm with the forest service—can I use it to report the fire?"

They climbed up the steps as Reuben used the fire finder and the smoke from the Davis Canyon fire to line up his best guess of the crash site.

Then he pinpointed Gilly's location.

The man reached the top, breathing easy. His dark hair curled out from his biking helmet, and with his lean, toned body, could probably bike for miles without stopping.

He looked at Reuben—bloody, filthy, sweaty—and stopped in the doorway. "You all right, man?"

"No," Reuben snapped. "I'm a smokejumper, my plane went down yesterday, I have two team members dying, one already dead, and my girlfriend"—yes, he said it—"is in the path of that fire." He pointed to the closest blaze.

The man just stared at him, then handed him his radio. "I'm not sure what range you'll get—"

Then Reuben's brain, for what seemed like the first time in his life, went blank. The emergency frequency simply slipped from his mind. Like butter, he couldn't get a grip on it.

But, in the space came the sudden recollection of Brownie's words—Patrick had a portable radio. And wasn't it Brownie's suggestion to use the emergency frequency?

Which meant if Patrick were smart, he'd be listening to the fire service line.

The only thing Reuben latched onto was a memory of the frequency listed on Conner's box. He turned to that frequency, listened.

"CQ, this is an emergency call to WB6KHP from…" He paused, then decided to break a few rules. "Reuben. Conner, you there?"

He waited, listening. Then again. "This is an emergency call to WB6KHP. Conner, come in."

He knew any legitimate ham operator out there would be cringing, but he didn't have time—or inclination—to care. He moved to the window, watching the smoke.

"I have binoculars—"

"Marshall, this is WB6KHP."

Conner's response through the line made Reuben brace his hand on the table, his knees turning liquid.

"Where are you?" Conner said. "We lost you on radar after takeoff. Sent in two planes—we can't find you."

"We went down just southeast of Davis Canyon, about nine clicks from Pete Creek, between Mushroom and Black Top." And this was why he'd called Conner. Because if Patrick were listening on the emergency frequency, he'd be heading exactly for his team's position.

"Roger that." Conner's voice betrayed no shock, but he imagined his friend's jaw tightening. "Sit rep?"

"Two injured, one casualty." He paused and then added, "Cliff O'Dell. We need aerial extraction. Call in PEAK Rescue."

"Roger."

Static on the line, then. "What is your position?"

"Garver Mountain Lookout Tower. We—Gilly and I—hiked out. We need a pickup on Forest Road 338 near the Pete Creek crossing."

"Roger that, on our way."

Reuben closed his eyes, refrained from adding *hurry*.

He handed the radio back to the man.

"Jim Rudini," the man said. "That's my girlfriend, Darcy."

Reuben shook his hand, nodded to Darcy. "Thanks, man. Reuben Marshall." He stepped back out onto the balcony, cupped his hand over his eyes.

It seemed the blaze near Pete Creek had doubled since he'd first noticed it, but that might just be his darkest fears alighting inside him. Still, the flames shot above the trees as the fire gathered strength, burning bright orange. Black smoke boiled up from the middle.

"That's quite a fire."

Jim held binoculars to his eyes.

Reuben barely refrained from ripping them from his hands. "Do you—could I—?"

Jim handed them over, and Reuben scanned the forest for any sign of Gilly's roost.

He located Pete Creek, then followed the creek through the trees, down toward the road, back into the forest.

No—*oh*—

As his eyes traveled downstream, the smoke thickened, a storm of flame washing over the cliff's edge.

Right where he'd left Gilly.

Reuben's throat tightened, a fist clamped around his heart. Especially when he spotted his rappel rope dangling down the edge.

As he watched, flames crawled out from the forest, chewing at the rope, running a smoky finger down the nylon.

Then the fire burst out of the forest, candling the trees, consuming brush, trees, moss, loam—

*Gilly.*

He was shaking.

"You said your girlfriend was down there?"

Reuben could barely nod.

"Need a lift to the road?"

If she died on this cliff, Reuben would never forgive himself. That much Gilly knew as she dragged herself to the edge.

The minute she'd woke to the smell of smoke, the fingers of gray drifting through the trees warning her of the advancing flames, she'd pushed herself to her feet.

Listened hard. She could hear it, the crackle and pop of sparks, the sizzle of bushes alighting, and behind it all, the roar of the wall of flames building speed as they consumed the forest.

She'd stepped out then and crumpled right there on the forest floor, her face in the dirt. Her cries echoed against the increasing roar.

She didn't know fires as well as Reuben or any of the other team members, but it didn't take an expert to figure out that she needed to move to safety, and fast.

For a long moment, she considered using the fire shelter, kicking it out, rolling into it. But without gloves, without fire protection, without the ability to hold the shelter down with her legs—and that meant her destroyed knee, too—she hadn't a chance.

She'd discarded the shelter and started to army crawl to the cliff, the smoke thick, tufting the air, turning the world to a war zone.

The roaring had turned to a locomotive thundering behind her. She'd glanced back, saw flames flickering around blackening poplars and birch, turning pine trees to bushy torches a hundred feet in her wake, bright through the smoke.

She'd gotten up on her feet, duck crawled, then pushed to a stand, moaning as the pain rocketed up her leg. She lunged from one tree to the next, tumbling out, finally, to the cliff's edge.

The rope dangled where Reuben had used it to rappel, and she lay on her stomach, looking down.

Fifty feet, and most of it just air, nothing to grab onto should she lose her grip.

Worse, she didn't have a clue where the harness might be. Or gloves. Or—

The fire hissed in the trees behind her, an earth-shaking explosion as a tree torched. The heat pressed a hand to her back, and she rolled over to see a great cottonwood crowning above her.

She had a minute. Maybe.

Die on the cliff or fall to her death.

*Oh, God, those couldn't be the only two choices!* Her heart turned to a fist, fighting to escape her chest.

The fact that she'd wanted to be a smokejumper seared through her. Laughable. What had possessed her to *ever* think she could save her team? She was going to turn to ash, right here on the edge of the cliff, a wretched reminder that she was no more cut out to be a smokejumper than she was a baker.

In fact, if she hadn't demanded to join Reuben on the hike out, everyone would probably be rescued right now.

*God* is *on our side, Reuben.*

Her words yesterday seemed caustic and stupid in the face of the inferno some twenty feet away.

*I'm sorry, Reuben.*

This would take him apart—knowing he couldn't be here to save her. The regret would gnaw at him, consume him whole.

All because she'd demanded that she had to save everyone instead of realizing—embracing—the truth. She was trying way too hard to prove herself, just like Jared, her bomber co-pilot had said.

And now she was in her over her head.

Reuben's words reverberated back to her. *That's why you're always trying to act like you don't need help, right? Because you're afraid if you do, God won't show up, because deep down inside you fear you're not worthy of help.*

Yeah, well, maybe she wasn't.

A broken branch fell near her, blackened, sizzling, and she scooted back along the edge with a scream.

She needed to get off this cliff.

She scrabbled for the rope but fire had caught it, and it began to sizzle. Even if she wanted to, she couldn't use it.

Smoke thickened the air, sooted her eyes, and they watered, blinding her. Her nose ran, and she coughed as she kept scooting along the cliff, her hand running over the rocky edge, dragging herself as the fire licked out from the forest.

In seconds the inferno would simply explode out over the ravine.

And burn her alive. Already her skin felt charred, and she

turned her face away as she scrabbled backwards along the cliffs edge.

*Just stand, do your part, and see the salvation of the Lord on your behalf. Right. Well, God, if you ever want to show up—*

Suddenly, Gilly fell back, as if the rock had given way. For a second, she thought she'd scooted right over the edge.

But no—she whacked her spine, and only then did she realize she'd fallen into a rivulet in the cliff.

She pushed herself out, rolled over, felt the rock, and discovered not a rivulet, but a crack, about a foot wide, parting the rock wall.

She could fit into it. And maybe if it went far enough down... She flipped around, backed herself into the space, wedging herself into the opening, searching for footholds. Tongues of flame lapped at her hands, and she clenched her jaw.

She finally ducked down, scrubbing her back against one side, her good knee against the other side, pushing against her hands as she lowered herself into the cleft of the rock. Moss and roots layered the granite walls, the smell earthy, thick with the heavy breath of trapped moisture.

Three feet, then five, then ten. She inched down. The crevasse seemed to be widening, but she kept going, working her way into the darkness. She scrabbled for nooks and holds for her hands, her legs. As she descended, the trapped, cool air cleared her eyes, her throat.

Above her, the fire roared, roasting the forest. Her heart thundered, but she didn't look up, feeding on the air from the creek bed, feeling the heat as it searched for her.

Twenty feet down, the crevasse opened up, and she wedged herself back onto a ledge, a lip of six inches, her mouth near the mossy, cool granite.

Only then did she look up. The fire had turned the sky a ghastly orange, cinders blowing in a tornado of wind, blaze, and fury. Embers blew down the crevasse, and she tucked herself back, letting them blow out to the river below. The water reflected the storm, glistening red and black, deep burnt orange.

Hell, right here outside her pocket of safety.

She wrapped her arms around herself, fighting the tremor that started in her gut, moved out to her chest, her breath.

Then she curled herself against the cool, solid embrace of the rock and wept.

# Chapter 8

R EUBEN HAD SIFTED THROUGH many a charred forest during his years as a firefighter. Usually, however, he did it while garbed up with gloves and armed with his Pulaski and his water canister to douse any remaining pockets of heat.

And never while crying.

His eyes ran, his nose thick with mucus, and he wanted to sink down into the ashy moonscape and howl. Let his grief ricochet off the blackened, skeletal remains of once bushy pine, formerly fragrant balsam fir. He kicked the ash at his feet, searching for anything—

He didn't know what was worse, the idea of finding Gilly's charred body or simply hoping she died quickly, the noxious air burning her lungs, suffocating her before the fire could burn her alive.

*Oh, God, no, please.*

Reuben longed for the febrile hope that she'd somehow made it out.

But he'd seen the fire, the mushroom cloud of black smoke that evidenced a fire frustrated, stunted.

Angry.

The kind of fire routed by the ravine and thus settled down to burn hot and thick, fighting its demise.

The forest still sizzled, smoke a ghoul as it moved in and out of the trees, searching for the unburnt.

He'd gladly commandeered Rudini's bike, shouldering it as he fled down the mountain. He hit the path and climbed on, grateful for the thick mountain wheels as he pedaled hard.

He should have flown off the mountain, broken something, but maybe God had heard his pleading, because Reuben had managed to muscle the bike over boulders, stay on the path, and find the bend where he'd emerged from the forest.

From there, he'd dropped the bike and begun to run.

He didn't remember much of the three-plus miles through the woods. He landed hard on the soft, loamy earth, turned his ankle a few times, slammed into tree limbs, hurtled boulders, and fell at least once with enough force to knock out his breath.

It barely slowed him, the smell of resin under fire igniting him.

He hit the ravine—he guessed it took him maybe an hour, but it felt like an eternity—and the moonscape of forest stopped him cold.

No one could have lived through the inferno.

He spied his rope downstream, burned, wrapped around a submerged tree.

"Gilly!" He'd let his voice echo into the air, closed his eyes, and leaned hard on his knees, listening.

Just the wind in his ears, the rasping of his breath.

The howl in his heart.

He didn't need a rope to descend—he found the place where he'd climbed up, scrabbled down, finally falling into the river.

And, just in case she'd done something crazy and flung herself over the edge into the river, he searched the water for her broken body.

No Gilly.

Which meant she was still on the cliff.

His chest turned to fire as he splashed downstream, past his rope. He examined it and realized he'd left the descender at the bottom. Taken off the harness and left it on the opposite shore.

He'd all but condemned her to die.

Reuben leaned over and lost it. His stomach emptied, his arms weak, he collapsed into the cool water.

But—she could be alive up there. The thought pulsed inside him, a fragile hope that had him finding his legs and searching for a place that didn't have an overhang, where he could ascend.

He'd never been good at rock climbing, but the primal urge to get up the face pushed him forward, his hands torn and bleeding by the time he reached the top.

But somewhere in there, he'd started crying.

He ran toward their camp—easily found it upriver near the camelback ridge of rocks.

When he'd left her, she'd taken out her fire shelter. He'd hung onto that hope with a fist as he'd careened down the mountain, bulldozed through the forest. *Please, Gilly, be under the fire shelter.*

Now that thought glimmered as he kicked up ash and cinder, skirting hot spots glowing in the loam, snags that simmered.

He reached the boulder.

He found the silver shelter wadded up, seared, melted

around the edges and—empty.

"No!" He kicked it into the wind, leaned against the rock, and pressed his hands over his face.

*God, she didn't deserve this.*

And then he didn't know why he was talking to God, because, please, what did he expect? He knew what God thought of him, and frankly, Reuben had done it again. Made the wrong decision and abandoned someone to die. He couldn't bear the thought of her alone, terrified.

Worse, his gut—no, his heart—had practically screamed at him to take her with him. To carry her on his back, even if she hated it. To protect her like he should have.

He got up, kicking through the debris, not sure what he might be looking for.

A reason, perhaps, not to despair.

His foot met a charred bundle, and he squatted, brushing away the ash.

Their gear pack. Melted down, the plastic clips a hard mass.

He picked it up, his breath heaving over itself.

He was going to be sick again. Instead, he turned and with a feral cry, the one building in his chest for the past two hours, he threw the deformed pack with all his strength toward the ravine.

His moan echoed into the scalded air, past the ravine, into the still green forest, and back, reverberating through him.

A howl of grief, and he let it shake him, send him back to the boulder.

He fell against it, his breathing hard, emitting moans he didn't know how to escape.

Then he closed his eyes and wept.

Why couldn't he have seen this? He should have known the fire would have run with the wind, east—

He'd left her here to burn to death. Just like he'd let Jock run back into the fire. Just like he'd walked away from his father.

If he'd been on the ranch, he would have been with the old man, checking fencing with him when he'd had his heart attack. Could have ridden back for help—

Maybe his father would still be alive.

*God, I screwed up. I screwed up bad.* Reuben couldn't breathe, the fist in his chest a vice.

*Reuben.*

He looked up, the voice so vivid he held his breath, searched for the source. *Keep playing your position.* His father's voice—it sounded so real Reuben actually got up.

*See the salvation of the Lord.*

He stilled, rooted, his pulse thundering. Remembering their conversation last night. Now he wanted to lean into the words, believe them.

"Reuben!"

He stilled, the voice thin, a barest hint against the wind stirring the scorched earth.

Gilly?

"Reuben, I'm here!"

He whirled around, definitely hearing something now, and he prayed it wasn't his heart, longing so much to hear her voice, he'd conjured her up.

"Gilly!" He didn't see her. Just an ethereal voice lifting from somewhere near the ravine. He started running, hope flashing through him.

"I'm down here!"

Down—he didn't see anything, just blackened trees, a film of ashy white over charred rock. He jumped over still-smoking tree trunks, came out to the edge of the cliff. "I don't see you!"

"I'm down here!"

He followed her voice, scrambling along the edge, looking over the side.

He nearly fell into the ravine. His foot kicked the far edge, and he tripped, landing on his hands. His leg dropped into the expanse.

"Don't fall in!"

He pulled himself out, backed up, peered down into the crevice. "Gilly?" There wasn't a hope that he'd fall in—he could barely fit his leg in.

There, in the darkness, about halfway down. By the looks of it she'd managed to wedge her entire body in this safe cavity in the earth, protected from the blaze.

He went weak with the sight of her, crouched on a ledge in the recesses of the crack. She looked a little singed, her face blackened, her eyes huge as she stared up at him.

"Are you all right?" he asked stupidly because he didn't know what else to say.

"I think so," she said. "The fire just—well, I climbed down here just as it blew up over the edge."

He swallowed back a rush of emotion that had the power to collapse him, rend from him another unmanly sob.

But he was just so— "I can't believe you thought of wedging yourself in this crevice!" He was leaning down now, trying to figure out how to get her out.

"I didn't—it just appeared. I thought I was going to die,

and suddenly I fell into it."

He had no words for the relief that gusted through him. "Let's get you out, huh? Can you climb?"

"My knee is…" She shook her head. "I'm sorry, Rube."

"Gilly, shh. No problem. Stay put. I'll be back."

"I'm not going anywhere." Then she smiled up at him, such a beautiful smile it took his breath away in a whole new way.

Joy. Right there in a tiny package that could fit in a slit in the ground.

*Thank you, God.*

Maybe the Almighty would just forget about that…earlier bit.

Reuben ran down the edge of the cliff to where he'd climbed up earlier and worked his way down to the river.

Found his rope, the remainder that hadn't burned. Still a good length—long enough, he supposed to pull her up.

He climbed up the cliff and returned to the hole. He sat on the edge and tied a harness into the end. He lowered it down to Gilly. "Put this around you. I'll pull you up."

She worked the rope around herself.

"Easy does it—don't fall."

She looked up, as if to snap at him, but instead just nodded.

Hmm.

He knew he should be roping in, securing his position, but frankly he could probably pull her up hand over hand. Nevertheless, he wound the rope around his waist, stood up, braced his legs, and began to pull.

She weighed nothing, or it could be sheer adrenaline, but she called out for him to slow down, to let her work her way up.

He slowed down, steadied his breath until her head rimmed the edge of the crack. Then in one quick move, he wrapped his arm around her tiny waist and heaved her up and into his embrace.

And then her arms were around his neck, as she held onto him, burying her face in his shoulder.

Shaking.

"Shh, you're okay. You're okay." He said it for himself as much as for her, backing away from the edge, then scooping her into his arms and sitting down. He settled her on his lap, holding her away from him enough to run his hands down her arms. He met her eyes.

Swallowed.

She was staring at him, so much vulnerability in her eyes, so much relief and just a hint of hero worship that his breath hiccupped.

"Rube—"

But he couldn't take it, couldn't listen, couldn't wait—he leaned in and kissed her. And not a soft, sweet, gentle kiss like before, but a full on, oh-I-nearly-lost-you move that had him tightening his arms around her, reeling at the emotions that suddenly turned him weak. He had his hands tangled in her hair, now dirty and knotted—

And she was kissing him back. Just as heartily, her hands fisted into his grimy shirt, pulling him closer, as if she couldn't get enough of him.

It slowed him down, and the relief shuddered out of him, until he softened his kiss, ending it sweetly, with a gentleness that he hoped showed her just how much he didn't want to frighten her.

Even though, yeah, he was suddenly very, very afraid.

He loved her. The realization washed over him, turned him a little woozy, scooping out his breath. Still, as he leaned back, meeting her eyes, her amazing smile, the truth poured into his bones, his heart.

Wow, he loved her. Her courage and her spitfire determination and even her resourcefulness. He loved the fact that, yeah, she'd risked her life for him at least twice—maybe more—but also that she could still look at him like he was her hero.

He loved her because despite him being a big man, with more bullheadedness than brains sometimes, she still trusted him with herself, this petite woman who had experienced pain and fear under the hands of a man out of control.

With everything inside him, he wanted to protect her. From everything—and especially Patrick and Brownie and fire and fear and—well, even his own crazy emotions. Because she couldn't possibly feel the same about him.

Unlike him, she hadn't exactly been pining for him for years.

Still, maybe they had a chance if he did this right, if he didn't rush her. Didn't scare her.

"What is it, Reuben?" She ran her thumbs over his cheeks. "You look like you've been crying."

He twisted his mouth, as if brushing her words away, but he couldn't quite manage it and just stared out over the ravine.

"You *were* crying."

"I just thought—"

And then she brought his face back to hers and kissed him again. So achingly sweet that he was in very real danger of bursting in tears again. He cupped her face in his big hands, caressed his thumbs down her grimy cheeks, so soft despite the dirt and cuts, and let himself sink into the wonder of her touch.

Gilly.

Making him feel like the guy who did things right.

She finally broke away, a smile in her eyes. Silence pressed between them, a warmth that had his heart thundering.

For a second he remembered the feel of her curled up against him in the night, and his body thrummed with an ache that he put away.

Preacher's daughter.

But he wrapped his arms around her and wrestled himself off the ground.

"What—"

"I got hold of Conner, and he's sending help. Sorry, Gilly, but we have a ride to catch, and I'm carrying you. No argument."

And maybe it was just the smoke fogging up her brain, but she slipped her arms around his neck.

Although, true to form, as he started off through the woods, she said, "If you tell anyone, I'll drop you out of a plane without a chute."

"I'll be our secret," he said, loving her even more.

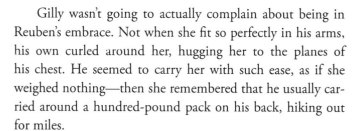

Gilly wasn't going to actually complain about being in Reuben's embrace. Not when she fit so perfectly in his arms, his own curled around her, hugging her to the planes of his chest. He seemed to carry her with such ease, as if she weighed nothing—then she remembered that he usually carried around a hundred-pound pack on his back, hiking out for miles.

He smelled like he'd spent a week fighting a fire—smoky,

the scent of a hard-working male, his whiskers rough against her hair. He still wore his bandanna, a little soiled from his head wound, the trail of blood into his dark whiskers.

Yeah, she could stay forever right here.

Besides, her knee did hurt, having been wedged in that hole for hours. She couldn't move her leg at all.

Still, "You can't carry me to the road. It's too far."

"I could carry you to Hawaii, Hot Cake."

She grinned, felt his words to the core of her body. "Okay, then at least let me climb on your back. You'll be able to go a lot farther if you carry me piggyback."

He looked down at her, met her eyes. Oh, he had devastating brown eyes, hints of gold around the edges, and so much compassion in them it could knock her off kilter.

Her gentle giant. With a hint of danger in his expression, of course, when riled.

"Then I can't see your smile."

And romantic to boot.

"You can see me smile plenty when we get back to HQ, and we have the team safely rescued."

He nodded at that then, and put her down. Crouched so she could climb on his back.

And yeah, her knee started to burn a little when he tucked his arms around her legs, but she hoisted herself up, clamped him around the waist, and knotted her hands around his massive neck and shoulders to help with the weight.

"How far to the road?"

They were traveling through the moonscape of the burned forest, smoke still rising from downed trees, puffs of ash lifting with each step. Thankfully Reuben was wearing his double-soled smokejumper boots.

Her skin crawled with grit and cinders, and she felt like she'd rolled in a campfire and added a layer of grime. But at least she was alive.

*Just stand, do your part, and see the salvation of the Lord on your behalf.*

Never did that feel more true than when she'd heard Reuben's voice, yelling her name.

She'd tried to yell back, but her voice died, stymied by the depth of the crevasse.

For a long, painful stretch of minutes, she thought she'd dreamed his voice.

And then, a feral, raw, gut-wrenching yell had echoed through the air, down through the ravine, and she knew.

The poor man thought she'd perished, the fire turning her to a corpse. And the pain in his howl had made her summon herself and shout his name with everything she had.

Twice.

And when he found her, the look on his face—so much disbelief, so much relief—turned her weak with the strength of it.

Not to mention the way he muscled her free, nearly yanking her into his arms.

And then his embrace—holding her so tightly, his entire body trembled. Or maybe that was her, she didn't know, but he just kept saying that she was okay. She'd be okay.

Words, she suspected, that were for him, too. Because when he'd looked her over for injury, she read it on his face.

He'd been weeping. Furrows cutting through the grime on his face, so blatant it made her own eyes well up.

This amazing man looked at her then, his heart in his eyes, and it was all she could do to say his name.

Until he kissed her.

And then she had no words for the way he pulled her to himself, claimed her mouth, as if she already belonged to him, or he needed her to. She gripped his shirt, and, for that moment, became his, surrendering, kissing him back, needing him to belong to her, too.

She loved the feel of his hands in her hair, tangled there, and the way his breath shuddered out when he released her, as if she'd stoked a fire in him.

He'd certainly stirred something in her. Longing, and more.

She couldn't call it love—not yet. Desire. Hope. A well of affection that went deeper than she could look. Because if she peered into it, she just might find that she could lose herself to this man. Could sink into his arms and simply stay there. Safe. Protected.

Loved.

She'd closed her eyes, buried her face in his shoulder.

"Are you okay back there?" He'd found a logging trail, was following it west. "I think we'll hit the road in about a half mile. And then we'll start walking toward Yaak. Conner should be able to find us."

She didn't want to ask about Patrick or Brownie.

She had no doubt that Reuben had already tumbled them through his mind. And if they got near her—them—well, she might see the other side of Reuben, the one who rode bulls and carried around a chain saw, the one who had let out the feral cry that could shatter her bones.

She loved that she knew both sides of him, the tough sawyer and the generous, kind, sweet man who had cried for her.

Except that same man was her, um, *teammate*. A guy she

had to work with, a man who had to let her do her very dangerous job of bombing fires.

The last thing she needed was him deciding that he didn't want his—what, girlfriend?—in danger. Yeah, Jed and Kate made it work, but they'd had their own identical set of troubles. Jed, not wanting Kate to die. Kate, being a fantastic smokejumper despite making the choice to go part-time.

This could get complicated, what with Reuben's off-the-charts overprotective gene.

Except the summer was nearly over, wasn't it? And then came a long, uneventful winter for them to sort it out.

Until then, Gilly would have to convince him to keep this—whatever it was between them—on a low simmer.

She was about to mention it when they emerged onto the road.

And, as if he knew exactly where they might be, there sat Conner, sitting in the cab of his truck, listening to his handheld ham radio.

Wearing a black JCWF T-shirt, he looked up at them, his blond hair swept back into a cap. Conner's expression suggested they looked worse than she thought.

"Holy cow, what happened to you two?" He came out of the cab and helped Gilly off Reuben, draping her arm around his shoulders.

She leaned into Conner, hoping to throw off the fact that she'd been perfectly comfortable snuggled up against the big sawyer.

Conner helped her over to the truck, and she braced herself on the driver's seat while he checked out the bloody scrape on her cheek. "Where did you get this?"

"Patrick Browning hit her," Reuben said, the slightest hint of exactly how he felt about Patrick in his voice. "Right before he tried to kill us."

Conner whirled around. "What?"

"We think Patrick could be our arsonist—or at least he has something to do with the fires. Who knows—it could be his father—"

"Brownie and Patrick? Setting fires?" Now Conner looked at her, and wore the same expression that she probably wore only twenty-four hours ago when she realized Patrick had his shotgun pointed at them

*Only twenty-four hours ago.*

"It's all about Tom. They say his death is our fault," Reuben said.

Conner drew in a breath at that, probably evaluating Reuben's words. Not for a minute did Gilly believe that his team was to blame, but she could imagine the three survivors had spent the last year in sleepless nights trying to decide that for themselves.

Maybe not coming up with the same conclusions.

"He tried to burn us alive in his cabin—ended up torching the entire forest. Gilly would have died if she hadn't found a way to hide from the fire." Reuben held a hint of pride in his voice, and Gilly wanted to amend his words.

Because she'd done exactly nothing to save herself.

But Reuben just grinned at her, something soft in his eyes.

*Oh boy.* Because she smiled back.

She simply couldn't help it when he looked at her like that.

"I've been thinking about it," she said, turning to Conner. "I'm pretty sure Patrick sabotaged the plane. If he put sand or oil into the fuel tanks, I would have still read them as full. Which I did."

Conner knelt in front of her now, examining her knee. "Is that what happened—you ran out of fuel? Because HQ lost you on the transponder shortly after takeoff."

"I wouldn't be surprised if he sabotaged that, too," Reuben said. "Maybe he was hoping the entire team would be aboard."

Conner had reached into his cab and pulled out a first aid bag. He dug around inside and pulled out an ice pack, cracked it, and placed it over Gilly's knee. Secured it with a Velcro strap. "Get in," he said.

She scooted into the middle while Reuben came around the side.

Conner was outside on the radio, calling in his successful retrieval of his teammates.

A few minutes later, he got in the truck, closed the door. "We're headed back to HQ. The PEAK Rescue team out of Mercy Falls is headed up to search for the rest of the team by air. And Pete, Ned, Riley, and Tucker are headed up to hike in. Do you remember the coordinates, Rube?"

"No. But I can show you on a terrain map."

Conner put the truck in gear and headed down the highway. "Satellite imagery suggests the Davis fire has grown to about fifteen hundred acres and headed east, through the canyon. We had significant wind increase this morning—"

"That's why the fire grew so fast," Reuben said, a tone in his voice Gilly didn't understand. "The wind kicked up after I left for the tower."

And then he did it. Put his muscled, protective arm around her in a very non-teammate move.

She stiffened, looked up at him.

He glanced down at her, gave her another one of those

soft smiles.

She longed to lean over, rest her head against his arm. Okay, so she supposed teammates did that, sometimes.

His thumb caressed her shoulder, an almost absent move that sent tingles racing down her arm, through her body in another very non-teammate-like response.

No, no— If Reuben started to baby her, to act like she needed help…

This wouldn't work. She shrugged out of his embrace then moved his arm off of her, sitting up straight in the middle.

She couldn't look at him, would hate the confusion on his face. But she had a reputation to keep.

"Hopefully Pete and the guys will locate the others soon," Conner said. "Then we can chopper them out. We'll deal with the fire after that."

Gilly let her head fall back and closed her eyes as she listened to Reuben give Conner the lowdown on the events. He started with the low fuel tanks, explained the crash, their determination to the hike out, how they ended up at Brownie's cabin, the cabin fire, then Reuben's race to the lookout, and finally her miraculous escape from the flames.

He left out, much to her relief, the kissing parts.

The very delicious, delectable, dangerous kissing parts.

Darkness descended around her, and it wasn't until the change in road texture when they pulled onto the gravel of the Ember Fire Base that she woke up.

Her cheek pressed against Reuben's shoulder. She might have even drooled, because her mouth hung open. Reuben didn't say anything as she pushed herself up. But he did look down at her and smile.

A curl of warmth started in her belly.

"Let's check in and see if they've found the team," Reuben said.

Good man, had his priorities straight.

Maybe this *could* work out.

He waited for her as she slid out of the truck but didn't make a move to pick her up. Instead, he offered his arm, and she leaned on it, limping into the office.

Miles stood over the giant relief map in the center of the room, running his finger along the edge of Black Top, down into the ravine, then further out toward Pete Creek. He held his radio, in contact with the rescue team. "Roger, Pete. PEAK Rescue is headed toward your position."

"I can see the smoke from here," Pete was saying. "I'm concerned their position is in the path of the fire."

Gilly came up to the table with Reuben and Conner and Miles glanced at them. "Pete, Reuben and Gilly are here. Stand by."

Then he holstered the radio and came over to them. "We were worried." He gave Gilly a quick hug, nothing but a perfunctory affection in it, but enough for her to confirm that Reuben's embraces were, well, not this.

Miles shook Reuben's hand, and they met in a man-hug.

"What's the sit rep?" Reuben asked.

Conner pocketed his sunglasses and leaned over the map. He touched the road where he'd picked them up. "You guys were here," he said.

"We hiked out along this ridge." Reuben trailed his finger along the south edge of Mushroom Mountain. "We crossed Pete Creek here, then hit the forest service road." He kept moving his finger north. "Brownie's cabin was about here." He pointed to a spot northwest of Garver Mountain Lookout Tower.

"What's your best guess as to where the plane might be?"

Before Reuben could answer, Gilly touched the thin blue creek line on the map. "I think they're here, at Beetle Creek, although it's dry now. Tell the PEAK team to fly up the creek bed at the base of the mountain."

Miles looked at her, his face grim. "They're covering that basin, looking. But the smoke from the Davis fire is really thick, the air currents rough."

She stared at Miles. "Are you saying the fire is too close—that they can't get in?"

"I'm advising they put down south of here, on this forest service road and hike in on foot—"

"But what if the fire finds the team first?" This from Reuben, who had walked over to the Doppler radar, reading the wind speed, the satellite images of the fire.

"It's through the pass, and from the looks of this, only a few miles from the team's estimated position," Reuben said quietly. He turned, and Gilly recognized his expression. The same one he'd worn when Patrick told him to sit down, to surrender.

Not a chance. Maybe Miles had forgotten who Reuben was, the grief he shouldered, but she could almost predict his next words.

"We need to go in after them, right now."

Yes. Exactly what she was thinking. She moved around the table, leaning hard on it, fighting the pain shooting up her leg. "Listen, I'll take a plane, drop retardant on the front edge, slow the fire down. That will clear a path for the chopper to get in."

Miles looked at her, and she could actually see the wheels turning in his head.

"It could work," she added. "Buy them time for Pete

and the guys to get in. The PEAK team could land in the creek bed, or maybe the smoke would clear enough for them to hoist them up." She took another step, drew in a quick breath, but masked it with a smile.

"And I know exactly how to fly that canyon—I've done it once already."

She meant it sort of as a joke, but it fell flat, with Miles's mouth tightening in a dark line. She looked at Reuben for reinforcement, but his jaw had locked so tight he could be grinding coal into diamonds. "Okay, too soon to joke, but really, I can do this—"

"I can send Jared. He'll get in there—" Miles started.

"No! Jared won't get low enough. The canyon winds—yeah, they're rough, but manageable. But a DC-10 will never make that run. Jared won't risk it—"

"And you will," Reuben said quietly.

She frowned at him. Of course she would.

"It's the only air tanker we have," Miles said. "The rest of the fleet has been routed to Idaho."

"We can take the Annie. It's fixed. I saw it before we left."

"Have you lost your ever-lovin' mind?" This from Reuben, who blew out a breath. She could read the disapproval in his eyes. "Let's, for one minute, remember who supposedly fixed the Annie, shall we?"

Her voice dropped, and she met his gaze. "Let's remember what he said in the cabin. This wasn't about me. I was just collateral damage. He was out to hurt you, the team. He wouldn't sabotage the AN2, because I'm the only one with the guts to fly it."

Reuben stared at her a long moment during which she thought he got it. The fact that this was her job, and their team needed her.

And when he turned to Miles, she expected a repeat of yesterday's blowout.

"No," Reuben said quietly. "Her knee is busted up. There's no way she can control the foot pedals, keep the plane steady through all those currents. Even if the plane holds together, she doesn't have the strength to keep it on course. You let her go, and we'll just have another casualty on our hands."

She had no words, her stomach dropping out from under her, her entire body numb.

He wouldn't look at her, just kept his gaze trained on Miles. Who looked between Reuben and Gilly, his shoulders rising and falling.

"Let me go, Miles," she said quietly, in a voice that she didn't recognize. Probably because her real voice was screaming in her head, words that she rarely used. She knew it, she *just knew* that Reuben would overprotect, not let her do her job.

So much for them sorting it out, finding a happy ending.

"If anyone is going to save them, it will be me, and you know it," she said stiffly.

More quiet from Miles. Then, he closed his eyes and gave a small nod.

"You've got to be kidding me!" Reuben roared.

"Thanks, Miles," Gilly said.

She didn't spare Reuben a glance as she gritted her teeth and limped down the hall.

But she didn't get far.

"Gilly—please! Don't do this." Reuben on her tail. She pressed her hand to the wall, drew in a breath, mostly to let out the coil of pain.

He stepped in front of her, a wall of frustration, anger—

and who knew what else.

Bully. Yes, that was the word for him.

"You can't go—we both know this. Even if the Annie is okay to fly, you're in no shape—"

"I'm going, Reuben. The team needs me." She started to push past him, but a needle of pain stopped her, made her catch her breath again.

"See—you're hurting—"

"And we'll both be hurting if our team dies out there!"

That brought him up like a slap. "Okay, fine—but let's get Jared—"

"He won't do it, and you know it. I can't leave them out there!"

"And I can't let you go!"

She recoiled, not only at his words, at his volume, but the expression on his face. Red eyes, his body nearly trembling.

"It's not up to you."

"Maybe not, but I can't watch another person I care about die! Not when I can say something, maybe stop it."

She looked away, her eyes hot.

"Gilly, please. I love you. I know it's fast—but I've probably been in love with you for a couple of years, and—*please don't go*. We'll find another way."

He loved her.

But she couldn't let his words stop her, derail her.

She closed her eyes, her throat thick. But she forced out the words. "If you love me, you won't make me choose between you and the team. You and flying. You and my job."

She looked back at him then, hoping he'd see the truth—

She wanted both. Tough and tender. Brave and beautiful.

But, no. Because his expression hardened, and he straightened up. Stepped back from her. "Because if I do make you choose, I won't win, will I?"

His words hit her like a fist, and she stood there, her mouth open, a fist around her heart.

*It was clear that the ranch meant more to him than I did.*

She swallowed. "I took them out there. It's up to me to bring them home."

And in that space of time, in the silence, Reuben's mouth tightened around the edges, his eyes filming. "Right."

Then he turned and headed down the hallway.

*Wait.*

But she watched him go without a word.

*What are you trying to prove?*

Jared in her head and behind that, Reuben's howl, reverberating through the forest.

Gilly turned into the flight office to plan her attack.

# CHAPTER 9

H E'D WALKED AWAY, AND she hadn't stopped him.

Reuben slammed his fist into the lockers. They shook under the power of his frustration.

"Hey, bro, take a step back." Conner came into the room. He had a map tucked under his arm, and was holding his gear pack. He set the map on the bench, opened his locker.

"What are you doing?"

Conner glanced at him. "I'm gearing up. I figure if Gilly is flying over the crash site, I'll jump from the Annie, connect with the team, see if I can give Pete and the guys a hand if the drop doesn't slow the fire down. We'll get them out on foot if we have to."

Right.

Without a thought beyond Conner's words, Reuben walked over, retrieved an extra jumpsuit from the surplus rack, grabbed a helmet, gloves, a letdown rope, and a chute pack, along with a fresh gear bag.

His hands shook, his entire body wanting to turn around, storm into the flight office, tell Gilly—

What? He'd already alerted the entire office to the fact that he loved her—what had possessed him to let that bit of information sneak out? He wanted to bang his head against the lockers, see if he could dislodge his stupidity.

The last thing she wanted was him stepping in to hover over her. And he knew that.

She was right—he *did* understand what drove her, and he should have seen that standing in her way would only get one of them hurt.

Stubborn woman. Her knee probably needed surgery. He knew without a doubt that it would also fail her when she needed strength to keep the plane on course as she drove through the super-heated canyon winds.

She couldn't hold the course, but he could. He could work the foot pedals in tandem with her, help her with the yoke.

*It's up to me to bring them home.*

No, it was up to *them.* He'd made promises, too.

He swallowed back a rise of nausea at just the thought of getting into a plane again—it rushed over him, and for a second he collapsed onto the bench.

"Rube, you okay? I'm not sure you should make this jump, pal. You're looking pretty frayed. That head injury looks brutal."

"I'm fine."

Conner held up a hand, backed away. "Ho-kay—listen, no one would blame you if you didn't want to go up in a plane so soon after—"

"And what would you do, Conner?" Reuben looked up at him. "Leave them to die? Let the fire run over them? I can't let that happen again."

Conner's jaw tightened.

"You were there when Jock ran into the fire," Reuben continued. "You heard them on the radio. Don't tell me that memory doesn't chew away at your gut all the time. Don't tell me that you don't wonder late at night if you did the right thing. Don't tell me you don't wish you could have gone back and done something—*anything*—differently. Stopped Jock, or maybe run after the team—"

"And died with them?" Conner's voice cut through the torrent. "Because that's what would have happened if we'd run back. If we hadn't obeyed Jock and kept going, we would have been caught by the flames running uphill and died on that mountain. Do you wish you'd died with them? Is that what you're saying?"

Reuben closed his eyes. "I just wish they hadn't died."

Conner blew out a breath. "We all do. But it doesn't mean we go back, keep reliving it. Or blame ourselves. At the end of the day, we have to hold onto the fact that we can't change the past. We have to just keep looking forward, toward hope."

Reuben winced, looked away. "I can't do that."

Conner slammed his locker. "Or won't. I get it. It feels almost—well, wrong for us to not live with that pain. To move on, be forgiven, set free. But that's now how God wants us to live. And if He's the one offering, it seems to me we should take it." He offered a wry smile. "Or try to, at least."

Conner picked up his helmet, tucked it under his arm. "God's not content to simply stand on the sidelines of our lives. But He isn't going to force his way into our lives, either. So He waits, He works, He protects, and He never leaves us until we open our eyes to see Him saving our sorry, stubborn hides. He waits until we choose him."

*Choose him.*

Reuben hadn't exactly chosen God that day he walked off the ranch—in fact, he remembered making a pretty clear decision *not* to choose God.

No wonder he felt like God wasn't on his side…he wasn't on *God's* side. And yet God had shown up to save him over and over and…

*My dad always preaches that we have to believe God when He says He loves us and has a good plan for our lives. That's how we get peace for today and bright hope for tomorrow, like the hymn says. But only if we trust in Him.* Maybe it was time to trust God, let Him set Reuben free.

No more hanging onto regrets or his hurt or even his fears and letting them steal his tomorrows.

Letting them steal Gilly.

He didn't want to make her choose—he wanted her to be free to have both worlds. Firefighting *and* dancing in his arms.

Conner picked up his pack, shouldered it. "It's not our fault Jock and the crew died. I hate it as much as you do. But we aren't responsible for their deaths, Rube. We did what we were supposed to do, and by God's grace, we lived. We just have to do what we are called to do and let God take care of the rest."

*Just stand, do your part, and see the salvation of the Lord on your behalf.*

Reuben shook his father's voice from his head, too angry to hear his wisdom.

"And that means letting God protect Gilly."

Only… what if…

Reuben grabbed his helmet. "I'll meet you on the tarmac."

Gilly was already out by the Annie doing her walk-through as a couple of hotshots filled the tanks with retardant.

Reuben watched her for a moment as she tested the new airplane struts then continued with the external check before turning to the fuel lines.

He had no doubt they'd be fully topped off before the plane left the ground.

He threw his gear into the empty cargo area of the plane beside two parachutes in the back of the tanker, probably left there from their previous run.

Then he climbed into the copilot's seat. Put his hand on the yoke. Heard his father, teaching him to fly.

*Just hold it steady, Reuben. Bring her home. Attaboy.*

He lifted his hands off the yoke, swallowed down the rise of memory. Except maybe not such a bad memory, either.

*Hold it steady. Bring her home.*

"What are you doing here?" Gilly opened her door, was trying not to wince—yeah, he saw that—as she climbed into the cockpit.

"I'm your copilot," he said in a tone that brooked no argument.

Apparently it worked, because she settled into her seat. "Don't get sick on me." She handed him a ringed binder.

He took it. "Preflight checklist?"

"Yes, please."

He read it off, starting with the prop, then the doorstop and oil can, moving on to the avionics.

"Magneto switch off."

"Check."

"Flight controls free."

Gilly moved the yoke, but when she went to move the pedals, Reuben added his own power.

She glanced over, and he drew his mouth into a tight line. "This is how it's going to be, Gilly. You and me. No choices made here—just us, together."

She stared at him a second longer, and suddenly, her eyes began to fill. She swallowed, looked down at the avionics panel. Wiped a quick hand across her cheek.

*Oh, Gilly.*

Reuben nearly reached out for her then, but Conner came up, threw his gear bag onto the floor of the plane, climbed in. He squatted on the bare cargo area, out of earshot.

"Thank you, Reuben," Gilly said quietly.

And he couldn't help it. "You got this, Hot Cake."

She gave the tiniest of smiles, and he managed one of his own.

"Air system charging valve," he said.

"Open."

"Air pressure."

"Check. Less than thirty."

"Parking brake."

"Set."

But not for long, because they moved through the list, then through the engine start list.

"Clear!" Gilly started the props, and the AN2 rumbled to life with the tremor of power. The cockpit shuddered with a roar of noise, and Reuben fitted on his headset as Gilly started the Annie.

A warm-up test, which the AN2 passed, and Gilly hollered at Conner to buckle in.

Then they were taxiing down the runway, the plane shuddering over the blacktop. Reuben glanced out at the biplane wings. They bounced along, catching the wind, no damage evident.

They might just live through this. All of them.

They lifted into the sky, his hands on the yoke, fortifying

Gilly's grip, adding strength to the rudder controls.

She called into the tower as they hit one thousand feet, lifting to three thousand, then five.

The transponder was working just fine.

"We'll be there in twenty minutes or less," Gilly said, pushing the airspeed above regs.

Reuben had left his stomach on the tarmac—or what felt like it—but maybe that was a good thing.

No airsickness yet.

They flew north, a beeline to the fire, which he could make out easily from up here. A thundercloud of gray smoke rising from the carpet of green forest filled the entire horizon, a smudge against the blue, dissipating as it reached for the firmament.

They soared over Yaak, and he recognized the forest road 338 below and then the blackened run of the Brownie fire farther north.

Gilly pointed them west toward the dark cluster of billowing white-gray smoke caught in a valley between two peaks.

As they got closer, he noticed the smoke hovered above a layer of gauzy dark-gray smoke threaded in and around the treetops, lodgepole pines, and towering cottonwood. Now and again, a flame licked out from the depths, igniting a crown.

Thankfully, it hadn't started a run across the treetops.

Even from here, however, Reuben could see how close it edged in to the crash site.

He got on the radio and called to Pete, and the team on the ground.

"Roger, we see you, Eight-Seven-Alpha-November," Pete

responded

"What's your position?"

"We're on the creek bed, hiking toward Black Top."

Reuben turned to Gilly. "Let's get Conner out of here. He'll drop down, hook up with Pete."

"I'm going to drop him right on the crash site," she said, her expression solemn. "I don't know how fast that fire is moving—flame lengths look to be about thirty feet—so if the wind stirs it up, it could get to them before Pete does."

Then she looked at him. "And what about you?"

He glanced at Conner, back to her. "I'm staying here."

She met his eyes, her mouth tight, and he knew she wanted to argue.

Instead, she nodded quickly and started her descent into the canyon, her run along the creek bed to let Conner off.

They descended to three thousand feet, and Reuben spotted Pete and the two others hiking. They waved. Then he unbuckled and headed to the back. Conner had his chute pack and helmet on and was working his way to the door. Reuben hooked his static line into the safety bar then opened the door.

Just for a second, the plane drifted to one side with the rush of air. He held on, used to it, but it didn't stop his stomach from jumping up, taking notice.

He leaned out and threw out a streamer. Watched the wind take it, send it east. It fluttered to the creek bed.

"Listen—" he yelled as Conner crouched in the door. "I know I should be jumping with you but—"

"I got this!" Conner shook his head, glanced at Gilly. "We all heard you back at HQ."

Oh.

Conner grinned at him, as if to solidify his meaning.

Perfect. Gilly would be thrilled.

Reuben pointed to the landing zone. "Aim for the creek bed. The crash site is about a quarter mile upriver." In fact, if he leaned out, he could probably spot it. Instead, he gave Conner a once-over, checking his gear, his helmet, his chute.

Then he tapped Conner on the shoulder, and Conner pushed out into the blue.

He'd strapped on a square chute for more maneuverability in the wind, and in moments it billowed out, a red patch of silk against the green forest below.

Reuben watched as Conner steered himself west, along the creek bed, apparently intending to drop at the foot of the waterfall into the arms of the crash site.

Reuben turned, searching for it, and as Gilly banked for her bombing run, he kept his eyes trained on the ground.

There—a patch of white, a flash of color against the forest.

Right about then, Conner disappeared into the trees.

Reuben closed the door, the roar instantly muted, and climbed back into the cockpit.

Conner's voice entered his headset, confirming he'd touched down.

"Now it's on us," Gilly said, moving toward the smoke. "We'll do a flyover, see where the head of the fire is, and then hit it crosswise, cutting it off."

She descended lower, to fifteen hundred feet, the air turning bumpy. "I'm sorry for the rough ride, but I need a test run—to see how the currents affect the plane."

His stomach had begun to revolt, but he swallowed it down. Closer now, he could see where the fire hadn't yet consumed the forest and could make out the flames at the front edge, leading the assault. Less than a mile from the crash site, by his estimation.

And gaining ground fast.

"We have two loads," Gilly said. "I'm going to start the run at the high edge of the canyon, then slip down into the saddle, drop the first load, and bank out to the southeast."

He just hoped to hold on. But she needed more than him just holding on. He reached for the yoke, added pressure with the foot pedals.

Gilly always made flying a sort of aerial ballet, the plane moving as if an extension of her body, up and over the trees, along the ridge, dropping into the canyon along the wind currents, almost effortless. She made it seem, well, easy.

Unless he glanced at her, took in the set of her mouth, her whitened grip on the yoke.

They dropped into the canyon, the heat rising around them, and suddenly their ride turned to washboard as they bumped along the gusts and flares of the firestorm.

"Hold on!" Gilly shouted.

Oh yeah. It was a good thing he hadn't eaten anything, because his gorge rose again. He tightened his grip on the yoke, following her lead, and fought with the pedals for control, shaking away the rising fear that they'd simply flip and nose down in a fiery ball, straight into the flames.

He couldn't help, also, a glance out at the right wing, just to make sure the new rivets still held under all this jarring. They were shuddering, but maybe Gilly was right—Patrick wasn't out to kill her.

Just Reuben and the other surviving smokejumpers from last year's team—Pete and Conner.

She did exactly as she said—ran them along the leading

edge of the fire. And just before they reached the head, she shouted, "Release!"

He'd already moved his hand onto the trigger, the button that would unleash a ton of slurry onto the fire. The syrupy, red liquid drifted out below them, dropping onto the flames, coating the trees, the bushes, the loamy, sizzling forest floor with a mixture of water, fertilizer, and clay.

White smoke sizzled up from the muted flames as Gilly banked and ascended out of the turbulence.

Once free, she came back around, surveying the damage.

"One more drop and we'll have that head shunted. At least until the fire can regroup—and by then the PEAK Rescue team should be able to get in."

She descended, heading again toward the far ridge, apparently for a repeat run.

"Young to Eight-Seven-Alpha-November, come in."

Conner.

Reuben toggled the radio. "Eight-Seven-Alpha-November, copy, Young. Come in."

"I've found them. They're all alive—and Pete's here. He's already called in the PEAK chopper. Just keep that fire out of our back pockets. Come back."

"Roger that. Over."

He glanced at Gilly, offered a smile.

And that's when he saw it. Something shiny and gray out of the left window, shooting across their airspace.

A bird—no—

Gilly let out an exclamation—more surprise than anger—banked hard to miss the projectile. Reuben slammed against the cockpit door.

"What was that?" Gilly leveled the plane, searching for

the object.

But Reuben recognized it too well—although disbelief turned him cold.

"A drone," Reuben said thinly. "It looks like the one Conner lost in the Cabinet Mountains a couple weeks ago."

Gilly shot him a look, wide-eyed, her mouth gaping. "You're kidding me—"

"Patrick's a mechanic. He must have found the drone and patched it up. And then listened to our radio transmission."

"And now he's trying to crash us. So much for him not trying to kill me," Gilly said.

Reuben's mouth tightened. "No. I think he's trying to kill *me*."

She came around to start her run—undaunted as usual.

He spotted the drone again, this time aiming right for their cockpit. "Gilly!"

She turned, saw it, banked hard left, and dove.

The drone missed them by inches, but with the plane banking, the right wing made an excellent secondary target.

The drone's impact shuddered the entire plane in an explosion of metal and chaos. The plane spun, inverted.

Gilly fought to right it, to roll them back.

Reuben slammed his hands into the cockpit ceiling, then grabbed the yoke.

"Foot pedals—Reuben, give me more right rudder!"

He also added heft to the yoke, and they managed to bring the plane back to trim.

But the wing shivered, and Reuben glanced out the window, searching for a tear in the rivets.

Yes. There, along the strut, weakened by the previous tear.

"We're going to lose the right lower wing, Gilly."

"Not before I drop this load."

They hit the leading edge of the fire, plummeting toward the flames, and the entire aircraft shimmied in the air.

With a screech, the wing fractured, the lower panel breaking free of the strut, flopping .

"The entire wing is going to sheer off!"

"I'm almost there." She was gritting her teeth, rattling in the seat as she gripped the yoke, pushing them toward the fire.

"Gilly—we have to jump—"

"No! Not before we drop this load. Then we'll be lighter and—"

"Gilly!"

His voice turned her then, and she stared at him, her eyes wide, ferocious. "What?"

He cut his voice low, solid, piercing the rattle of the plane. "We go now, or we die."

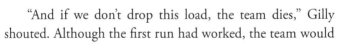

"And if we don't drop this load, the team dies," Gilly shouted. Although the first run had worked, the team would stand a better chance with another dump of slurry.

She glanced at him, and he stared at her, his mouth a tight line of disbelief. "Get out if you want," she said then. "Just go—"

His eyes narrowed slightly, and he shook his head. "I can't."

Okay, she got it—they were over the fire. And too low. So she turned back. "We'll drop the load, and I'll get you up to three thousand, and then you can go."

"I can't without you."

She frowned, his words reverberating through her, but she didn't have time to argue.

Not with the gusts threatening to roll the plane, rip it apart.

"She'll hold together, Rube! Trust me!"

She could taste the smoke in her mouth, her eyes burning as it invaded the cockpit.

"Fine—dump this load, and then let's get out of here."

"I need to get lower. If we drop now, it'll dissipate and do nothing."

His jaw tightened, but he didn't argue, so she turned back in the seat, staring down at the smoke. The flames licked up through the treetops. The plane shook with the descent, and if she didn't pull up, they'd simply arrow down into the blaze, causing another fireball.

She eased back on the yoke, fighting against the pressure of the damaged ailerons from the lower wing.

Next to her, Reuben worked with her, pulling the yoke back in tandem.

The AN2 threatened to shake apart as it surrendered. Her altimeter approached five hundred, and she could have leaned out and spit on the fire. "Ready?"

"Always," he said.

Ho-kay. She trimmed it level— "Release!"

Again, the slurry fell, this time in thick blobs that dropped on the fire like paste. She could almost hear the blaze sizzling, choking, fighting for life.

Then she pulled back on the yoke once more, heading to the skies. One thousand feet, fifteen hundred.

And that's when she heard it. The shudder of the lower

wing finally losing it. It broke free of its mount and sheered away, dangling from the body of the plane.

Ripped free.

The plane yawed to the right and Reuben was on it, fighting the rudder to straighten it out.

Miraculously, they were still climbing.

But a horrible rush of wind behind Reuben's seat suggested— *No*! Gilly looked and confirmed.

The lower wing had taken with it the mounted right wheel, tearing a hole in the fuselage. She could see flames, trees, smoke, and sky from the hole behind Reuben's seat.

Which meant they weren't landing.

Heat filled her eyes, but she kept climbing.

Because she didn't know what else to do.

A hand on her arm—solid, a grip she knew—turned her.

"Get us to three thousand. Then, Gilly, we jump."

She drew in a breath, shook her head. Turned back to the blue skies.

"Honey—listen. You'll be fine."

"I can't, Rube—I—"

"Yeah, you can. Because you'll be with me. I'm not going anywhere without you." He unbuckled and, hooking himself to the overhead bar, made his way to the back. He returned at twenty-seven hundred feet with an empty harness, his own chute already attached.

"Put this on." He climbed back into his seat, took the yoke.

She stared at it, back to him. "Where's the chute?"

"I'm getting you out of here if I have to carry you, Hot Cake."

Her eyes burned, probably from the smoke.

No. She couldn't do this. Tears turned her world hazy.

Reuben leaned towardher.. "I know you don't want to hear this, but I think God sent me here to protect you. Because you're right—He *is* on our side. And we're getting off this plane, together, and alive."

She looked at him then, and he held her gaze, he was exactly what she'd always known about him—solid, dependable. Strong.

*I love you, Gilly.*

The words he'd spoken at the base. Even though she didn't deserve it.

"Okay," she said, and reached for the harness.

She tugged it on while he topped off the plane at three thousand feet. What remained of the right wing had started to wobble, shake, and tremor its way free.

Probably they had seconds before they simply fell from the sky.

No autopilot on an AN2, but it didn't matter. He motioned her to the back, and she tumbled into the body of the plane, nearly in the fetal position.

Reuben climbed back and grabbed the door.

For a moment Gilly thought it wouldn't budge, mangled by the destruction of the wing. Then Reuben tore it away as if it were made of paste and fabric. Which, really, it was.

Then he climbed behind her, his big legs around hers, tucking her into his embrace. She felt him buckling her in, attaching herself to him, tandem.

The plane had started to lose altitude.

He plunked a helmet on her head and snapped the chin strap. "When we jump, keep your arms around yourself—I'll do all the work. Just enjoy the ride."

Enjoy throwing up, maybe.

But with the plane shimmying…

He moved them over to the door, one arm around her waist, the other on the edge of the door. "You tell me when," he said.

She looked at him. "No—just push us out."

"No! You have to do this, Gilly. It's time for you to fly."

*Time to fly.*

And with his legs around her, his body against her back, his arm around her waist, yeah, she could.

She glanced at the ground.

Then out at the pure blue sky with only tendrils of the suffocating fire, the vast, green-furred Cabinet Mountains spread out like a blanket.

*Strength for today and bright hope for tomorrow.*

The words slipped through her, ribboned around her heart.

*Yes, Lord.*

It *was* time to fly. She drew in a shuddering breath, put her hands on the door, and with a scream, she pushed.

The wing separated from the plane. It tore off just as they left the edge, the metal screaming.

Then they were all falling. The wing, the plane suddenly nosing down, then over and over, rolling, its beautiful white belly up as it screamed to earth.

Gilly hung from Reuben's arms, her own suddenly flung out. She stared at the world below as she gulped in the cool, brisk air. The fire, simmering to the west, her poor Annie plummeting over a ridge, disappearing into the green.

Reuben tucked his arms around her, clasped his legs

around hers and pulled the chute.

They arrowed up fast, and her breath caught as their fall arrested.

She looked up, watching as the square billowed out, a deep indigo against the ocean of blue.

And then they were floating.

Just soaring above the treetops. A quiet rush of wind filled her ears, but really just silence here, fifteen hundred feet above the earth.

Not silence. Peace.

Strapped to her parachute—actually, strapped to her, well, *man*—the fear drifted out of her chest like a slow exhale.

"What do you think?" Reuben asked, his deep voice against her helmet, in her ear.

"Breathtaking. Is this how it is every time?"

"Not every time," he said. And then he took her hand and guided it to the parachute toggle. "You drive."

She took the other toggle in her hand, and, just like in the simulator and how she'd learned on the platform, she steered them toward the creek bed.

A gust of wind blew them away from their destination, but Reuben's hands went up to cup hers, right there to guide them back.

The crash came into view, her Twin Otter in pieces. She spotted Pete, Riley, Ned, and Tucker attending to Jed and CJ, strapping them to litters. Next to them, on the rocky bed, sat the red-and-blue PEAK chopper from Mercy Falls. An EMT crouched beside CJ.

"We're not going to roll," Reuben said as the ground came up to them. "Just land with me, I'll cushion our fall. Don't worry, I got you."

She knew that. But the creek bed wasn't a grassy field, and as she landed, pain speared up her leg and she cried out. But he did have her—his arm went around her waist as he pulled her on top of himself, landed beneath her.

Breaking her fall. She leaned back into his arms as the chute fell over them.

A silky blanket of blue.

She didn't kick if off. Instead, as Reuben unhooked her, she pulled off her helmet. Then she turned in his arms, lifted his visor, and as he blinked in confusion, she kissed him.

An awkward, less-than-effective kiss, but he was all in, his arms closing around her, kissing her so sweetly, she knew… tangled up with Reuben Marshall was exactly where she was supposed to be.

She let him go and met his eyes.

"Wanna go again?" he said.

She raised an eyebrow.

"I meant the jumping part, but, yeah, I like how you think, Gilly Priest."

She laughed, and then someone yanked the blue silk off of them, and she looked up at Pete, standing over them.

"Do you mind?" Gilly said. "We're having a sort of private moment here."

Pete frowned.

"Team meeting," Reuben added and reached for the chute.

But they couldn't stay wrapped up together on the ground with the team in need of help, so she pushed herself off of him. He helped her climb to her feet.

He braced his arm around her and helped her over to the team.

Their team.

Jed was white faced but awake as the PEAK EMTs carried him to the chopper. Kate held his hand. Gilly watched as Reuben went up to them, grabbed Jed's other hand, and leaned into a one-armed hug from Kate. "I told you I'd be back," he said.

"I never doubted it." She kissed his cheek then followed Jed into the chopper.

Reuben helped Gilly over to CJ, wrapped like a package in the litter, an IV attached to his arm. He was drifting in and out.

"We're taking him to Kalispell Regional Medical Center, if you want to follow us," said the female EMT. Blonde, shapely even under her blue jumpsuit, she crouched to pick up one end of the litter.

"Hey, Jess, let me help with that." Pete came running over.

They carried CJ to the chopper.

Hannah appeared pale but stronger than when Gilly had left her. "You okay?"

Hannah managed a smile. "Now we are. But you—you don't look so good."

Indeed. A glance at both of them suggested, well, a plane crash, a gunshot wound, a forest fire, and maybe something else.

A happy ending. Yes, that was the expression Gilly saw on Reuben's face as he looked down at her, a spark of something in those brown eyes that had her thinking they should probably get back and cleaned up.

So she could put on the blue dress.

# Chapter 10

"Don't be afraid. I'm here to protect you." Gilly reached over and touched Reuben's hand, whitened on the steering wheel.

He released it and wrapped his fingers through hers, letting a low chuckle rumble out of him. "I feel so much better."

"I thought you would," she said, grinning as he turned under the arched entrance to the Triple M, located ninety minutes southeast of Ember.

Gorgeous. A long gravel-and-dirt drive curved toward a two-story log lodge in the distance. The lush, rolling open range filled with sage and grass undulated as far as the eye could see, dissected by groves of aspen and ragged, dark-green Douglas fir. The entire landscape butted up to the jagged, snow-tipped mountains along the eastern horizon.

Cutting through the land, the lazy, impossibly blue Geraldine River, bordered occasionally by willows and towering cottonwoods, reflected a cloudless sky.

Truly, Big Sky Country.

Reuben slowed, bumping over a cattle gate, and Gilly spotted a field with freshly cut alfalfa in rows, ready to be raked into stacks or baled.

Black Angus lounged in the grass, their tails swatting the

occasional fly. Others roamed the pasture, grazing.

"How big is the ranch?"

"A little over nine thousand acres. We also have a private lake, although my cousin Ned calls it a pond. But he's a Minnesota lake snob."

She laughed. Ned, the rookie, had left for home a few days ago, eager to get back to his small town of Big Lake for Labor Day weekend.

"We also have about six miles of excellent trout fishing on the Geraldine River. Which was named, by the way, for my great-great grandmother."

"Wow."

"The Triple M was started by my great-great grandfather Marshall when he came over from Scotland back in the late 1800s. He had three sons, so he named it the triple M, probably intending to pass it down to them, in three parts. But the oldest returned to Scotland, and the youngest decided to find his fortune in Alaska, so my grandfather inherited the ranch. He expanded it to five thousand acres, and when my father took over, he bought out two neighboring ranches. We run about three hundred fifty head of cattle."

"Did your grandfather have any other sons?"

"Oh, yeah—my father wasn't even the oldest. He was just the one who loved ranching. My grandfather had seven sons. They've mostly left Montana—are scattered all over the world and in Minnesota, Colorado, and California. We even have cousins in Maine and Alaska. But only our family stayed in ranching."

"Wow. But…" She squeezed Reuben's hand. "It might account for why your father passed the ranch on to Knox. Maybe he thought you wanted something different."

Reuben glanced over at her. "I've been thinking about

that. I was pushing pretty hard to play football—mostly because I didn't want to let him down, but maybe he thought that's what I wanted, that by letting me go, he was doing me a favor."

Gilly knew what it took to confess that, baby steps to forgiveness, even acceptance, and she couldn't help but reach up, touch his face.

He'd clipped the beard down but hadn't shaved it off, and now she ran her fingers through it gently. The doctors had shaved his hair short in one area at the hospital to add stitches, but Reuben wore a baseball hat today to cover it. Black waves curled out the back. In his dark-blue T-shirt and faded jeans, only the cowboy boots gave him away as a rancher.

He caught her hand, pressed his lips against her palm. Released it. "Thanks for coming with me."

"A chance to buck hay? Are you kidding me?"

His brown eyes were rich with emotion. "I just love you."

She drew in her breath, her throat thick. Nodded and looked away. And felt the silence drop between them.

Behind that quiet, brooding demeanor was a true romantic, a man unafraid to tell her how he felt, and that surprised her.

Scared her, just a little, at the amazing depth of his love for her. The fact that he said it without reserve, without fear.

And of course she loved him back. How could she not love him—this amazing, handsome, broad-shouldered, indefatigable man who risked his life over and over for her?

Who showed up to protect her for no other reason than he loved her.

He squeezed her hand, then, and she looked at him. Warmth in his expression, so much of it, it stirred the low burn inside her.

But once she admitted her feelings, then there was no taking it back. No turning around, retreating to her tough, not tender, world.

"So, are those cupcakes really homemade?" He indicated the box on her lap.

"Juliet helped, but…yeah."

He squeezed her hand again.

They drove past a large corral into the circular drive and pulled up to the lodge, a beautiful, two-story, hand-hewn log structure with a towering stone-covered entryway. A long porch out front hosted rocking chairs and a long wooden bench topped with a basket of dried purple lavender and daisies.

The place had charm written all over it.

"My grandfather built this house by hand," Reuben said, not a little pride in his voice. "My dad added the wing with the new kitchen and great room. He hand stacked the fireplace—trust me—I carried in the stones. Wait until you see the views from the back."

She was already blown away.

Gilly got out, taken by the smell of the towering ponderosa pine that cradled the house and by the view of the mountains, craggy and bold in the distance.

Not far away, a traditional gambrel roof horse barn, painted a deep green, confirmed what Reuben said about it being a working ranch with traditional horses.

Two pickups sat in the driveway in front of the four-car garage.

The front door opened.

"Reuben!"

Gilly turned to the voice. A woman about sixty years old

with her shoulder-length dark-brown hair, deep hazel-green eyes, and a smile that resembled Reuben's—the kind that could light up her entire face—stood on the porch. She wore a flannel shirt cut off at the shoulders and tied around her waist, a hint of a tank top underneath, and a pair of jeans and cowboy boots.

She held out her arms, and Reuben nearly engulfed her with his embrace, picking her up, swinging her around. She laughed, and he put her down.

"Mom" he said, kissing her cheek. "You look good."

"Now that you're here," she said, and patted his cheek as if he might be ten and not towering over her by a foot.

He took her hand. "I want you to meet Gilly. My…girl-friend."

Gilly dumbly held out the cupcake box, which his mother neatly ignored. She wrapped Gilly in a hug. She smelled of chili spices.

"Call me Gerri," she said, letting go.

Gilly found a smile.

Gerri took the box. "Your sisters are helping me in the kitchen. But the boys are in the barn," she said to Reuben. "Go tell them it's time for lunch."

Gilly might have only imagined Reuben's slight flinch.

She took his hand, squeezed, meaning her words earlier. "Really, I'll protect you."

He gave a slight grin, but held on as he led her off the porch to the barn.

She didn't know what she expected, especially after his story of the fight. A bunch of hooligans, perhaps, wrestling in the barn or maybe armed with pitchforks.

Instead, they were huddled over the engine of a very ancient, green tractor, the hood open. All four of them. She hadn't a clue how to guess their ages—they all looked nearly as big as Reuben, the oldest, although two had sandy-brown hair, one with Reuben's dark features, and the final one, the one crouching in front of the engine, was a dark redhead.

"Did you check the spark plugs?" Reuben asked casually as he walked in.

The redhead looked up, and for a second his expression drained, his shoulders tensing.

Then the look vanished as he got up, wiped his hands on a rag. "Rube. Uh—"

"I can't believe it!" This from one of the other brothers, the one with the scruff of copper beard. "Mom didn't say anything!"

"Wyatt," Ruben said and dropped Gilly's hand to give him a hug.

"And you brought a friend," said the darker one, the spittin' image of Reuben.

"Yeah, and she's taken, Tate," Reuben said, meeting his hand. But he grinned.

The other one, with the long tawny brown hair held back with a baseball cap like Reuben's, came over to her. "Ford Marshall, ma'am."

He reminded her of the rookies, wide-eyed, eager to please. She shook his hand. "Gilly Priest."

The redhead holding the rag glanced at Reuben with dark-green eyes. If she wasn't mistaken, she saw a hesitation in them. Then he extended his hand. "Knox."

"Hey, Knox," she said, injecting warmth into her tone as she took his hand.

Knox glanced at Reuben, and she ached for them, the rift that had torn them apart. And from Reuben's expression, he was replaying it, a tiny tick in his eye.

And then, suddenly, the memories seemed to break away, and Reuben smiled. "Bro."

He reached out and Knox met his hand.

Reuben pulled him in for a one-armed hug.

She could almost feel the brothers exhale as Reuben let him go.

Gilly took a look at the tractor's engine. "So what seems to be the problem?"

Knox glanced at Reuben, who lifted a shoulder. "She knows what she's doing."

And see that's why she loved…okay, yes. Loved him. Because although he protected her, he also trusted her.

"Engine just seized this morning."

"And you checked the oil?"

Knox gave her a look, and she grinned.

"Just checking. Let me take a look." She fiddled with the wires, acquainting herself with the engine. Asked Ford to turn it over, just to check spark and fuel flow. She took the rag from Knox for her fingers, stepped back, and hadn't even realized how much time had elapsed when she heard Gerri from the door of the barn.

"Seriously? Reuben, you're a terrible messenger."

Gerri stood there, looking anything but angry, however, grinning.

And it wasn't hard to figure out why—all her children back in one place.

"You can fix the tractor after lunch. It's getting cold."

Gilly finished wiping her hands as she followed the boys out. Until she noticed Reuben standing near the tack room, as if transfixed.

And then his mother walking up to him. "He left it here for you," she said.

Gilly hadn't a clue what Gerri meant until Gilly joined Reuben, looked inside.

Hanging on the wall was an old, battered Pulaski, not unlike the kind Reuben used.

"And I thought you might like to read this." Gerri pulled out a folded envelope and handed it to Reuben. "I found it in your father's belongings recently." She touched his back. "I'll heat up your bowls when you get in." Then she headed to the house.

Gilly walked into the tack room, took down the ax. "This was your father's?"

He nodded, opening the letter. "I used to play with it when I was young. He caught me and was afraid I'd chop my foot off and took it away. Hid it. I haven't seen it since…"

He was reading the letter, and something in his expression caught her, ran a hand around her throat.

His jaw tightened, his breath turned shaky.

"Rube?"

He looked up at her, and she stared nonplussed at his wet eyes.

"Are you okay?"

He handed her the letter. "It's from Jock."

Jock?

"My dad must have written to him after I left, maybe when he heard I'd joined the Jude County team."

He ran a knuckle under his eye. Turned away and walked over to a stall. One of the horses met him, and he ran his big hands over the muzzle, almost absently.

She looked at the letter. Jock's tiny, blocked handwriting—she recognized it from so many reports and whiteboard directions.

*Simon—*

*Yeah, he's here, and he's fine. Working on the hotshot crew—one of the hardest workers I've ever seen. Has shown some interest in joining the smokejumping team, like you suspected. I would guess he'll try out next year.*

*Following, apparently, in his father's footsteps.*

*He's everything you said—stubborn, tough. Smart. Good instincts. He'll make a great leader someday.*

*I know you didn't ask, but yeah, I'll look out for him.*

*I know you're wondering if you made the right decision, telling him to go. From my perspective you did. He was born for this. Not surprising—he has it in his genes.*

*You're right, you have a lot to be proud of.*

*Best—*

*Jock*

Gilly folded the letter, slipped it back into the envelope, and walked over to Reuben.

He had his forehead pressed to the soft nose of his horse.

She touched his back, and he drew in a long breath.

"You okay?"

He said nothing for a long time. Then, "I will be. Yeah."

He turned, reached out, and touched her cheek. His eyes betrayed a hint of red, thick with emotion. "I'm glad you're here."

"I'm glad I'm here, too." She touched his hand, so much love overflowing for this man, who only weeks ago could barely speak to her. Now it seemed with everything he did, from inviting her to his family's ranch, to taking her in his arms, to even the way he looked at her and spoke to her. Told her she was strong and beautiful and cherished.

She took his hand and brought him over to a nearby hay-stack. Then she climbed on it, raising herself to his eye level.

He smiled at her, meeting her eyes. "What are you do-ing?"

"Telling you I love you. That when I'm with you, I feel invincible. But also that I know I don't have to prove it—you already see me like that."

He wrapped his arms around her waist, tugged her against the hard planes of his body. "Absolutely. But maybe you could let me, every once in a while, protect you anyway? Just for my male ego?"

"We'll see," she said and leaned down to kiss him.

A nice long, delicious, off-season kiss, the kind that stirred the slow burn into a fire that caused her pulse to rush, her knees to weaken.

Then, because every time he kissed her he made her be-lieve she could fly, she let him lift her into his arms. Cradle her against his amazing, broad-shouldered, work-toughened body. She flung her arms around his neck, drinking in the sense of the big sky, a smoldering fire, and the open spaces of their tomorrows in his touch.

And in her heart, she swooned.

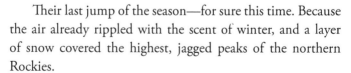

Their last jump of the season—for sure this time. Because the air already rippled with the scent of winter, and a layer of snow covered the highest, jagged peaks of the northern Rockies.

Reuben waited as Kate indicated with the spotting rib-bon where they might land. "See that clearing, off to the right of the river? You have a nice put-down there."

The wind tugged at her jumpsuit, but she was strapped in to the plane.

Jed had made sure of that. Because this trip wasn't for Kate. Or Hannah, or Ned, or CJ, or Tuck, Riley, or even Gilly.

This was for Conner. For Pete. For Reuben.

And led by Jed, because it was only right.

Pete ducked out first, his square opening against the scope of blue, the jeweled tones of the western edge of the Kootenai Forest. Just beyond the closest rise of mountains lay Canada, Brownie and Patrick's destination, as figured out the best the team could from Conner's patchwork hack into their personal finances. Conner had tracked the fugitives across Montana, starting with a brazen stop for gas and a beer at the Yaak River Tavern, then gas along 508, and a motel stay for a week at Golden Nugget Cabins in southwestern Montana, where the duo had probably planned their escape into Idaho.

Pete had pulled in some favors from his brother Sam's law enforcement buddies who raided the place. Unfortunately, the pair had escaped, probably due to a tip off from Patrick's portable scanner.

Reuben decided they wouldn't make that mistake again. Next time, they'd sneak in, keep their attack on the down low.

They'd tracked the Brownings into Idaho through a short stopover at Moyie Springs, where they'd withdrawn cash.

After that, they'd dropped off the grid.

Conner had set about using his techie skills and tapped into weather satellites to search forest service roads that traveled north to the border.

It had taken two more weeks, but this morning they'd gotten lucky with the sighting of their red station wagon on a remote forest service road in Idaho about a mile from the

Canadian border.

Yeah, they should have possibly alerted local police.

Except this was personal.

Besides, they had Conner, who, before he ever started jumping fires, jumped into war zones and trekked up desert passes to find the bad guys.

It always helped to have a former Green Beret on the team.

And, at this moment, Conner looked very military. No Kevlar jumpsuit for him. He wore a tactical, all-black jump-suit, a matching helmet, and body armor.

Reuben expected to see him armed with a semiautomat-ic machine gun, maybe an AK-47, or HK 416. But Conner only carried a very utilitarian Colt M45. Strapped to his leg.

Just in case Patrick still had the shotgun.

Conner also carried a backpack, like the rest of them, probably filled with camping gear. And all the necessities of an overnight, or even week-long trek into the wilderness.

Because they weren't coming home without their targets. Not after they'd pieced together the evidence, the clear truth.

Patrick had been out to take down the team since before the season started, tampering with the chutes, his first efforts at retribution.

After Kate's heroic save of Pete during their first jump of the season, she'd discovered the sabotage, so Patrick had had to turn to something else.

Conner's drones proved the perfect device. Patrick had been interested in them from the beginning, watching Reu-ben test them in early spring.

He'd even helped Conner with the avionics of the con-troller, discovering, no doubt, the frequency. They guessed that was how he figured out how to jam the signal and send a drone crashing, its transponder disabled.

Not unlike how he'd disabled Gilly's transponder.

Then it was simply a matter of trekking out to the woods, following the trajectory, and picking up the drone. He waited until his targets were all listed on the go-chart in the office, and then sent the drone out with flammables to ignite a fire.

One that would call in the jump team.

Maybe, then, fate would take over.

It seemed, however, he'd gotten tired of waiting.

Or weary of luck turning against him, because the smoke-jumpers just kept surviving.

Which meant Patrick probably became desperate and turned to sabotaging the plane. Only problem—the wrong jumpers got on board.

But he'd still managed to inflict pain.

Jed was gritting it out to go on this trip, only three weeks after being injured. Thankfully, the metal bar narrowly missed a kidney. But he couldn't sit still while the rest of the team went in search of justice.

Reuben understood that completely.

CJ had broken his pelvis, dislocated his shoulder, broken three ribs, and nearly died waiting out the night for rescue.

Hannah had kept him from going into shock, and only then did she reveal she was in her third and final year of nurse's training, the smokejumping gig a long-awaited dream she wasn't sure she would still pursue. No one blamed her.

They couldn't guess when and how Brownie got involved, unless it had started when one of Conner's drone went missing on Brownie's land, a buffalo pasture near the base. Although, if Patrick's revenge started at the beginning of the summer, then Brownie's might have also.

But no one forgot why.

Nearly a year had passed since the fire that took Jock Burns, Tom Browning, and five other firefighters.

And yeah, that kind of grief could drive a man crazy.

So they would bring Brownie and Patrick in for a fair trial. In front of the town of Ember.

Reuben considered that it might not, in reality, be so fair.

Kate tapped Conner's shoulder, and he flung himself from the plane. His canopy billowed out, a light blue against the vault of the sky.

Jed went next, and Reuben watched him fall, nodding to himself when Jed's square opened.

Kate put a hand on Reuben's chest before he could go out the door. "Bring him home," she said.

He nodded, but looked over his shoulder at the pilot, who had her hair pulled back in a cute ponytail.

She glanced back at him, her blue eyes in his. *I love you. Come back.*

Or he imagined that's what she said—mostly because she'd said those very words this weekend as they rode together through the moonlit fields of the Triple M. His second time home in two weeks, this time to attend Ford's football game, the kid following in his big brother's footsteps.

Then, later that night, under the cascade of stars, he'd taken Gilly in his arms in the barn and asked her to dance.

Keeping his promise. Knowing, finally, exactly what he wanted, no looking back. This life as a firefighter. Gilly. A tomorrow without regrets.

*Strength for today and bright hope for tomorrow.*

But all of this, of course, *after* they found justice for the

Jude County Smokejumpers.

He leaped out into the blue, the rush of wind galvanizing him, stirring his pulse. He fell, soaring, arms out, counting.

*Jump Thousand.*

They'd get on the ground, sneak through the woods and, using Conner's latest high-tech drone, find Patrick and Brownie.

*Look Thousand.*

He spotted Pete already on the ground below and Conner drifting out over the landing zone.

*Reach Thousand.*

Reuben's hand went around to his chute pull, and he wrapped his grip around the pull, the other hand still out for balance.

*Wait Thousand.*

Wait and take in the view one last moment. Conner landing safely, Jed drifting down in his wake. The view of Gilly soaring off to his right.

*Blessings all mine, with ten thousand beside!*

*Pull.*

# A Note from the Author

Our mistakes plague us, they haunt us and keep us from pursuing our happy ending. Right? You know what I'm talking about… just when you think you want to reach for your dreams, a little voice says…silly you! What are you thinking. You don't deserve to be happy. Or forgiven. Or to have your dreams come true.

So you pull your hand back.

Worse, what if your mistakes weren't even your fault? But you feel like they are, because you have no one else to blame. You tell yourself you're simply not enough.

Lies. But they hold us captive, and it isn't until we, well, crash land into a place we don't want to be that we start to see the truth.

You can be more. You are enough. Your mistakes don't define you.

Reach.

Gilly is a woman who longed to be a smokejumper. But because of her very real fear, she failed herself. Still, she determined to be the next best thing—a pilot. She reminds me of mighty mouse, fighting to carry her own weight, save her people, refusing help even when she needed it. And poor Reuben—he knows he made a gigantic mistake, but has no idea how to rewind time and fix it. Reuben is a true hero, self-sacrificing, loyal—I pictured Reuben as the guy on the defensive line who always holds his position, does his job, for no glory for himself, but for the good of the team. The kind of guy you want to have by your side.

Both Gilly and Reuben have refused to believe that they could have more. That they can reach out, past their failures, fears and mistakes to what might be waiting for them.

God doesn't want us to stand on the sidelines, haunted by our mistakes, paralyzed by fear. He wants us to strap our parachute harness onto Him and jump. To gulp in freedom as we believe His love, his faithfulness, his forgiveness. His delight in us.

That's what, strength for today and bright hope for tomorrow, is all about.

God loves you. Full stop. Hold onto him, breathe in the truth and jump out of the plane.

My deepest gratitude goes to Ellen Tarver, Barbara Curtis, David Warren, Lacy Williams and my sweet husband who is the guy who learned to dance, for me. Gotcha, you said. And you do.

Thank you for reading the Summer of Fire trilogy. There's a Christmas story, too! CJ and Hannah…they survived the crash, but what's next? What happens after the summer is over…and the winter storms in? Discover their story in Oh! The Weather Outside is Frightful, a Smokejumper Christmas Novella.

Until we meet again—**Go in Grace!**

*Susie May*

# Montana Rescue

## Book One
## Wild Montana Skies

*Sneak Peek*

# Chapter 1

Kacey didn't want to raise eyebrows and alert the entire town to her return. She simply hoped to tame the beast that had roared to life when she spotted the billboard for the Gray Pony Saloon and Grill, off Rt. 2, on the outskirts of Mercy Falls.

The home of the best hickory rib sauce in the West.

From the look of things, the hangout on the edge of town hadn't changed in a decade.

Dim streetlights puddled the muddy parking lot, now crammed full of F-150s and Silverado pickups. The twang of a Keith Urban cover swelled as the door opened. A cowboy spilled out, his arm lassoed around a shapely coed, probably a summer intern for the park service. She wore Gore-Tex pants, a lime-green Glacier National Park T-shirt, and a too-easy smile on her face. Kacey watched as the cowboy wheedled her toward his truck. She tugged his hat down, and he braced his hands on either side of her, leaning down to steal a kiss.

The sight had the power to stop Kacey cold, reroute her down the country road of regrets.

Maybe she should simply keep going, head north to Whitefish, back to the anonymity of a town that couldn't catalog her mistakes.

Still, the brain fog of two days of driving, not to mention the drizzle of a nagging rain, could be the recipe for disaster on the winding roads that journeyed north through the foothills.

The last thing she needed was to drive headfirst off the highway and die in a fiery crash here in her own backyard. Some welcome home that would be.

Kacey parked just as thunder growled, lightning spliced the darkness, and rain began to crackle against her windshield. The soupy night obliterated the view of the glorious, jagged mountains rising in the horizon.

Another pickup rolled up next to her, the running boards caked with mud. A fleet of what looked like army types piled out, garbed in mud-brown shirts and camo pants. Fatigue lined their grimy expressions, as if they were just returning from a two-day march in full field gear.

With the nearest army base over 150 miles away, the appearance of soldiers had her curiosity piqued. She watched them go in, and a reprimand formed on her lips about donning utility wear off duty. But, like her army psychologist had suggested, some time away from her fellow soldiers might help her heal.

Keep her from derailing twelve years of distinguished service with an ODPMC discharge—or, to her mind, the old Section-8, Maxwell Klinger designation.

She wasn't crazy. Just...exhausted. Maybe.

She couldn't let the war follow her home. Let it destroy the best part of herself, the part she'd left behind in Montana.

The part of her that desperately needed a definition of life that included words like safe and normal.

Instead of, oh, say, deployment and Afghanistan.

And acronyms like PTSD.

Which meant she had to start living like a civilian and keep her military secrets safely tucked away if she intended on putting herself back together and returning to base, healed and fit for duty, by the end of the summer.

Kacey scrubbed the sleep out of her eyes, then got out, hunting ribs and a frothy homemade root beer.

The Pony might not have updated their exterior, with the rough-hewn porch, the Old West style sign, and neon beer ads in the windows, but inside, they'd overhauled for the next generation.

The honky-tonk tones of some country musician met her as she opened thick double doors, and she walked into the distinct intoxicating aroma of hickory barbecue.

She glanced to the front and almost expected to see cowboy crooner Benjamin King on stage at the back of the room, past the gleaming oak bar. Work-hewn muscles stretching out his black T-shirt, one worn cowboy boot hooked onto the rung of his stool, and wearing his battered brown Stetson over that unruly dark blond hair, Ben would grind out a love song in his signature low tenor, wooing every girl in the room.

His devastating blue eyes fixed only on her.

Kacey blew out a breath, letting the memory shake out, settle her back into reality.

Stopping for dinner at the Gray Pony would be a very bad idea if Ben hadn't long ago sprung himself from the grasp of Mercy Falls, his guitar slung over his shoulder, nary a glance behind. No, she wouldn't find him, a big star now with the country duo Montgomery King, back in this one-horse watering hole tucked in the shadow of Glacier National Park.

Now, Kacey scanned the room, getting her bearings. Roy had kept the taxidermied moose, rainbow trout, and black bear still posed over the bar, but the rest of the joint, from the themed barrel tables to the sleek leather barstools, suggested an upgrade. Along the wall, every few feet, flat screens displayed sporting events—bull riding, a UFC fight, a golf tournament, and a fishing show. And the adjacent hall that once hosted a row of worn pool tables now sported a shiny mechanical bull riding pit.

Judging by the cheering of the fellas gathered at the rail, more than a few wearing Sweetwater Creek Lumber Co. shirts, the girl in the center of the ring offered up quite a show.

The saloon seemed to have upgraded their clientele from the obligatory cowboys and park workers to a large conglomeration of army, local law enforcement, and even what looked like young, long-haired hippies hoping to spend their summer in yurts and hiking the craggy routes of the Rocky Mountains, cameras hanging from their necks.

Waitresses squeezed through tables packed with hungry patrons, their trays stacked high with wings, onion rings, and nachos. An "oo-rah!" rose from a table of soldiers as one of the UFC fighters went down.

She recognized no one, which, of course, could be providential. Because they might not recognize her, either.

Kacey squeezed past a group of hikers perusing a map and nabbed the only empty barstool. She climbed up, took a napkin, and mopped up the remains of a frothy beer puddling on the counter.

"Sorry about that." This from the woman behind the counter, her dark hair pulled back in a long braid, her brown eyes quick as she surveyed the activity behind Kacey. She took a rag and wiped the counter. "I think the person sitting here stiffed me." She glanced at the door.

"Where did she—"

"He. I dunno. I don't see him. He wasn't in uniform, but he could be with the guard." She tossed the rag under the counter, grabbed a coaster. "We have specials on tap—"

"Do you still have the house root beer?"

A hint of a smile. "Home brewed, my daddy's recipe."

Her daddy...seriously? Ah, sure, Kacey saw it now. Hair dyed black and about fifty pounds thinner. And of course, a decade in her eyes, on her face. She couldn't help but ask, "Gina McGill?"

The woman frowned. "Do I—"

"Kacey Fairing. I used to—"

"Date Ben King, yeah, wow, how are you?"

Kacey was going to say that she'd sat behind her in Mr. Viren's biology class, but she supposed Gina's version might be an easier association. "I'm good."

"I haven't seen you since, uh..." And there it was. The prickly dance around Kacey's mistakes. The ones that had driven her out of Mercy Falls and into the army's arms.

"Prom," Kacey filled in, diverting, trying to make it easier for both of them. "Nice of your dad to let us host it here. One of my favorite high school memories."

"What are you up to?" Gina said, pulling out a frozen mug from the freezer, filling it with frothy, dark, creamy root beer from the tap.

"I'm a chopper pilot. For the army."

"Really? Wow. I suppose they called you in, huh? Rescuing people off rooftops?"

Kacey frowned. "Uh, not sure what you're talking about."

Gina set the mug on the coaster. "Oh, I thought you were here with the rest of the National Guard. The Mercy River is flooding, and all these guys are working twenty-four-hour shifts sandbagging upriver all the way down to the bridge."

Ah, that accounted for dinner in their field dress.

Kacey took a sip of the root beer, let the foam sit on her upper lip a second before licking it off. "Nope. Here on leave for the summer, although, yeah, I'll be doing some flying for Chet King's PEAK." See, that came out easily enough, no hitch, no hint at the past. No irony.

And no suggestion that she might not be fit to fly. Keeping her chopper in the air had never been her problem, thank you.

Besides, she needed this gig, if only to keep her sanity during the daylight hours. Too much idle time only invited the memories.

Gina offered her a menu. "Well, don't be surprised if Sam Brooks comes knocking on your door. The Mercy Falls EMS department has the PEAK team on full alert, and he's recruiting volunteers for the sandbag brigade."

Kacey perused the menu offerings. "Why is Sam doing the recruiting? Is Blackburn still sheriff?"

"Yeah. He'll be in office until he retires, probably. Sam is the deputy sheriff. So, the smoked BBQ ribs are half off now that it's after 10:00 p.m., and I think I could score you a basket of the fried calamari on the house."

"The ribs sound perfect, thanks, Gina," she said, handing her the menu. "And I'm game for the calamari too."

Kacey grabbed the mug, sipping as she turned in her chair, glancing at the band on stage, the lead singer now leaning into the mic, plucking out another Keith Urban ballad.

"I'm gonna be here for ya, baby..."

Young, dark-haired, and not a hint of Ben's resonant twang. And yet just like that, Ben showed up, almost tangible in her mind, even after all these years. The smell of fresh air in his flannel shirt, his arms around her, lips against her neck.

Nope. She wrapped her hands around the cool glass.

She should probably also remember that Ben had made her believe in a different life. In the full-out happy ending. She should probably hate him for that.

On the dance floor, the cowboy and the coed from outside locked themselves in a slow sway. A few more couples joined them, and Kacey turned away, rubbing her finger and thumb into her eyes, slicking away the exhaustion.

"Working the flood?"

She looked up into the striking, almost teal eyes of the man who had slid onto the stool next to her. Brown, neatly trimmed hair and a smattering of russet whiskers, neatly clipped but just long enough to suggest a renegade attitude in a cultured life. He wore a camel-brown chambray shirt open at the neck, sleeves rolled up over strong forearms, a pair of faded jeans, scuffed hiking boots, and the smell of money in his cologne. A rich, cowboy-wannabe tourist. And he had a low, rumbly voice that should have probably elicited some response, if she weren't so tired.

Really tired. "Nope."

From the end of the bar, a huddle of hikers roared as one of them landed a bull's-eye into the dart target. The man seemed to follow her gaze, frowned.

Huh.

"I suppose the rain's cutting short your vacation," she said.

This got a laugh. Or a harrumph, she couldn't tell. "Naw. I'm over the park."

"That's a shame. So much beautiful country."

Did she imagine the shadow that crossed his eyes? Maybe, because in a blink it vanished. Instead, "Gina talked you into the calamari, huh?"

Gina had deposited the deep-fried squid, sided with creamy aioli.

Kacey reached for a twisty piece. "Why? Something I should be worried about?" She took a curl, dipped it into the spicy mayo.

He shook his head, took a sip of his own root beer. "I tried to tell Roy that nobody north of Denver has ever heard of calamari, but he wanted to add it. Something for the tourists..."He lifted a nicely sculpted shoulder. "I think I'm the only one in five hundred miles ordering it."

So, not a tourist. But not exactly a local either.

"Rubbery." She wrinkled her nose. "Yeah, probably Roy should have stuck with cowboy food." She shoved the basket his direction. "Help yourself."

"Not for you?"

"I'm spoiled," she said, rinsing down the flavor. "I've spent the past year in Florida, seaside."

He seemed like a nice guy—maybe the right guy—to help erase old memories, find new ones.

Not that she was looking, really, but maybe, away from her rules on base, and with a longer stint home than normal, she might...

A shout on the dance floor made her turn, and she saw that the cowboy she'd seen before on the porch was tussling with one of the hippies, this one wearing a park-logoed shirt.

Oops. Apparently that cute coed in his arms had cuddled up against the wrong demographic.

"We're dancing here," Cowboy said.

"And she's not your girlfriend!" retorted the hippie.

Next to her, the man, Mr. Rumble Voice, rose. "That's

not pretty."

She glanced at him. "They'll be fine."

He wasn't the only one on his feet, however. A couple of the hikers on the far end of the bar separated from the group and edged toward the dance floor.

And the table of UFC fans stopped cheering, eyes on the spectacle.

She took another sip of her root beer.

The voices raised, a few expletives thrown.

When Cowboy pushed the hippie, Rumble headed toward the dance floor.

And, shoot—like a reflex, Kacey found herself on her feet, as if still on duty, the cool-headed soldier she'd been for twelve years.

Stay out of it. The voice simmered in her head.

"Hey, guys," Rumble said, moving closer, hands up. "Let's just take this outside—"

Cowboy threw a punch at the hippie, and the room exploded. The hippies emptied their table, and of course Cowboy had a few hands he'd dragged in off the ranch.

And just like that, Kacey was dodging fists, zeroing in on the coed who started the mess. The girl held her mouth where someone had accidentally elbowed her.

Kacey maneuvered through the fray, caught the girl, and pulled her back toward the stage. "Are you okay?" If she remembered correctly, there was an exit just stage left...

"I didn't mean to start this."

Kacey threw her arm over the girl's shoulder and ducked, heading toward the exit.

She didn't see it coming.

A body flew into her, liquid splashing over her as the

weight threw her. Kacey slammed into the stage; pain exploded across her forehead.

The room spun, darkness blotchy against her eyes.

She sat there, just a moment, blinking.

Pull back, Kacey! Your position is compromised!

She shook her head to rid it of the voice but felt a scream rising when arms circled her, lifting—

"Oh no you don't!" Kacey shouted.

She thrashed against the embrace, elbowing her captor hard.

He made a sound of pain, but she followed with a hard uppercut to his jaw.

And landed on the floor.

The jolt of hitting the floor, the sense of movement around her, brought her back.

"What—?" She blinked, clearing her vision.

Rumble peered down at her, holding his jaw. "You have quite a right hook, honey."

Oh. Boy. She made a face, but her forehead burned, and she pressed her hand against the heat of a rising bump. "Sorry. But—"

"My bad. But you need to get off the floor."

Voices now, loud, punching through the tension in the room.

He hesitated a second, then held out his hand again.

She made a face, shook her head, and climbed to her feet. "I don't need help, thanks."

But she swayed, trying to find her feet on the wooden floor.

"Seriously, you look like you could go down."

"I'm fine." Only then did she realize the wetness down the front of her white T-shirt. And...oh no. The odor of beer from her soaked shirt rose to consume her. That would play well when she arrived home. She pulled the shirt away from her body and removed her hand from her head. Then, "Wait...that girl—"

"Jess has her."

Jess? She looked around and found the girl being led to a table by a pretty blonde, one of the hikers.

Rumble seemed to be debating grabbing her am, but she gave him a look, and he simply led the way back to the counter. On the dance floor, the factions had separated, the musician was setting his mic back to rights. The hippies, angry, a few of them holding back their champion, congregated at their table. The cowboy stalked out of the bar, holding his hat, his posse shouting epithets as they trailed.

"The flood has everyone keyed up," Rumble said.

A man walked by, wearing a two-day scraggle of whiskers, dressed in a tight black shirt, Gore-Tex pants. Another one of the hikers. "Thanks, Ian," he said, clamping her not-needed rescuer on the shoulder.

Ian nodded after him. "Miles."

Apparently, this guy knew everyone in the saloon. "Ian? That's your name?"

He nodded while reaching for a napkin. He fished ice from his water and folded it into the napkin. "You've got a nasty bump there." He made to hold the makeshift ice pack to her head, then simply handed it to her.

"Thank you." Kind. She should have seen that earlier. "Sorry I hit you. It's a...well, a reflex."

"What, from your years cage fighting?" He raised an eyebrow, and she couldn't help a smile.

"No. Just...nothing."

He frowned a second, but it vanished.

She anchored the ice pack in place, too aware of the fact that she should be attracted to this man who seemed so clearly interested in her.

Or maybe she was simply so out of practice she didn't know how to flirt, or what flirting even looked like. Maybe he was simply being nice.

And she looked like a fool. She knew better than to dive into the middle of a barroom brawl—resurrect all her nightmares in broad daylight, or at least under the dim lights of a bar. Her specialty was picking up the pieces, not preventing the disaster in the first place.

Or at least it had been.

"I should go," she said, pulling the ice away, fingering the bruise, testing it. "I still have an hour of driving tonight."

Ian raised an eyebrow. "I don't think so. You're injured, and you've been drinking."

Huh? "Hardly." She picked up her glass. "This is root beer. Besides, I've been hurt worse than this and still managed to airlift eight marines out of a hot zone. Trust me, I can keep my Ford Escape between the lines from here to Whitefish."

"You still can't go."

"Enough with the gallantry. Listen, I'm exhausted, I've just driven for two days without sleep and I have to report for my new job in the morning." She turned to Gina just emerging from the kitchen with her ribs. "Can I get those to go?"

Gina nodded, turned back to the kitchen.

"You don't understand—" Ian started.

"No, dude, you don't understand. I'm simply not interested, and frankly, you don't want to get messed up with me.

Trust me on that one."

He frowned then, but then reached out and cupped his hand over her key.

And that was just...it. So what if he had six inches on her, looked like he worked out regularly, and knew how to handle himself. She only appeared helpless.

She schooled her voice, kept it even but with enough edge for him to take her seriously. "Ian. I know you don't know me, and right now, I sort of wish we'd never met, but trust me...You let go of my keys or that little altercation on the dance floor will look like a warm-up."

And he actually, seriously, smiled?

"Huh. Okay." She slid off the stood.

"Slow down, I'm not trying to start another fight." He moved his hand. "You can't go home because...you can't. Highway 2 is washed out just north of Mercy Falls. Unless you want to drive three hours back to Great Falls, then two hundred miles to Missoula, then finally north on 93 for another one hundred or so miles and end up arriving home around dawn, you're hunkering down here tonight."

Here. In Mercy Falls. She sighed and found the fist she'd made loosening.

"I was just trying to save you hours of driving."

Gina came back out, plunked the bag of ribs on the bar. "Okay, here you go. By the way, Dad says hi. And that dinner is on the house for your service to your country. I didn't know you won a bronze star."

Kacey glanced at Ian, who raised an eyebrow. She turned back to Gina. "Tell him thanks." She didn't follow up on the medal comment. Because, really, she had her doubts about the validity of giving someone who'd just barely kept it together a medal.

"Listen," Ian said. "The hotels from here to Great Falls are full of National Guardsmen and volunteers trying to keep the river from flooding. Why don't you come home with me? I have a ranch not far from here."

She stared at him. "You've got to be kidding me. What— do I have the word desperate tattooed on my forehead? Or easy, perhaps?" She grabbed the bag, her keys. "This may be a shocker, but no, I won't come home with you, thanks." She slid off the table, bumped her way through the crowd.

"Kacey!"

She ignored him, skirting past his friend Miles, who turned at his voice. She pushed outside, gulped in the fresh air. Wow, did that go south fast.

Apparently, it still wasn't over because Ian emerged through the doors right behind her. "Stop, Kacey."

She rounded on him. "And now this is starting to get a little stalkery. What's your deal?"

But the way he was looking at her, something like determination in his eyes...Now a little concern reached in, tugged at her. Her breath caught. "How do you know my name?"

"Take a breath. I'm not a stalker." He held up his hands as if in surrender, his jaw tight. "But I'm right, aren't I? You're Kacey Fairing?"

She found herself stepping back, wishing she had a side-arm. She dropped her takeout bag onto a bench.

He noticed and softened his voice. "This is my fault. I should have explained myself better. I heard you mention PEAK and then figured it out when Gina mentioned the medal, which is, of course, exactly what Chet said when he told me about you."

She took another step back. "Chet King told you...about me?"

Which would only stir up questions, she had no doubt. The last thing she needed was for her reputation to precede her.

"What did he say?"

"That you were exactly who we needed to take over flight ops for PEAK. Military hero…"

Oh. That. Still, that meant maybe she was safe from anyone grounding her based on false assumptions. Just because she was a little jumpy didn't mean she couldn't still handle a bird.

Ian lowered his hands but kept them out, away from his body, where she could see them. "You are the new pilot for PEAK Rescue, right? The one Chet hired to replace him and Ty?"

She nodded.

"Let's start over. I should have introduced myself earlier." He stuck out his hand, as if meeting her for the first time. "Ian Shaw. Local rancher and, well, founder of the PEAK Search and Rescue team."

Founder.

She swallowed, wrapping her brain around his words, even while reaching out to take his hand.

He rubbed the other hand over his jaw, now red, even a smidgen swollen.

"In other words, I'm your new boss. Welcome home."

And don't miss Susie May's
newest series,
Montana Rescue!

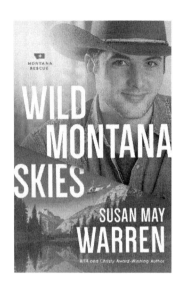 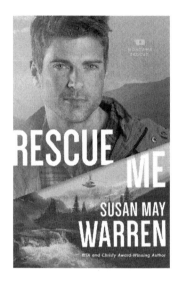

Made in the USA
Columbia, SC
13 March 2020

89160664R00155